ROSEMARY BOY

AMY COOMER

ROSEMARY BOY

AMY COOMER

First published in 2025 by Popcorn Press,
an imprint of Fair Play Publishing
PO Box 4101, Balgowlah Heights, NSW 2093, Australia
www.fairplaypublishing.com.au

ISBN: 978-1-923236-37-0
ISBN: 978-1-923236-38-7 (ePub)

Cover design by Asher Reed
Typesetting by Ana D. Nedeljković

All inquiries should be made to the Publisher via hello@fairplaypublishing.com.au

For my dad

In this terrifying world, all we have are
the connections that we make.

—BoJack Horseman. Season 3, episode 6.

JANUARY 2017

Chapter 1

I was watching television when I saw myself die.

I mean, it wasn't actually me. But it could have been. The unfortunate features. The messy brown hair. The resemblance was almost uncanny. The only difference was *this* seventeen-year-old had died in a car crash last night, and I was sitting on my lounge room floor eating shortcake.

"Mum—" I was cut off by the sound of my mother's cake dish hitting the floor. It cracked like a porcelain universe into two uneven pieces.

The word sat in the air. *Mum.* The longer it did, the stranger it began to feel. How does a word you've said a million times suddenly feel so wrong? For most of us, it's the first word we ever say. Our first point of connection in the world. Our first moment of recognition.

You are Mum.

The next few hours were a blur. Hell, the next two *weeks* were a blur. My life as I knew it was unravelling before my eyes, like a spool of thread that just kept going. And going, and going, and going.

Mum began to pace, and the house dissolved into a swirl of earth tones. I imagined her pulling her hair out like a character in a cartoon. I imagined the strands floating to the floor like silky brown feathers.

Mum sat next to me on the carpet. She took my hands in her tiny ones, and that's when she started to cry. "Everything that I have done…" she said, in between these huge, terrible gasps. "It has been for you. It has all been for you. I love you, Jules." She leaned in close. She nuzzled her face into my hair. "Please… Please forgive me."

She must have rehearsed those lines in her head a thousand times. It wasn't until much later that I could contemplate the stress she would have been under. From the moment she took me, and each little lie that followed, starting with *You are adopted.*

I wanted to say something, anything, but my gaze kept drifting to the TV. To the boy who looked exactly like me.

His name was Jack Rosemary. There was media interest in his death because of what happened to his mother, Pamela, the night he was born. One of her babies had been kidnapped from a hospital in Brisbane. Jack's twin.

Mrs Rosemary has issued a statement to police. 'My heart is burning. I can't put into words how this feels, to lose one child only to bury another. Please, keep my family in your prayers tonight. Jack…and my missing angel, Nick. Two boys taken from me before I was ready. May we all meet again one day.'

I stared into the eyes of the woman on TV. That was the first time I ever saw my real mother.

I don't remember much of the next two weeks. Even now, I recall them like the dark dregs of a nightmare. A revolving door of people in uniforms and psychologists asking me endless questions. A DNA test. Sitting alone in waiting rooms, in the back seats of cars. Watching the streets of Fremantle roll past my window, a strange caricature of the town I used to know.

"It will all make sense soon," said the woman in the driver's seat—my court-appointed social worker, Eloise. She was driving me to the airport.

I didn't answer her. I just stared out the window at the soulless streets.

"Just think of it this way, Jules. There is a woman out there who has been longing for you since the moment you were born, and even long before then. Now you get to be reunited with her."

"As her replacement son."

"You are her son, Jules. Just as much as Jack was. You were always her son."

Then who the hell is that woman I was living with for seventeen years? I kept the question to myself. Eloise seemed like a nice lady. She didn't need to be on the receiving end of my existential angst.

"What if she doesn't like me?" I asked instead. The question came out softer than I meant it to.

"She's not just your natural legal guardian, Jules. She's your mother. Your mum." I felt her glance at me. "None of this is your fault, Jules. You are a victim here. A survivor."

I resisted the urge to roll my eyes. I didn't feel like a survivor. Angela had always treated me with love, but now I was being told to view it as something else. That what I had gone through with her—growing up, being nurtured—was something criminal and abhorrent. I'd watched her turn herself over to the police two weeks ago like she deserved to be punished. *For being my mum.*

"I just...I want to go home."

"You'll be in Brisbane soon," Eloise told me, but I was talking about my home in Fremantle. With Angela… My *other* mother.

"Are there going to be reporters?" I asked her. "I don't want to be in the media. I don't want everyone knowing who I am."

"We've managed to get a gag order—at least until Angela is formally charged. And police have assured us that this will be after Jack's funeral, once you've settled in."

"What's a gag order?"

"It means the media can't publish your name, photo or any other identifying information about you until the order is lifted."

"What happens when Mum is charged?" I gritted my teeth. "When…when *Angela* is charged. What happens to the gag order?"

"It's a unique situation," Eloise said. "Since you're under eighteen, we can extend the gag order to protect your identity, but given that you're Jack's identical twin, the public already knows what you look like. Quite frankly, it's going to be very hard to keep your identity a secret." She met my gaze in the rear-view mirror, her eyebrows pulling together. "We're all doing our best to protect you, Julian. Usually, Angela would be extradited to Brisbane because that's where your kidnapping took place, but the court has agreed that it's best to keep her in Perth for the time being, so that you and your birth mother have as much space as possible to navigate this situation. You'll have a new social worker once you arrive in Brisbane. His name is Elijah. He's a lovely man, and he'll be there to help you every step of the way. From there, you'll have a grief counsellor named Yong, who you'll meet with once a week."

I tried to smile at her. *Cue the smile. Cue the courageous young man who's about to brave his new life.* But I couldn't smile. I couldn't even cry. The psychologists kept telling me it was okay to cry, almost like they were encouraging it. I felt like I was disappointing all the adults in my life for being so dry-eyed. I found myself trying to scrounge up tears just to make them happy, but whatever look crossed my face in those moments only seemed to concern them instead.

I guess I wasn't so good at being around other people. I could never seem to be what they wanted me to be, or do what they wanted me to do. Which was fine. Two weeks ago, none of that was an issue for a home-schooled kid from a small town.

But now, thanks to Angela and every news reporter in wider Australia, I was about to have more fame than I ever could have imagined.

Chapter 2

I was alive, but I was dead. My heart was beating, but I was staring at a picture of myself on a memorial pamphlet with the words 'Forever Young' written in cursive above my head.

I always hated that song. Angela had downloaded a selection of songs onto an iPod shuffle for my eleventh birthday, and that one had been fourth on the list. I'd always skipped it, but there was no skipping it today. Today, it was the official funeral song for my dead twin brother.

The funeral was in a place called Regents Park, and Elijah and I were given strict instructions to arrive before 7 a.m., three hours before the scheduled start. This was to avoid the media, and to ensure that my first moments with my real family were uninterrupted by camera flashes. We'd been told to meet them inside the church, but so far it was just Elijah and me. There was nothing but an empty church and some guy in a dark grey suit handing out pieces of paper with my face on it.

He'd done a double take when he'd handed it to me. "Oh," he'd said. I could practically read his mind. *You look just like him.*

It had already happened once. About a week ago, when I was leaving a police station in Fremantle. The guy had only been a few years older, and part of me had been astonished that so many young people were tuning into the news these days. The other part of me had been completely mortified.

I took the pamphlet. Grey Suit didn't say anything, but he didn't need to. He'd already set the tone for today. He'd already penetrated my subconscious.

"Just ignore them," Elijah said. "You're going to get a lot of stares today—some of them good, some of them weird, like that guy. Just smile and do your best, okay?"

So far, I liked Elijah. He was a large Māori man who didn't sugar-coat anything. In fact, he was rather forthcoming about the ways in which my life was about to get seriously screwed up. I appreciated that. I appreciated the honesty.

"Come on," he said. "Let's get away from that fucking rubberneck."

He also swore a lot. I appreciated that, too. The fact that he treated me like an adult and not some fragile little kid.

We walked away from Grey Suit and found a spot under an air conditioner. It was already hot as balls in Brisbane; Fremantle was hot, but this place was like stepping into an armpit. Elijah started typing something on his phone, and I stared down at the picture of my face— *our* face.

Jack Rosemary was seventeen, like me. He'd had that same stubborn curl at the end of his hair before he'd cut it, whereas I'd begged Angela to let mine grow. He'd listened to the classics, according to the rest of his scheduled funeral songs. Red Hot Chili Peppers, Queen, Nirvana. I liked to listen to the hum of my ceiling fan.

It's almost like finding out you've lived a second life. That somewhere, under the same sky, the same star, a person wearing your face had made a mark on the world. Perhaps they'd broken hearts, or they'd fallen in love, or they'd had sex with people. I certainly hadn't done any of those things. Maybe Jack had all the charm and charisma; maybe he'd absorbed all of those shiny things in the womb, leaving me a weaker, lesser version of him.

But he's the one who's dead.

"I've got to take a piss," Elijah said. "You need to go?"

I shook my head. "Already been three times this morning."

Elijah laughed softly, patting me on the shoulder. "You'll be okay here for five?"

I nodded.

A car arrived outside. I turned away as the people entered, watching them take their pamphlets in my periphery, watching them cry. It occurred to me that these people were probably my family. People I was supposed to love. People who were supposed to love me. I hated Angela in that moment. Not for kidnapping me. Not for lying to me. I hated her for putting me in such an awkward fucking situation. For making me meet over fifty family members and strangers at the same event.

At the moment, there were only four. A man and a woman and two young children. The man—David Leman, according to the papers—looked to be around his late forties, with tan skin and a silvery blonde beard. He was tall and broad-shouldered. The woman looked like she was made of twigs and her eyes focused on me—light blue eyes, impenetrable. She looked like she was about to collapse at any moment, like even the air conditioning was painful on her frail limbs.

My heart dropped. I recognised her from the papers. Recognised her from my dreams.

My mother.

Pamela Rosemary. Thirty-Eight. According to Elijah, she'd

been an aspiring actress before becoming pregnant, and she's been a stay-at-home mother ever since.

She didn't look like me. I didn't look like her. I wasn't in denial; I could admit that Jack looked like me. We were *identical*. But this woman, this woman with her yellow blonde hair and her long, birdlike features… She didn't look like me.

I saw the word form on her lips: *Julian*. A silent greeting. She wiped the tears from her face, but they were instantly replaced by fresh ones. I could see them shining in her eyes, even from here. It was like her body was threatening to cave in on itself.

Suddenly, the two young children were bobbing around her waist. They pulled on her black dress and one of them, the girl, demanded to be picked up.

I walked over to them, slowly, my heart trembling with each step. *Where the hell is Elijah?*

"Mumma!" the little girl beamed, pointing at me. "Mumma, it's Jack!"

I froze, unsure if I should take another step. This was probably as terrifying for them as it was for me. In all the madness, I'd forgotten there could be *children* here. Children that were related to me, and who had only a rudimentary understanding of death.

Pam looked mortified, before quickly kneeling to put her one free arm around the little boy. She hugged both children, whispering urgently. "No, no, no, this is Julian. The boy I was telling you about." Pamela smiled nervously at me, and it simultaneously healed me and tore me apart. "This is your new brother."

Tentatively, I took another step closer. The kids just stared at me, wide-eyed.

"Julian, this is James," Pam said, nodding to the boy. "And

this is Tanner." She gestured at the little girl in her arms, who frowned at me like I was some kind of cartoon character.

"It's nice to meet you guys," I said. My voice broke on the word 'nice'.

The man cleared his throat. He was looking back and forth between Pam and I in a way I couldn't quite pinpoint. His jaw was tight and he kept sighing through his nose, almost like he was frustrated by the situation.

Finally, he extended his hand to me. "Nice to meet you too, Julian. I'm David, your, uh…stepfather, I suppose."

"David," Pamela said quietly. She seemed to instantly regret it.

He shrugged his shoulders. "What? I *am* his stepfather."

"We just—" Pamela took a deep breath, turning to me. "We don't want to overwhelm you. It's going to be a lot, once the media arrives."

"I'll say. I've had reporters calling me nonstop. I'm surprised we weren't trailed leaving the bloody house—"

Pamela turned back to David with a look I couldn't see. "Honey… Can you take the kids to get a snack or something? There's some food in my car."

"Fine," David said. He nodded at me. "See you later, Julian."

David ushered the children back toward the door. They stared at me with big eyes and then reluctantly walked outside.

Pamela and I just looked at each other for a moment. For the first time since all of this happened, I wanted to cry. I wanted to fucking weep at this woman's feet.

I wanted her to let me.

"Julian…" she said, and the rest of her sentence was choked off by a sob.

I needed Elijah. I needed help. After all, most kids don't ever have to meet their parents; they just know them. They're not some stranger on the street that they have to approach—some awkward handshake or aborted hug that they have to endure. Some foreign voice on the other end of the phone call. There's a sea of broken adults who have to know this feeling, but not kids.

"Forgive him," Pamela said. "David is…blunt, at the best of times." She nodded toward the car. James is only six, and Tanner just turned four. They're a bit confused by all of this."

"Join the club," I said. I tried to laugh but it sounded wrong. Everything sounded wrong. I'd never been so unaccustomed to the sound of my own voice. I cleared my throat. "It's, uh, really nice to meet you, Pamela."

She sniffed, wiping her nose. "Call me Pam, please."

"Sorry," I said. "Pam… Most people call me Jules."

She smiled at me, tears still swimming in her eyes. "Jules, you are…you are exactly how I imagined you'd be."

I didn't know what to say to that. I couldn't even look at her, so I stared at the thick bushland outside the door. How did you look at a stranger you were supposed to love?

And then she opened her arms. She opened her arms and I stepped into my mother's lukewarm embrace. We were the same height.

She ran a perfunctory hand up and down my back. The whole thing was remarkably numb—for both of us, it seemed.

"It's nice to meet you, too," she whispered. "I met you once, briefly, but you were crying too much to let me hold you."

"Sorry," I said. Again.

She laughed into my shoulder. She had a nice laugh, a rare

laugh that was softer than her voice. "We're going to have to fix that." She leaned back, looking at me. "You don't have to feel uncomfortable here, Jules. You're not a stranger. You're family. You're…you're my son."

Her eyes started to well again. I looked at the floor. I wasn't good with other people crying, either. Watching people cry was like staring directly into the sun.

Thankfully, at that moment, Elijah decided to make his court-appointed reappearance. "Shit," he muttered. "Sorry, Jules. I had to track down a key for the toilets." He extended a hand to Pam. "I'm Elijah, Jules' social worker."

"I'm Pam," she told him. The words *Jules' mother* went unsaid.

We all stood awkwardly. In that moment, it dawned on me that I didn't have a biological father—in either reality. According to Angela, I'd been adopted as a baby. She'd been an only child and my grandparents had died before I was born. I'm sure she dated men, but never seriously, and she never brought any of them back to the house.

A couple of weeks ago, thanks to Eloise, I finally found out the truth of my identity. Pamela Rosemary was my mother, and my biological father was a random man she'd met on a holiday. He'd died shortly before Jack and I were born—work accident at a warehouse. Over the years since, many media outlets had falsely assumed that David was our real father.

I felt cheated, in a way. All of this drama, two mothers, a half brother and sister, but not a single father—just a *David*.

"The service starts at ten," Pam told us. "David has warned us that the media will probably start arriving well before then, so we'll have to keep the door closed while the others arrive."

I glanced at Elijah. "Wait, but—I thought there was a gag order?"

He looked at Pam, and then at me. "Unfortunately, they can still take your photo. They can still hassle you as much as they want, but they just can't publicise any of it until you turn eighteen."

"The rest of us are fair game," Pam said. "They'll just blur out the faces of anyone underage."

"Oh," I said. "Right." There was just so much information being programmed into me the last couple of weeks—new relatives, gag orders, kidnapping laws, the Child Protection Act—that I was having trouble retaining all of it. I knew the media would be hassling some of the adults; I just didn't think they'd be hassling *me*.

"I know it doesn't seem fair," Elijah told me. "Because it's not. Unfortunately, this is just the way our world works, Jules. People feed on sensationalism—on the misfortune and pain of others."

"But why do they care?" I asked him. "They don't even know me."

Elijah and Pam just exchanged another look. For some reason, I got the feeling that there was some big cosmic truth that I wasn't understanding.

"On the bright side," Pam said, "there are a lot of wonderful people who will be eager to meet you."

"Great," I said. *Fuck.*

Elijah placed a hand on my back. He squeezed it once, giving me a knowing smile. "You got this, mate."

The next three hours were an endless loop of tension and

drudgery. We mostly just sat together, waiting for things to happen. After about an hour, the funeral staff began setting up flower arrangements. Then policemen started setting up barricades around the funeral to keep out the media, or so Elijah told me. I knew it was a protective measure, but it felt strangely punitive—like they were encasing me inside with nowhere to escape. Part of me wanted to escape, to run into the bushlands and to finally be alone. To *breathe*.

Pam was dry-eyed right now, but I knew it was only a matter of time before she'd start sobbing again. Grief was confusing like this. One moment, everyone was fine, and the next Pam was hyperventilating and snapping at David and the kids. I wasn't really sure how to act, given that I didn't actually know Jack, or anyone who had died.

Eloise told me that wasn't true. She said that, in a strange way, *Angela* had died a few weeks ago, and what I was going through now was a complex kind of grief. Grief for a person that I thought I knew—and grief for someone I should've known, but never would. Because of this, I was more prone to something called CPTSD, or complex post-traumatic stress disorder.

Honestly, it all just sounded too confusing to me, like a puzzle I couldn't make any progress on. But maybe that's what grief is: a never-ending puzzle—one that only we hold the answers to solving.

One of the funeral staff brought out a large photo display of Jack. I stared into his calm, confident face, and I felt the puzzle inside me shifting and rearranging once more. For a brief, dark moment, I wondered if maybe there is no solving this puzzle—if my life would forever be missing pieces.

Chapter 3

If I had to guess, I'd say the cosmic truth is that humans are no better than animals. We just have thumbs now.

Seriously, all that evolution and for what? So someone could create a camera we could take to record ourselves being dumb? Being in pain?

I looked out the window and a flash dazzled my eyes. A sea of zoom lenses and flashes. One seemed to set off the other, and then suddenly they were all flashing at once—each of them just slightly different angles of the same thing. I wasn't doing anything particularly interesting other than standing there, trying to hold myself together. But they held up their cameras the way they did whenever one of those big athletes was about to take their turn at the Olympics. I was a gold medal contender; Pam was silver, anyone crying was bronze, and so on, and so on. That's the only way my brain could think to explain it. A month ago, I'd been a nobody, and now a photo of me was as precious as a photo of Michael Phelps…or whoever that guy was who was always winning things.

The windows were stained glass, so they had no hope of getting any good photographs or usable footage through one of those. The smart ones knew their only real hope was to wait for each opening of the church doors (which lasted roughly five seconds per arrival), and then launch their cameras blindly into the air.

Luckily, the police barricades meant that they were about twenty metres from the church on all sides, so their photos would probably be as ambiguous as the patterns on the windows. But that didn't stop them from *trying*.

There were no seats left inside anymore—just a rickety-looking stool parked up next to a man I was pretty sure was my uncle, so I assumed everyone had arrived. I had been at the front, but I'd needed to use the bathroom (not really, I'd just wanted to have five minutes of peace to myself), so now I was trying to find my way back. Elijah was talking to someone I didn't recognise, and he made a move to head over to me. I shook my head at him, telling him to stay. The priest was already beginning the service.

"Friends…family…" *Biological twin that was separated from your family at birth.*

I noticed a white rose amid a sea of black. I found that to be a beautiful sight, despite everything. Cameras flashed against the tinted windows as I weaved my way through the crowd, eliciting a few double takes when people saw my face.

That's him. That's Julian.

Oh, my word. He looks just like him.

How eerie.

How beautiful.

Like a ghost.

I finally reached the front. Pam didn't stir when she noticed me, just let out a heavy sigh and held my hand. I knew the sobbing would start again soon, probably with the priest's sermon.

Jack Gregory Rosemary was a celebrated scholar. He was at the top of all his classes at Sparks High School. Many of his peers and teachers would call him an overachiever. He was somebody of pure heart.

Someone else began crying behind me. It was all I could hear and see—crying and camera flashes, each punctuating the other like a dissonant song.

Jack's life was cherished by all those he knew. Whether it be the love from his parents, Pamela and David, the adoration from his long-term girlfriend, Chelsea, or the popularity afforded to him by his many friends at Sparks High School... This was not a boy who had any shortage of affection in his life.

I stared at the picture of Jack behind the priest. It was painted onto a canvas and surrounded by flowers, like the rose in that girl's hair. It was the only photo of him that didn't look like me. It didn't look like me because he was smiling *this smile*—this cool, half smile that I didn't even know our face was capable of making.

But sometimes, no matter how much we love someone, they still leave us. And to lose someone is terribly painful, but it does not diminish the love you felt for them. It does not diminish the love they felt for you.

I didn't really listen to the rest of the service. I'd started to think of Angela, and my life that wasn't my life, and a part of me thought I might cry. I imagined the roles being reversed—if Jack was the one attending my funeral. I'd had no girlfriends. No friends at all, really. Just a dog called Rusty, but he'd died of cancer at the ripe age of fourteen. He'd slept on my bed nearly every night of his life, and I still missed him like I'd lost a family member.

All in all, I'd lived a simple life. I hadn't made anyone fall in love with me. I hadn't pissed anyone off. And now here I was, starting over again at seventeen.

Only, as I gazed around the room of crying faces, I felt like

I wasn't starting over at all. I was continuing a life—somebody else's life, and a life that would never be just mine again. It was theirs now: every relative who didn't know how to talk to me. Every member of the public who would tune into the news over the next few weeks. Every nosy person in this congregation as they peered at me and pretended to listen to the service.

That's the real curse of tragedy. You don't just grieve for everything you've lost—family, home, privacy. You grieve for yourself, too.

The person you once were. The person you will never be again.

I didn't think anything could be more uncomfortable than attending Jack's funeral. But I was wrong. Attending his *wake* was even worse. Not just because those fifty-odd family members/strangers were now packed into a three-bedroom home and backyard in Chambers Flat, but because they were packed into *my* home. My home that I had never seen before, on a street that was also barricaded by police. Only local residents and people on the pre-approved funeral attendee list were allowed access. It's a good thing Pam and David lived in a semi-rural suburb in South Brisbane, otherwise we'd probably have more than a few prying neighbours trying to see over our fence right now.

"How long do we have the barricade for?" I asked Pam. She was on her way to the kitchen, always busying herself with something.

"We pulled some strings with the police. We'll have it for a few days, at least—until you're properly settled in here."

"And after that?" I asked her.

A sad look settled over her face. "We figure it out as we go."

Her words hung in the air. There was a lot to figure out, starting with what to do now that she had disappeared into the kitchen. I wrung my hands together, staring around the hallway, and I nearly choked on my own spit when I noticed the walls.

There were photos of 'me' everywhere, just with a slightly different haircut. Jack had kept his natural dark hair all throughout his life, whereas I'd been rocking a bleached crew cut for the majority of my childhood. It was only in my late teens that Angela finally gave in and let me grow out my natural hair. Looking back, I suppose it made sense why she'd had me looking like a mini army cadet.

She didn't want me to look like Jack.

I still did, though. If you really looked at these photographs. It was my face in all of them. My face in these photos with my arms around my half-siblings. My face in these photos of my fourth birthday party. My face in these photos of me playing cricket, even though I'd never picked up a bat in my life.

"We'll need to get you out on the field," someone said, clamping a hand on my shoulder. "See what those hands can do. You a batsman or a bowler?"

"Um, not sure," I muttered. I wished that Elijah was still here to save me from this conversation, but he was gradually giving me more and more space.

"That's all right," the man said, shaking me a little. "We've got time. We'll figure out what you're good at." He winked at me. "Grab you a beer?"

"Ray, he's seventeen," Pam said from the kitchen. She had her hands full with four different casserole dishes, her fringe falling over her eyes.

"Jack was sipping from my beer at ten years old," *Ray* said, winking at me again.

"Yes, well, Jules is not Jack."

The whole house seemed to go quiet at that moment. It was jarring, after what I'd just experienced at Jack's funeral. The brief journey from the church doors to Pam's beat-up red Ford— roughly thirteen steps—had been the most adrenaline-fuelled moment of my life. The cameras. The shouting.

Ray scowled at Pam, and then led me away from the kitchen. "I introduced myself earlier, but you've probably forgotten. I'm David's brother—your uncle, if you wanna get technical." He held out his hand. His skin was rough, and his eyes were so blue they were almost white.

"I remember," I told him.

"You look just like him," 'Uncle Ray' told me. He seemed insistent on that title, even though there was no blood relation between us whatsoever. "It's…uncanny. Eerie. Wow."

I just smiled awkwardly.

"No, really," he said. He was still shaking my hand, still staring at me.

I looked around the wake. There was a line of people beginning to queue behind Ray. I hoped their handshakes wouldn't be as strenuous.

"You're not as tall, though," Ray said. *Great.* "You've also got a few more freckles."

"Too much sun," I said. I tried to pull my hand away.

"That's a good thing though," Ray said. He leaned in close

to me, and I could already smell the beer and cigarettes on his breath. It wasn't even 2 p.m. "At least we know that woman wasn't keeping you locked up in a bunker somewhere doing God knows what."

He squeezed my hand tighter. I stared over his head and saw the white rose from earlier, floating gracefully above a sea of relatives. I still couldn't see the girl's face.

"You hear about those stories," Ray continued. "See it all the time at work, too. I'm a senior sergeant—not sure if Pammy told you."

I kept my gaze locked on that rose. I didn't know why. Maybe I just wanted something to look at other than Ray's worn-out skin.

"Anything sketchy you wanna talk about, you talk to me. But it seems like you got lucky, all things considered." Ray shifted his weight to one foot. He was in my line of sight again. "I don't mean to be *insensitive* or anything, but it seems like you were taken care of. Seems like you got fed. Plus, you can talk, so we know she taught you some things. Home-schooled, right? She couldn't have you going to a school and getting recognised. Bet you hardly had any friends, did ya?"

"Not really," I said. But that wasn't true. I'd had friends—just not as many as a normal kid, apparently, or any that were age appropriate. I'd been good friends with our neighbour and her ten-year-old son. There was my home-school teacher, Helena, and my seventy-year-old babysitter, Mrs Goddard. There was our paperman, and Angela's work friend who sometimes came around with chicken casserole. There was also a girl across the street who'd been my first kiss, and who'd shown me the internet. I had a phone for emergencies, but I wasn't allowed to have the internet. When I'd asked Angela why, she said that the internet and social media were some of the biggest dangers to young people. According to her, home schooling was the only way to guarantee that I'd grow up healthy, and not indoctrinated by a system that produces clones instead of free-thinking individuals.

I finally got my hand back from Ray. I rubbed it on my pants and tried to find that white rose again. It'd disappeared. *She'd* disappeared.

"Plus, you know, not to *generalise*," Ray said, "but it's better to be kidnapped by a woman instead of a man—statistically speaking."

"Yeah," I said, "exactly. Hey, Ray, sorry to cut this short—"

"Uncle Ray, please," he said. "You're just as much my nephew as Jackhammer was."

Not really, I thought. I just smiled at him. "I'll catch up with you later, okay?"

He pointed a finger at me. "I'll hold you to it. There are so many things I want to know, starting with whether you're a good shot! Jack and I used to go shooting all the time out in Blackwater—"

"Sounds great, yeah," I patted him on the back. Then I made a beeline for Pam, ignoring the line of relatives waiting to meet me. I almost heard their collective sigh as I passed them, their hushed whispers.

"Pam," I called out.

She turned around. So did the girl standing next to her.

"Jules," she said. "Have you met Jasmine?"

Jasmine stared up at me. She had these huge brown eyes— and now that I was up close, I realised she was White Rose Girl. The flower balanced delicately on her dark hair—long, shiny hair that was only a few shades darker than her skin.

"No," I said. I held out a hand, and it was almost comical—Jasmine's smooth skin in comparison to Ray's. Like sticking my hand in a jar of honey.

"Julian," she said. She looked to be around my age, and she was staring at me from beneath an overgrown fringe. She was staring at me like I was a ghost.

"Jules," I told her. It occurred to me then that I wasn't shaking her hand. I was just holding it. The thought made my stomach swell like a balloon.

"Jules," she corrected.

I dropped her hand immediately. It was too much all at once. Her skin, her eyes, her voice.

"I've got to check on the roast—" Pam said, but she was cut off by a blonde girl barrelling her way toward us. She broke down in tears before she reached me, almost crumbling to the concrete like a wet tissue.

"I can't believe it," she said, or at least I think she did. It was hard to hear her with her face tilted toward the ground. "You look just like him—"

Oh, no.

I recognised this girl from the photos in Jack's funeral montage. I recognised her wide, teary eyes…

Jack's long-term girlfriend.

Chapter 4

I'd read her statements in the papers. The girl-next-door turned grieving girlfriend. Straight-A student. Captain of the girls' volleyball team. She looked up at me with sparkling green eyes and made a noise that didn't sound entirely human.

"Chelsea," Pam said, "this is Jules."

I held out a hand toward her, and she launched herself into my arms.

"*Jules*," she breathed.

I stared at Jasmine over her shoulder. She was watching us with a strange expression, almost like she wanted to laugh. I lifted my arms to Chelsea's back and she hiccupped into my shoulder.

"Jules, Chelsea was Jack's girlfriend for two years," Pam said. "They were incredibly close."

I started to pull away, but Chelsea held me even tighter. This wasn't a hug. This was Chelsea gasping for air.

"I'm sorry," I told Chelsea.

"You sound like him, too." She finally pulled back, wincing. Her tears had melted into my shoulder, and it felt like someone had just doused my suit jacket in water. I wasn't just watching her grief anymore; I was *wearing* it.

I cleared my throat. "Uh…"

"Chelsea, do you mind helping me with dinner?" Pam asked.

Chelsea looked mortified by this idea, by the idea of leaving me. She was still clutching my suit jacket, and I realised I'd never been touched by so many different people in my life. It was oddly claustrophobic, like all these touches were a different piece of clothing that were being piled onto me. Each touch left me heavier than before, and Chelsea… Chelsea's touch was like a cement scarf around my neck.

"Chelsea," Pam implored. "There will be plenty of time for you and Jules to talk later, but for now we should let him get to know the other people in Jack's life. This is all a bit overwhelming for him."

Chelsea still seemed hesitant. Her gaze drifted from mine to Jasmine's, and I realised she wasn't just reluctant to leave me. She was reluctant to leave me with *Jasmine*.

Jasmine sighed beside me. She moved deeper into the hallway, and this seemed to placate Chelsea. She sniffed, gave me one last violating stare, and then took Pam's outstretched hand. The two of them headed inside the kitchen, and suddenly I was alone. Alone with walls that were completely foreign to me, and more questions than I could ever have answers to.

"She doesn't like me."

I flinched slightly. Jasmine was staring at the photographs on the wall, her face completely devoid of emotion.

"Why not?"

She shrugged. "You'll figure it out."

"Will I?"

"Maybe."

We stared at each other for a long time. I didn't know what to say at the best of times, but right now I was especially stumped.

"I like your rose," I told her.

She frowned at me, like she wasn't expecting me to say that. Maybe it was an odd thing to say. But why else did people wear things like that, unless they wanted people to comment?

"I, uh…noticed it, during the funeral. It was like this sea of black, and then a single white rose. I…" I waved my arm, almost spilling my Sprite. "It was cool."

"Cool?" Jasmine repeated.

Oh my god. What was I saying? I could never understand girls. Not even the girl from across the street. She said she'd only kissed me because she felt sorry for me—and back then, that seemed like a good enough reason to me.

Jasmine's gaze drifted back to the walls, to a large painting of a river. "It's kind of fugly, right?"

"What?"

"The house. It was built in the 1930s. I think most of the décor is still the same. Looks like it, anyway." She scrunched her nose up.

"It looks fine," I said. "Homely." The word I really wanted to use was *creepy.* In all honesty, the home looked like a dollhouse erected in the middle of a forest. It was an off-white, almost yellowish colour with a blue roof and a front patio with broken floorboards. On the inside, it looked like someone had vomited on the floor and then decided they liked the pattern.

Jasmine snorted. "No one can hear you, you know. You don't have to be so proper."

"I'm not being proper. I'm just not being rude." I turned to walk down the hallway, and then realised I was heading straight into what I assumed was a circle of Jack's high school friends. I stopped. There was a tall, dark-haired girl with a septum piercing giving me a strange look. I was certain no girl had ever made that face at me before.

"Watch out for that one," Jasmine said in my ear.

"Another girlfriend?"

"Not officially."

I swallowed, adjusting my tie. "How do you—?" A couple came around the corner, and we shuffled to let them pass. I ended up standing far too close to Jasmine again. She'd moved the rose from the back of her hair now to the front, so that it was tucked innocently behind her ear. "How do you know so much about Jack?"

She scrunched her nose, staring at another painting. "You know, I never understood why Pam didn't sue the hospital for big money after all that shit went down."

I glanced down the hallway, making sure no one overheard her. "She got some money, I heard." There had been a settlement between her and the hospital for an undisclosed amount, according to Elijah.

"Yeah, but nothing life-changing."

I took a step back from her, and my heart started to return to a normal rhythm. "What else do you know?"

"About your family?"

"About everything."

She seemed to think for a moment. "Well, if you value your personal space, you'll avoid Chelsea at all costs. If you value your sanity, you'll drop *Uncle Ray* like a drunken potato." She leaned in closer to me again. The rose in her hair looked fresh and clean. "His whole uncle act is total BS. He had nothing to do with Jack. They never went hunting or played cricket. He hardly even knew him. I'd say he's just playing it up for the other relatives, or to get some media attention. He probably thinks he can make some money out of you or something."

I swallowed. In that moment, I wondered just how many people in this room I could actually trust. How many of them were just playing up their relationship to Jack for fame? For money?

"His high school friends, Bradley Huxtable and Gavin Lewis…total scumbags. The Serbian girl with the septum piercing…that's Mindy. Be careful: I'm pretty sure she gave Jack herpes in tenth grade. She *will* want to give it to you, too."

I turned to her. "You go to Jack's school?"

"Yes. Is that surprising?"

"No," I said. "You just…you don't seem…"

"Educated?"

"No. You seem too mature to be a high school student."

She raised an eyebrow. "Oh, so I look old?"

"*No,*" I said. "Christ." *Why am I so bad at this?*

She stepped closer to me again, and my heart stepped with her. "What do I look like to you?" she asked.

We stared at each other. She had freckles—small dark ones in the corners of her eyes. They looked like tiny black stars.

"You just look like a girl," I said.

She tilted her head up, gaze still locked on mine. "Haven't talked to many of those, have you?"

I shook my head, and she just stared at me, almost like she couldn't comprehend what she was seeing.

"You seem pretty normal," she told me. "I mean, for someone who's had such an abnormal life… Raised by an imposter. Home-schooled, no friends, no internet and no social media, I'm assuming. And yet here you are, able to carry a conversation."

"My mother wasn't a psychopath," I whispered. I gazed around the room, making sure no one heard me. For some reason, it just seemed important that *Jasmine* heard me. "She took care of me. I didn't need social media. I had books."

"No TV either, I'm assuming?"

"What makes you say that?"

"Well, surely you would have seen all the crime shows on the kidnapping. They were on all the time for, like, ten years. There were a lot of different theories about what happened to you."

I pressed my lips together. "No," I admitted, and I felt a strange need to defend my upbringing, to defend Mu—Angela. "Angela said TV rots your brain, and I think she was right about that. Anyway, we ended up getting one when I was fifteen."

"So, you never watched any films? You've never seen any of the classics?"

I shrugged. "I watched a lot in the last year or two."

"Like?"

"I liked *The Shawshank Redemption. One Flew Over the Cuckoo's Nest. The Truman Show…*"

Jasmine was looking at me like I was the most interesting science experiment she'd ever seen. "What else did you do? Before TV?"

"I read books. I did home schooling. I played with the kids next door. I spent time with Angela, and we talked about the world. I swam. I read more books."

"Sounds like a simple life."

"It was."

"She really did you a favour, all things considered."

We stared at each other for a long moment, like neither of us could be sure she'd just said that. "Maybe." I shrugged again. "Can't miss what you never had, right?"

Jasmine nodded. She wasn't looking at me anymore, and her brows were furrowed like she was deep in thought. "I'll see you 'round, Julian."

She disappeared after that, and it was as if the house became stripped of all colour. I was left standing in a monochrome hallway wondering what the hell to do with my hands, and how to feel about everything that had happened to me.

She really did you a favour.

There was no longer any reprieve from Ray, just a lot of tears and misplaced guilt. People I'd never met before were coming up to me and apologising for all that I'd endured, even though I didn't realise I'd endured *anything* up until two weeks ago. They were offering me foods I didn't like, claiming that it had been Jack's favourite.

You must be hungry, they'd said, like I'd been starved for the last seventeen years. *This must all be so strange for you.*

I'd just shook my head at them. *I'm adjusting well. Really, I am.*

But I wasn't. I wasn't adjusting well and I couldn't tell a single soul. For some reason, I wanted Jasmine to come back here. I wanted her rawness. Maybe that was her true appeal: she was someone I could say anything to. A valve to release tension.

I imagined myself talking to her by the windowsill. *I'm not well. I don't want to live in this house. With these people... I don't feel like I exist anymore, or that I ever existed... I hate everyone, and I want to go home.*

Elijah had checked in a few times, but he'd disappeared

again to talk to Pam and David. I know they were discussing the logistics of me moving in here, and that was important, sure—but couldn't he see that I was drowning right now?

A man sat down next to me. I regarded him like a stranger—a small nod, a cursory smile, and then I realised he was probably my uncle or older cousin or something.

"Not a family member," he said. "Don't worry, you can relax."

I exhaled. "Sorry."

"Don't apologise, Jules. Can I call you Jules?"

"Sure."

"It's a pretty fucked-up situation," the man said, and my gaze snapped up at his words. He was drinking a whiskey and frowning out the window.

"Yeah…it is."

"I bet this is probably the last place you want to be. Surrounded by strangers… You probably want to be with the one person closest to you, who knows you better than anyone, and you can't. You're not allowed."

I stared at this man, feeling my eyes start to burn. He reminded me of Jasmine, just in less of an antagonising way.

"I'm Brett," the man said. He was wearing a suit and had a beard that made him look slightly older, but underneath all that he looked no older than his early forties.

"How'd you know Jack?"

"I was his footy coach."

I studied him briefly. Despite the scraggly orange beard, he seemed relatively put together. "Were you guys close?"

He smiled. "Yeah," he said. "I like to think we were."

"I'm sorry," I told him. "It seems like he meant a lot to people."

"He was a good kid. He had his troubles, but he was a good kid."

"Troubles?"

Brett took another sip of his drink. "Growing up without your real father is tough."

I thumbed the edge of my Sprite can.

"How are you really feeling, Jules? I'm not a reporter. I'm not a family member. You don't have to hold back."

The words were already there from my imaginary conversation with Jasmine. They were already bubbling at the surface. "I feel angry."

Brett watched me. "That's understandable."

"I don't want to offend anybody, but I really don't want to be here."

"That's understandable, too. These people are strangers to you."

I frowned at my hands. "They're my family."

"Not yet, they're not. Family isn't just blood, Jules. Family has to be earned."

I took a sip of my Sprite. It burned in the empty pit of my stomach. "Yeah?"

"It may happen in a few months. It may take longer. You may find that you have absolutely nothing in common with these people, and that's okay too. You didn't grow up as Pam's son. You grew up as your own person."

It was a relief to hear someone say those words. To know that someone didn't just expect me to love my family.

"And hey, if you're ever feeling alone, or like an imposter, come down to the field one day. You can sit in on practice. It might give you a little break. Jack even helped me coach some days. It was a good distraction for him."

I wanted to ask him how well he knew Jack. I wanted to know if Jack ever confided in him the way I was right now. But people were starting to crowd around us again, and I had the feeling I was about to get pulled away again by another distant relative.

I just smiled at him. "Thanks, Brett."

He clinked his whiskey glass against my Sprite can. "Take care of yourself, Jules."

I watched him disappear into the crowd, and soon enough, some old lady started tugging on my arm. She looked sweet enough, but I couldn't ignore the fact that the only two people I had any interest in talking to had disappeared, and I had no idea how to contact either of them.

The old woman cooed at me, pinching my cheeks. "I always knew you were still out there." She frowned, inspecting my face. "*Julian*. Pammy was always set on calling you Nicholas."

I smiled at her. "I heard."

She grinned, pinching my cheek again. "Such a pretty face. Both of you."

After about ten minutes of talking to my Great Grandma Marie (who I soon realised had dementia), I made an excuse to step away. I walked into the kitchen to grab another Sprite, and unwittingly put myself back in Ray's line of vision.

"Jules!" he said. He leaned over my shoulder, reeking of some kind of alcohol. "Did I see you talking to Coach Finlay before?

"Coach Finlay?" I frowned at him. "Oh, you mean Brett?"

"Stay clear of him, Jules."

I took a sip of my new Sprite. "Oh? Why's that?"

Ray swayed slightly on his feet. "He's always sticking his nose where it doesn't belong. Always fussing over Jack. You'd think he was trying to be his father or something." He knocked back the rest of his whiskey. "You don't want him doing the same shit with you. Messing with your head."

"I think my head's messed up enough."

"Don't talk like that." Ray levelled his gaze with me, his face hardening. "Don't let your mother hear you talking like that either. Not after everything." He pointed around the room. "I swear, if she has to go through that shit again, it'll kill her."

"I wasn't—"

"I'm serious, Jules. If you want to cry or scream or hate the world, you come to me. You don't go crying to Brett or Pammy about it. We'll have a drink. Get it out of your system."

I just stared at him as he poured himself another drink. I had no intention of even speaking to Ray again, much less crying to him. I also couldn't help but wonder what *shit* he had been referring to. Jack's death? Something before then?

He clapped my shoulder. "We'll get through this Jules, you and me."

I closed my eyes. I'd never wanted to hit somebody so bad in my life, but I just smiled, and I remembered Elijah's words.

You got this, mate.

Chapter 5

I'd started helping Pam clean up after the wake, but I must have done something—said something a certain way, or held her gaze a little too long, or washed a dish in a way that was just a little too reminiscent of Jack—because she'd gone up to her bedroom to cry and she hadn't come out since.

"Let her rest," Elijah told me. "It's nothing personal."

We were on the way to a motel in Browns Plains. That's where I was staying the night, as apparently the notion of staying with Pam and David my first night was too overwhelming. I'd argue that attending my dead twin's funeral and meeting over fifty family members had *also* been too overwhelming.

But these things had to be done, I suppose.

"Just one foot in front of the other," Elijah was telling me. The two of us were trudging up the stairs to our room. A part of me was relieved to be away from everything, but the other part knew that it was all waiting for me. That part niggled at the back of my brain, at the edges of my heart. *It's only going to get worse.*

There was moving in with the Rosemarys/Lemans. Then there was my first day at Sparks High—a normal high school full of normal kids who didn't grow up learning about maths at their kitchen table. Normal kids that had never been kidnapped, and who would most likely be freaked out by the fact that I looked identical to their dead classmate.

"One step at a time," Elijah told me. *Just one step at a time.*

I took a bath while he was having a cigarette, and all I could do was stare blankly at the white tiles until the bathwater ran cold. Angela had run me baths like this all the time. She'd put Radox bath salts in to help my muscles. But there weren't enough Radox bath salts in the world to fix whatever was happening inside of me now. There was no soothing the devastating weight of what was to come.

"I'm going to try my best to stay awake," Elijah said from outside the door, "but if I nod off…"

"It's okay," I told him.

By the time I came out of the bathroom, Elijah was indeed asleep. He was a lump of sweat and body hair atop the motel sheets, and he was snoring almost as loudly as the television set by his feet. There was some kind of talking horse on TV—an animation.

I sat on my bed as the theme song started to play.

Back in the '90s, I was in a very famous teeeeeevee show. Ah! I'm BoJack the horse—BoJack! BoJack the horse, don't act like youuuuuuuu don't know.

Maybe it was the numbness, or the fact that TV programs—particularly animations—were still such a novelty to me, but I found myself completely hooked. I was oddly entranced watching this talking horse destroy his life. I laughed. And a little toward the end of one of the episodes, for whatever reason, I started to cry.

Elijah and I got to Pam and David's around eight the next morning. The police let us through the barricades, and the street was oddly quiet without the clamouring of a dozen reporters. It was like someone had turned the volume down on my life.

The house was also oddly quiet without fifty people mourning inside it.

I still had no idea where anything was. In all the hysteria, Pam had neglected to give me a house tour yesterday. I suppose I couldn't fault her for being preoccupied. This had all happened to her as miraculously as it had happened to me, and it wasn't like there was a manual for how to induct your estranged biological son into your life while you're still grieving another son.

As it turned out, her house only had three bedrooms. Tanner and James shared one room, and Pam and David shared another, so that meant that the third bedroom was mine. Jack's room.

"We thought about swapping the rooms around," Pam said. "Having you sleep in Tanner and James' room…"

"It's fine," I told her.

But it wasn't fine. There were echoes of him in every corner. The records on his bookshelf. The pictures of him and Chelsea on his nightstand. The corded phone shaped like a pair of red lips. According to the priest's sermon, he'd been a big fan of Full House. He'd even convinced Pam to name his sister Tanner—the surname of the characters in the show.

"I hope it won't be too strange for you…" Pam hovered by the door. Elijah was somewhere downstairs talking to David. I was just sitting on the edge of Jack's bed, but I still felt like I was doing something wrong—like I was disturbing something. A shrine, perhaps.

"Really. It's fine."

She sighed. "I just wish I had another room to give you."

I wanted to ask her, then, about her court case against the hospital that Jasmine had mentioned. I wanted to ask about why she took such a small settlement. She could have had a house with a dozen rooms. But it just didn't feel right to ask. It felt like asking a stranger these intimate questions, not my mother.

"It's fine," I told her again. "It's…good."

We stared at each other for a moment. I could only imagine what she was thinking, seeing me in this room. It was probably similar to what I was thinking *being* in this room. *This could have been my life. This* should *have been my life.*

"I should check on the kids," she said.

"Okay."

"Let me know if you need anything. What's ours is yours now."

I nodded. Pam closed the door and I lay back on the bed. I closed my eyes, and for a brief, shining moment, I couldn't see my surroundings. I couldn't see Jack.

I could hear him, though. In my head. I could hear him telling me to get the hell out of his bed, to get the hell out of his house. This was his life, not mine. Those people had been *his* family. Chelsea has been *his* ex-girlfriend. Brad, Gavin and Mindy had been *his* friends. Jasmine had been *his*…whatever.

A sharp ringing sound cut through the silence. I froze, my muscles tensing beneath Jack's sheets.

I stared at the novelty lip phone. Whoever was calling obviously wasn't looking for me. Nobody knew I lived here but Pam and the long list of distant relatives who attended the funeral yesterday. Was it one of them calling? More uncomfortable well-wishes?

I pulled the phone apart, pressing the top lip to my ear. "Hello?" I whispered.

There was a rush of air on the other end of the line.

"Hello?" I repeated. "Who is this?"

Silence. And then, "It's me."

"Who?"

"It's me, Jules. It's Chelsea."

My heart sank into my stomach. "Oh," I said.

"Aren't you happy to hear from me?"

"No," I said, grimacing. "Of course I am."

"Jack and I used to call every day," she told me.

"How nice."

"You sound just like him."

I swallowed. "So you've said."

"Do you think—?" she started, then stopped. I already knew where this was going.

"Chelsea, I don't think—"

"Just talk to me," she said. "Please. Just talk."

I rubbed my eyes. "What do you want me to talk about?"

"Anything," she said. "Ask me anything."

I stared at the ceiling. The seconds were torturously long. "How do you get through the day?" I asked her.

"It hurts a lot."

"I know," I said.

"Jack used to write a lot. Did you know that?"

"No, I didn't."

"This one time, when my cat died, he wrote me this note. It said, *Someday, sometime, I will meet a version of myself that's no longer in pain, and together we shall leave this rotting shell behind.*"

"That's really nice." I looked out the window. It had started to rain lightly, and Chelsea's breath was soft in my ear. "What else did he like to do?"

"He read a lot of books. His favourite was *The Count of Monte Cristo*."

"I've been meaning to read that one."

"It's a redemption story. I think he thought about that a lot. Redemption… The idea of disappearing for a while and then coming back when he was stronger and wiser. Getting revenge."

"Revenge on who?"

"I'm not sure. He was angry, though. I know that."

The rain crackled against the tin roof of the house. I took a deep breath, closing my eyes.

"You have the same initials now," she told me. "J.R."

I hummed. "I don't know if I'm taking that last name."

"The media seems to think you're a Rosemary. They've started calling you *Rosemary Boy* since they can't print your real name."

"I don't really feel like a Rosemary," I told her. "Elijah and Pam have been discussing whether or not to keep Angela's last name."

"What do you feel like?" she asked me.

I thought about it for a moment. "Like an alien."

"If it makes you feel any better, I think a lot of people feel like that sometimes."

"They do?"

"Everyone's questioning who they're meant to be. I question it every second."

"You know your name though. I think it would be all right—I mean, I think it would be okay, at least—if I just knew my name.

If I didn't have to think about it."

"You'll get used to it," she told me.

"To what? Being a Rosemary?"

"It's just a name, Jules. People change them all the time."

"Well, apparently my birth certificate isn't even real. The one that says Julian Edwards was forged. My real birth certificate says Nicholas Rosemary, Twin 1."

"I like the name Twin 1."

"Even my birthday was a lie. Angela always told me it was the 4th of May, 1999. The fourth of the fifth. Turns out it's the 5th of April, 1999. The fifth of the fourth. I'm an Aries."

"You feel like an Aries."

"I don't even know what that means."

"You're strong."

I hummed again. Her voice was so calming, I was almost drifting to sleep. "I don't want to change my name. I am who I was. Or who I was told I was. Julian Edwards…"

"So, go back to that," she said. "Be an Edwards."

"But I'm not that either. Not anymore…"

"No last name, then. You can just be Jules."

"Jules," I said.

"Jules. Screw the rest. Edwards, Rosemary, Smith, it doesn't matter. You don't need anything else."

"You think the government will be cool with that?

"If Prince did it, so can you."

"Who's Prince?"

"The musician who changed his name to a symbol."

A smile broke out on my lips. It was unexpected, to say the least. "Thanks for calling, Chelsea."

"Any time, *Jules*. I'll see you tomorrow, right?"

"Tomorrow?"

"Yeah, it's Monday tomorrow. Your first day at Sparks."

My eyes flew open. "Oh, right," I said. "School."

Fucking fuck.

There was a knock at the door. "Chelsea, I gotta go—"

"Okay," she told me. I could physically feel the pause on her end, could feel all the words she was holding back. *I love you. I miss you.* All the words she wanted to tell Jack. "Talk soon," she whispered.

I hung up the phone, slamming the two lips together with more force than necessary. I stared at the door, rubbing my eyes. "Yeah?"

"Jules, it's Elijah."

"Come in."

He walked inside with a solemn look on his face. Then he shut the door behind him, which could only mean that this was bad news. (Lately, it was all bad news.)

"How are you, Jules?"

"I'm okay." I wish people would have stopped asking me that. I was running out of words. *Fine. Okay. All right.* Usually, it was just Angela asking me that after a long day. Now it was every adult in my immediate vicinity.

"Between the wake and the funeral, I know it was a lot to take in. I really don't want to add more stress onto you."

I nodded, staring at a brown mark on Jack's wall. "What happened?"

There was a long pause. Where Chelsea's breathing had been dainty footsteps, Elijah's was leaden stomps. "Angela's been charged. They were waiting for your DNA test to come back to make it official."

The words knocked me up and down. My eyes blurred, and my chest constricted, and I couldn't breathe, *couldn't think—*

"Jules, did you hear me?"

I bit my lip. "Yeah, I heard you. I just, I didn't think… I knew it was happening after the funeral, but not this soon. I—"

"They were eager to get it done. Especially after what's happened to Jack."

I nodded again. I blinked the tears out of my eyes, and I kept staring at that spot on the wall. "Is she… I mean, is she…?" *Is she going to jail?*

"She confessed, Jules. She will plead guilty in court and be sentenced, but that won't happen for a while. But she'll still be in jail while she's waiting for her court date. Legal processes take a while."

I kept nodding. It felt like someone had stepped into my body and kicked all of my internal organs. I held a hand over my mouth, trying to keep it all contained, trying not to be sick.

"The good news is that you won't need to be involved. The prosecution will use an agreed statement of facts, and Angela will be sentenced. You won't have to watch it all unfold. She was very adamant about you not being brought into the courtroom."

"What…what's she been charged with?" I asked him.

"Kidnapping, for a start. She's also been charged with multiple counts of fraud and violating the Child Protection Act. They may go easier on her, since she turned herself in. We just don't know."

I wiped a hand over my face. I kept nodding silently to myself, trying not to cry. "Can I… When can I visit her?"

Elijah sighed. "Not right now, Jules. Not until you're a legal adult at eighteen. She's being held in Melaleuca Women's Prison in Perth, and it looks like she'll remain there."

"For how long?"

"We don't know yet. But…it's looking like a maximum sentence of fourteen years."

I gritted my teeth together. "Okay," I whispered.

"Jules," Elijah said.

I couldn't speak. If I spoke now, I knew it would all come out. Everything—all my questions, all my anguish.

"I want you to be careful tomorrow. At least, don't check the news. There may be some stories written about you, even though we have that gag order and they can't name you or show your picture yet. They'll probably do everything else they can until then. We've done our best, but with the media circus that's surrounded you and Jack… There's just no way we'll be able to keep this contained."

I ran a hand through my hair. Every corner of my heart was on fire. "Yeah, no, I get it."

"I'm only a call away, Jules. We've got our scheduled appointments, but I want you to know that you can reach out to me whenever. Day or night."

It sounded nice, in theory. To believe that Elijah would coddle me for as long as I needed, and that he would sacrifice his own life just to reconcile mine. But I knew that it wasn't true. I was alone in this. Completely alone.

"Thanks, Elijah."

"You've got this, mate. I haven't known you for long, but I know you're stronger than you think."

I blinked my vision back into focus. Each breath felt like a train squeezing through my chest. I wanted to throw up but I hadn't eaten anything today—despite Elijah and Pam trying to force-feed me food from yesterday.

Elijah stayed with me for a while, and then eventually he had to go. I told him I was fine. *Fine. Okay. All right.*

Chapter 6

I woke to the sound of a screaming child. For a moment, I thought I had fallen asleep with a movie on. But there was nothing playing. There wasn't even a TV in this room.

As it turned out, the screaming was coming from a real-life child—my little half-sister, Tanner. She was screaming because James was using her favourite orange plate for breakfast. I'd floated down the stairs at about 6 a.m. and stumbled upon the scene: Tanner (red-faced); eggs strewn over the table; superhero toy dunked in a glass of juice.

Pam smiled at me, tired circles under her eyes. "Welcome to breakfast at our house," she said. "Help yourself to some juice. I think one of the glasses doesn't have anything floating in it. Tanner says they're baths for her toys."

"*My* toys," James said. "She keeps stealing them!"

"You two share your toys," Pam said. "Just like you share that plate, otherwise you can go without. Tanner can have everything until you learn some manners."

James huffed, crossing his pale little arms. "Tanner always gets everything."

Pam looked me up and down, and her body froze. "Uniform looks good," she muttered, turning to face the kitchen. "I was going to order a new one for you once I knew your sizes, but that looks like it fits well. I was worried, with Jack being a little taller…"

"Uh, yeah," I said, glancing down at my grey button up and shorts—*Jack's* grey button up and shorts. Neither of us commented on just how morbid it was that I was wearing his uniform to school. That I was sleeping in his bed, wearing his face. When I woke up this morning, I'd put on this uniform and simply stared at myself in the mirror. For a moment—a strange, inexplicable moment, I'd found myself looking directly into Jack's eyes. I'd never felt more like a carbon copy of someone, even though his shorts were slightly too long, and the sleeves were down to my elbows.

Pam just sniffed, like she was trying hard not to cry. "Breakfast?"

"Uh, no, thanks," I said. "I should get to school."

"Do you want a ride? I know Elijah said he'd take you, but I'm happy to do it. I just need to dress the kids—"

"That's okay. I'll be fine with Elijah."

Finally, Pam turned around. Her eyes were red-rimmed, and she was avoiding my general direction. "I get it. First day at a new school, don't want to be dropped off by your…"

We glanced at each other. The word 'mother' seemed to hang in the air, heavy and unspoken. She cleared her throat. "Need some money for lunch?"

I didn't. Not really. But she was looking at me with this look in her eyes, this ache. I nodded my head. "Sure. Thanks."

She walked over to her purse and grabbed a twenty out of her wallet. When she gave it to me, she curled her fingers around my hand. "Have a good day," she said softly.

"Thanks, Pam."

The word shouldn't have sounded like an insult—it was her name, after all. But anything other than the word 'Mum' felt undeniably cruel. I picked up my faded green backpack and grabbed a croissant from the table. I didn't want it, but it eased the look on Pam's face.

"Bye, Jules!" Tanner called out.

"Bye," I said, and I smiled at her. *I have a half-sister.*

It was a strange picture: this table full of mess and life and colour. Breakfast at Angela's house had never been like this. She'd home-schooled me herself until age nine, and then a lady named Helena had taken over. As far as the police were aware, Helena had no knowledge of my identity, nor did the few trusted adults that Angela had allowed into my life. My mornings in Fremantle were slow, uneventful: just Helena and I banging out mathematics over a bowl of soggy cereal.

As I sat in Elijah's car, I stared out the window and contemplated this new life: people in suits crossing the road, phones to their ears, cups of coffee spilling down their hands; car horns blaring like we were driving through a parade instead of morning traffic; the pain that had made a home in my body, with no answer as to how long it would remain.

Logically, I knew that pain never lasted, but I'd also never lost the things I'd just lost. How do you promise yourself pain won't last when it's one you've never felt before? As I stared at my reflection in the window—a reflection that was no longer just mine, I felt like perhaps this pain would last. At least a small part of it, forever.

Elijah pulled onto Sparks Road, and dread settled in my chest. Sparks High was a public school nestled in the middle of a suburb called Marsden. It was a lump of concrete, not a school, and there were news reporters crawling over the car park like ants.

"Shit," Elijah muttered. "Keep your head down. They may not see you."

We slowly edged forwards. We'd almost made it into a parking space near the school gates when I heard muffled voices through the car window, almost like they were talking underwater.

"It's him!"

"Go, go!"

It was peak hour in the school drop-off zone, but all the reporters still made a beeline for Elijah's car. It was like they were impervious to being run over, like they'd lie under a wheel and *die* for this meagre headline. *Rosemary Boy Goes to School*!

"They'll only be trying to get a statement from me," Elijah said, like he was trying to reassure me. He turned the engine off, but I noticed his hands shaking. "Just ignore them. They can't get to us once we're inside the school gates. Just take a deep breath, and we'll get you in there."

I took a deep breath. *In. Out.*

I climbed out of the car, tears welling in my eyes.

The questions came thick and fast from all directions.

"Are you a relative?" Elijah was asked.

"Sir! Can we get a quick comment for the Sunday paper?"

"Angela Edwards confessed this morning. Does Rosemary Boy know about that?"

"Do you think she should receive the maximum sentence? Fourteen years?"

My stomach churned.

"No comment," was all that Elijah said.

I kept my gaze locked on the road as we walked. I was trying so hard not to look up that I hardly had time to take in my surroundings. Right now, I didn't feel like a teenager having his first day at a real school. I felt like a freak who had just murdered his wife and children. I held a hand over my face.

Finally, we reached the oasis of the school gates. We had probably only walked thirty metres, but it felt like an eternity. We took a couple of minutes to gather ourselves.

"All of this media stuff will die down soon," Elijah reassured me. "We just have to take it one day at a time."

One day at a time. Right.

He put a hand on my shoulder. "Let's get you settled into your first class. English, with Ms Morè."

Turns out there was a mandatory assembly before my first class. An assembly with the entire school cohort that I couldn't avoid, despite my pleas to Elijah. Granted, he did allow us to stand at the back of the horde of students, and I was able to hide behind his broad shoulders once the principal began talking about Jack's death. He went through it all: the entire, fucked-up situation, as if I hadn't been replaying it in my head every second of the last few weeks. As if every student in this auditorium hadn't read the same story a dozen times from every news and media outlet in the country. He emphasised the dangers of being on the roads, and how crucial it is for new drivers to be extra cautious. He also explained that Elijah would be on hand in the school office for anyone requiring any extra support over the next week—that he was an experienced social worker who helps adolescents and young adults during times of loss or other significant change. The words *Jules' babysitter* were thankfully omitted.

After that, Elijah walked me to class and I swear I ended up sitting at Jack's desk. I had to be. It was the only empty desk in the classroom, and it was right next to Chelsea's. It also had J.R carved into the edge, and the words 'Tender age in bloom' written in Sharpie.

I'd been the first person in the classroom. Elijah had stayed with me for about an hour, and he'd filled me in on the basics of conventional schooling. Most things I had already gathered from talking to my neighbours, but there were a few surprises. Mainly, there were going to be over thirty-five students all crammed into the one room. One teacher for all of us. How the hell was one teacher supposed to command an entire classroom? Some days, Helena even had trouble commanding *me*.

Soon, students started funnelling into the room. They tried to act normal; at least I think they did. They tried to keep their eyes on their books and not on the reincarnation of their dead classmate. Honestly, I couldn't really blame them for staring. I was a ghost, after all. But I just wished I was more interesting… More attractive… More *something*—something to warrant all the attention I was getting.

This small, sick part of me couldn't stop worrying that they were *disappointed.*

"I'll leave you to it," Elijah told me, typing something into his phone. "Ms Morè was supposed to be here early to talk to you, but she's running late. She's going to talk to you after class instead."

"Wait—" I told him. Dread was curdling in my stomach, and a bunch of students were listening to me. I swallowed, feeling my face burn.

"It's okay, Jules. If you're overwhelmed, just excuse yourself and go outside for a few minutes. I can also stay, if you'd prefer."

I glanced around the room. An entire room of strangers—people my age—who were sitting by themselves. They didn't need an emotional support person just to get through a day of class. "It's okay," I told him. "You can go."

"Are you sure?"

I nodded, and the pressure in my chest only worsened.

"Okay. I'll be working from the school staff room, so I'll be on hand if you need me at all throughout the day." He clapped my shoulder. "Remember: you got this, mate."

I watched Elijah walk away just as Jasmine entered the classroom. She looked from him, to me, and I quickly glanced down at my desk. Jack's desk.

When the teacher finally entered, I expected her to draw more focus onto me. But she didn't. She just started the class like it was any other day, like Jack wasn't dead. Like I wasn't an imposter sitting in his seat. She was an Indian woman with ochre-coloured hair. Pretty. She turned around and wrote her name on the board, presumably for me. *Ms Morè*.

"I'm going to go easy on you guys today," Ms Morè said. "It's the first day back. You're all tired. You'd all rather be somewhere else."

"*I* wouldn't want to be anywhere else," said a boy with a dark afro. He had a slight British accent and wore his tie loosely around his neck. I recognised him—he was the guy standing with Gavin and Mindy at the funeral. "You're our favourite teacher, Tarini."

Ms Morè smiled. "I appreciate that, Bradley. It's Ms Morè, by the way."

"My apologies, Ms Morè." He smiled at her with the whitest teeth I'd ever seen. "It's Hux, by the way."

That Gavin guy snickered. I heard Jasmine sigh behind me.

"Your apology is accepted, Bradley." Ms Morè locked eyes with me, and a kind expression settled on her face. She looked like Jasmine would if she'd grow up to wear blazers and smile sometimes.

"You're all going to be writing an essay about your summer holidays. I trust that you can each come up with at least one interesting thing that happened to you over the last couple of months."

Gavin snickered again. "Jasmine might struggle coming up with something."

My stomach soured. Both Gavin and Hux looked like overgrown toddlers giggling at their desks.

"You should write about the time you pissed yourself at Gavin's party," Jasmine muttered. "Oh, wait, that was last holidays."

A few of the nearby students laughed. Some of them gasped. Ms Morè just turned around to write on the whiteboard, seemingly oblivious.

Hux's smile disappeared. "Simmer down, Jas." He swallowed, tapping his fingers on his desk. "That's not what happened."

"My mistake. I must have heard the story wrong eight times."

"Yeah, you must have. Don't worry, though. It's hard to know what happens at parties when you never get invited to any."

Gavin barked out a laugh. He covered his mouth.

"It's not like they're shrouded in secrecy," Jasmine said. "Gavin's house is three houses down from mine. And you pissed yourself in the gutter."

"All the more embarrassing that you weren't invited." Hux raised his eyebrows at her. He had this look in his eyes, this sadistic gleam. For some reason, probably multiple reasons, I wanted to spear tackle him into his desk.

"All right, save the passion for your essays," Ms Morè said. When I looked up, she was glaring at Jasmine, not Hux. There seemed to be a strange connection between them, and I couldn't put my finger on it. "I know high school politics seems like a priority right now, but it won't be when you're all unemployed in your mid-twenties and lacking basic English skills."

Hux blew Jasmine a kiss, and the action made me strangely uncomfortable—annoyed, even. Everyone opened their notebooks, but I snuck a glance behind me at Jasmine. She was just sitting back in her chair, staring out the window.

"Jules," Chelsea whispered, snapping my attention back. She smiled at me. "What are you going to write about?"

"I don't know," I said. For whatever reason, I decided to crack a joke: "I guess life's been pretty dull lately."

She looked like she didn't know whether it was a joke or not. She grimaced, tilting her head. "Did you see any movies?"

Ms Morè shushed us both, and Chelsea bowed her head. I guess you weren't allowed to talk to other students during class.

I stared at my blank notebook. I thought about being smart, about being that messed up kid who takes his pain and shoves it in someone else's face. *Holiday break... Holiday break was interesting. Holiday break was the summer I died.*

Instead, I crapped out something about how I'd gone to an aquarium for the first time. I had gone, actually—Angela had taken me. I'd seen a dugong and thought it was the most remarkable thing I'd ever seen.

The bell rang before I could finish. I was going to linger and wait for Jasmine, but she shot out of the room before the bell had even stopped ringing.

"Jules?"

I looked up. Ms Morè was staring at me.

"Uh, yes?"

"Could you hang back a second? I just have some orientation things I need to run through with you."

Chelsea touched my shoulder. "I'll catch up with you later."

I watched her walk out of the classroom, the last of the herd. Soon it was just Ms Morè and me.

"Jules," she said, clutching the edges of her desk. "How are you doing?"

I nodded. "Fine."

She pursed her lips together. "Listen…" she said, "I know Gavin and Bradley were close with Jack, but it doesn't mean that you have to be."

I frowned. "Is that advice?"

"Let's call it a gentle reminder."

"Got it," I said. There was a lull, and I started packing my books into my backpack.

"There's another thing," she said.

I looked at her. "More orientation things?"

She smiled at me. "I imagine things must be…overwhelming. If you ever want to get away from all of that, and earn a little extra money, there's a job for you."

I frowned at her. "Here?"

"No, no, definitely not. It's at Beacon Heights Nursing Home.

Just some general administration work. Jack used to work nights there, and they're looking for someone."

"I don't know why they'd want me," I told her. "I don't…I don't have any experience. I've never had a job in my life."

"Neither had Jack." Ms Morè walked closer to me, picking up one of my textbooks that had fallen on the floor. "I understand if it's morbid."

"I just don't think I'd be very good at it," I said. "Being around more people…"

"Well, in my experience, being around elderly people is a lot different to being around your peers. It's a bit more…peaceful." She shrugged. "Perhaps it might be useful for you."

"They'll probably just think I'm strange," I told her. "Everyone seems to."

We were quiet for a moment. I don't know why I'd told her that—not that it wasn't obvious. There was something about her that made her easy to talk to. There was a calmness about her. Her eyes gleamed even when she wasn't smiling.

"I can imagine it feels that way." She handed me my open notebook. My essay was right there on the page. My story about the aquarium.

"Thank you," I said, stuffing it in my backpack.

"You're welcome. And by all means, say no. But the manager of Beacon is a close friend of mine, and I think she'd really like you."

I stared at her. Her eyes were the exact same as Jasmine's. Brown with a little bit of green. She sounded like her, too. Had the same warm, lilting voice.

"She might be disappointed," I said. "I don't think Jack and I were very similar."

"Of course not. Twins are still different people."

I zipped up my backpack. I was running out of things to do with my hands, running out of places to look other than Ms Morè and her familiar eyes.

"But I do know it was very good for Jack. It was quiet, and the residents really loved him. He loved them, too."

"Everybody loved Jack."

Ms Morè tilted her head, like she wanted to disagree with me. She just frowned slightly, and the move was so reminiscent of Jasmine that I could hardly believe it.

"Are you Jasmine's mother?" I asked her. Actually, I didn't ask. I blurted out the words like an ill-mannered child.

"I am," she said.

I wanted to ask her more about Jasmine, but I didn't want to seem weird. I was already the weird guy. The kidnapping victim. The living half of two people.

"I have to get ready for my next class," Ms Morè said. "But let me know if you'd like me to pass your name onto Barbara. She's the manager of Beacon."

"Sure," I said. I slung my bag over my shoulder.

"Jasmine works part-time there after school. It might be a good chance for the two of you to bond. She could use some more friends."

I stopped halfway to the door, turning to look at Ms Morè. "Jasmine works at Beacon? She worked with Jack?"

"For a year or so, yes."

A million different images rushed through my brain. Jack and Jasmine. Jasmine and Jack. "Oh," I said.

"Yes, well, let me know—"

"I'll do it."

Ms Morè's eyes lit up. "You will?"

"Yeah, sure. I'll be a receptionist…admin…person…" I waved a hand. "How hard can it be?"

She grinned. "I'll call Barbara today. She'll get in touch with Pam and you can go from there."

"Great," I said. "Later, Ms Morè."

Ms Morè patted my shoulder gently. She was so kind. So soft and gentle and *not* Jasmine. But still so Jasmine. It was like talking to her from the future.

"Oh, and Jules? Please don't tell Jasmine that I arranged this. She'd be mortified if she knew I was the one recruiting students for Beacon. Let her think it's just a happy coincidence."

"A happy coincidence," I said. "No problem."

Chapter 7

My first lunch break of the day was not in my kitchen, like it had been with home school. It was outside on a wooden bench, in front of a hundred or so different students all pretending not to stare at me.

It felt like I was eating my sausage roll on stage, like there was a constant spotlight trailing me on every spot I decided to sit or stand. There was also an audience of people watching everything I did—each squirt of sauce that missed my mouth, each stubborn swipe of my hair when the wind decided to ruin it, each time Elijah glanced at me from across the courtyard and offered a hopeful thumbs up.

"Oi—stop staring!" someone yelled. It was that Gavin guy. He had spiky black hair and he smiled at me like he knew me, like we were friends. "Bloody hell, Jules. You'd think Chris Hemsworth was in town."

"Nope, just me," I muttered.

He sat at the end of my table. There were now four of us sitting here, but he was the only one who had the nerve to talk to me. "You're the *Brisbane* Chris Hemsworth," he clarified.

"I don't know who that is," I told him. *Was that the Thor guy?*

He tossed his head back and laughed. "You're funny. That's a good thing, Jules. Jack was always too serious. He acted like he had the entire world's problems to deal with. What with all the media attention from you being gone. Kind of like what you're going through now." His eyes widened. "Shit, sorry. That's a bit insensitive, isn't it?"

I shook my head. "It's cool."

He shoved his hand in my direction. "I'm Gavin, by the way. Everyone calls me Gav. You met Hux and Mindy yet?"

"Uh, no. I haven't really met anyone."

He squinted at me. "Saw you talking to that Jasmine chick at the wake. Two words: Stay. Clear."

I nodded. The other people at the table were staring at us, and Gavin hissed at them to *fuck off*. They got up instantly.

"I'll give you the rundown," Gavin told me, moving to sit directly in front of me. "Mindy and Hux are good company. The rest of this place is shit. Yeah, Jasmine is cute and all, but she's bloody annoying. One of those girls that are prettier before you get to know 'em, you know?"

"Sure," I said, but I didn't really know what he was talking about. So far, I was learning that it was easier just to agree with Gavin. On everything.

"School's pretty shit, but it must be better than home schooling. It has to be. You must get a bit weird when you stay cooped up like that. No one to talk to. No *girls*."

I shrugged. Honestly, regular school seemed weird—like a corporation or something. A corporation for teenagers… Everywhere I looked, there was a soulless grey classroom, and another student wearing a soulless grey uniform—another one that couldn't stop staring at me. My schooling experience consisted of one student (me), but there were at least a hundred in this area alone. I even think some of them were taking pictures of me.

"Jesus," Gav said. He seemed to be smiling for someone's

photograph, and he spoke through his teeth: "I'm hot property sitting with you!"

"I don't think it's the kind of attention you think it is," I told him.

"Any publicity is good publicity, Julesy Boy."

I frowned at him. He was entirely too cheerful for someone who had just lost a good friend. I'd seen him shed a couple of tears at the wake, but now it was like he'd reverted back to his factory clown settings.

"Mindy will probably take a liking to you," Gav said. "She's pretty hot, and easy, if you know what I mean." He glanced over his shoulder, and I followed his gaze to where a group of people were standing near a basketball court. It was that girl from the wake that Jasmine said would give me herpes. She was staring at me, but it was different to the way everyone else was staring. Without warning, she held up her ring and middle finger and made a V against her tongue.

"Case in point," Gav said, taking a bite of an apple. "Honestly, you're lucky. *So* many girls had the hots for Jack. You should have seen all the crying going on when the news broke."

"Wasn't Jack dating Chelsea?"

He winked at me. "Yeah, Monday to Friday, if you know what I mean." He smirked, and then he must have seen someone walking over to us, because he hid his smirk with his apple. "Don't repeat that. Hey, Chelsea!"

"Hey, Gav. Jules..." Chelsea smiled at me.

"Well, I'll leave you guys to it," Gav said. He tilted his head at us. "I'm sure you have a lot to catch up on..."

I gritted my teeth. Gav disappeared and suddenly Chelsea

was hugging me, pressing her nose into my hair. I thought her touching me had just been a one-off at the wake—an unrestrained moment of passion. But she kept touching me like she'd done it a thousand times before.

"How are you?" she asked me.

"I'm good." I gently unlocked her arm from around my neck. *Great*, now people probably had pictures of her inhaling my hair.

She sat down next to me. "You look a bit tired. Did you sleep okay?"

"Uh…" I looked around, searching for an exit to this conversation. I stared over Chelsea's head at a group of students sitting at another table. They all looked the same: grey, dull heads…except for a singular white rose sitting gracefully in someone's hair.

"Jasmine!" I called out.

She turned sharply, brown eyes meeting mine. Her entire body bristled.

"Don't take it personally," Chelsea said, and I watched Jasmine turn back around. "She's like that with most people."

"She seems to be worse with me."

Chelsea pursed her lips together. It seemed like she wanted to say more, but she was too sweet to say how she really felt. Instead, she just said, "She was like that with Jack, too."

"Mean?"

"Standoffish."

I didn't know what that word meant. I just hummed.

"Hey, lunch is nearly over," she said. "Do you want to have our second lunch together? It's longer…"

"We have two lunches?"

She laughed, and then she must have realised I was being serious. "Yes, we do. Three classes and two lunch breaks. You want me to come find you next break?"

I stared at the sea of grey fish. "I guess, yeah."

"Great," Chelsea smiled. She seemed better today. Less... weepy. Then, without warning, she squeezed my hand. It was so quick I didn't have time to react—like when a mosquito lands on your arm and bites you before you can swat it. She instantly lifted her hand away, like the move had been reflexive more than anything. "I'll, um... I'll see you later, okay?"

I watched her walk away, her ponytail swaying like a blonde pendulum. It was one of the strangest moments of my life—being there, at a normal high school, holding hands with a girl who felt sort of like my girlfriend, feeling guilty that I didn't *want* her to be my girlfriend.

There was also the fact that I couldn't stop staring at someone else. Someone who clearly didn't like me very much. I felt like I was betraying Chelsea every time my gaze strayed to her table. Every time I searched for her perfect white rose in a sea of grey.

This time, when I looked back, the rose was gone.

I was alone. Again.

"Jules?"

It was an older guy's voice. At first, I thought it might have been Elijah, but then I turned around and realised it was that guy from the wake—*Brett*? It was hard to recognise him at first, but he was wearing a white polo shirt and a navy cap that said 'Coach Finlay'.

"Thought that was you," he said, almost like *he* didn't recognise *me*. It was doubtful, given that I had one of the most recognisable faces in the country. But I appreciated it anyway. I think he was trying to make me feel normal—as if he hadn't been staring at me just like every other person in the courtyard.

I got up from my table. "Coach Finlay," I said, shaking his hand.

"Call me Brett."

I nodded. "What are you doing here?" I asked him.

"I teach physical education here sometimes. They call me a supply teacher—I work a couple days a week throughout the year. It's a good gig. Some of the senior footy boys have got a lot of talent. There's a fair bit of potential here."

I wondered if Jack had the same potential. For a brief, dark moment, I wondered what happened to all that potential when people die—especially kids. Where does it all go?

"How are you doing, anyway?" He glanced down at my uniform. "This has all got to be a bit overwhelming. New high school and everything. Or just a high school in general."

"It's a bit weird," I said, and for some reason I felt tears pricking at my eyes. *Suck it up*, I told myself. *You're not at home. You can't go crying anymore.*

I'd cried, once, during one of Helena's home-schooling sessions. We'd had to put Rusty down the day before. All I could do was stare out the window at where he used to be. I cried into my sleeve and Helena just sat behind me and rubbed my back.

If I did that here, someone would probably film me. Kids like Hux and Gavin would probably make fun of me and then sell the footage once I turned eighteen.

"You okay?" Brett asked me.

I nodded. The prickling sensation was overwhelming, but I

had enough faith in myself to hold it together. I'd barely cried since leaving Fremantle, and there was no way I was going to cry here, at school with Coach Finlay of all people. *Call me Brett.*

"I can see that you're okay," Brett told me, and he really was a rotten liar. He gazed over my head, as if he was offering me a reprieve from his gaze. "But, you know, it's okay if you're not."

I stared at his moustache. I'd never been able to grow one at all, and I wondered whether Jack had. I wondered if thoughts about myself would ever stop encompassing him, if my mind would ever be just mine again. Sometimes my self-perception felt fractured, and other times, it was like he and I had merged into one amorphous being. *Jack Rosemary. Jules Rosemary. J.R.*

A bell rang, which apparently meant that lunch was over. First lunch, anyway. People began syphoning back into classrooms, somehow all knowing exactly where to go, exactly how to exist with each other. I watched them in a strange daze.

"Kids treating you okay?"

"No one really talks to me," I muttered. "A few people have come up to me, almost crying. But most of them just…stare."

"Well, you're a pretty remarkable young man, Jules."

"But I didn't do anything," I told him. "It all just…happened to me."

"Sure, you could look at it that way. Or, you could look at it in a way that's a little bit closer to the truth: that you've survived some incredibly tough days, situations that 99% of people on this Earth will never have to experience. Situations that I'm certain many other people wouldn't be handling as gracefully as you are."

"Am I only handling it that way 'cause I'm not normal?"

Because I'm a freak? Emotionally stunted?

"What's normal, Jules?"

"I don't know," I told him. "Everyone else…"

"Who? All those people who are staring at you?" Brett folded his arms. "You want to be like them?"

I shrugged. "I just want people to stop talking about me."

Brett seemed to consider this. It occurred to me that I was late for my next class, but I figured I had a free pass for…pretty much the rest of my time here. Finally, he said, "Do you know who those people are, Jules? The ones that nobody talks about?"

I shook my head.

"They're the ones that talk the most about other people."

I suppose that made sense. People who were busy with other things probably didn't have much time to consider the lives of strangers.

"Yeah, some people may be saying things about you," Brett said. "And some of those things might not be very nice, but you know what? They're talking about you because you're noteworthy, and the most noteworthy thing those people are ever gonna do is get attention for talking about people who are noteworthy. I know which one I'd rather be."

"I'm noteworthy for being kidnapped."

"No," he told me. "You're noteworthy for surviving."

Noteworthy for surviving. A few weeks ago, I was noteworthy for being the only seventeen-year-old kid on the street without a learner's permit. (Angela had kept making excuses, telling me there was no reason for me to have a licence seeing as I didn't go anywhere.) Now I was *noteworthy for surviving.*

Brett leaned in closer, and suddenly I didn't care that he was looking directly at me. He squeezed my shoulder and he said, "That's one hell of a thing to be."

For dinner that night, Pam made pumpkin soup from scratch. Angela would always just heat it up from the can. I noticed little things like this. From the moment I woke up to the moment I laid my head on Jack's lumpy pillows. All these little differences. The things that make up a family. The things that separate them.

"How was school?" Pam asked me.

It was a rare moment of quiet. Rain was falling gently on the windowsill and James and Tanner were watching cartoons in the other room. The kitchen was dimly lit by candles. Angela hated candles. She said they made her nose itch.

"Good," I said. I picked up a piece of garlic bread before the kids noticed it was there. "It was good."

"I got a call from your teacher this afternoon… Something about a job?"

"Oh," I said, taking a bite of bread. "Ms Morè?"

"You must have made quite the impression. Jack didn't get offered that job until well into grade ten."

"I think she probably feels sorry for me," I said.

Pam stopped stirring the soup for a moment. She looked at me over her shoulder, and then she looked away. "Yes, well, nevertheless, they want you to come in for a trial one Friday after school. I told them I'd discuss it with you and get back to them in the morning."

"Tell them I'll do it," I said. "I mean, that's cool. One Friday will be fine."

Pam chuckled. "I've got to say, I thought a seventeen-year-old boy would be a little less keen on hanging out with old people during his spare time. God knows Jack needed persuading." She started pouring the soup into bowls. "It wouldn't have anything to do with the fact that Ms Morè is Jasmine's mother, would it?"

I shoved another piece of garlic bread in my mouth. I could barely close my lips around it. "Huh?" I said.

She set a bowl down in front of me. "Jasmine. You were talking to her a lot at the wake."

"Oh, yeah, Jasmine. She's cool."

"She's a nice girl," Pam said. "Headstrong, clever." She grabbed a mug out of the pantry; for the first time, I noticed three bottles of vodka and a half-empty bottle of whiskey lined up behind the glasses. "You want a drink?"

"Of vodka?"

"Just a little nip," Pam said. "Jack and I used to have a little nightcap sometimes before bed."

I glanced at the clock. It was barely 6:30 p.m.

"I'm okay," I said. I'd never been offered alcohol before.

"Suit yourself." I watched her fill the mug to the top. She took a sip as she sat down next to me. "David left this morning," she told me. "He had to go away on an urgent business trip, but he'll be back at the end of next week."

"Oh," I said. "Cool."

"He's a little serious, David. You know those corporate types…" She trailed her finger around her mug, and I wondered whether David leaving her right now made her sad.

"What does he do?"

"He's in real estate."

I hummed. I assumed that meant he sold houses, but it felt silly to clarify.

"He got you something," she told me. She reached into a bright yellow bag on the table and pulled out a white rectangle. It was a new phone. An iPhone 7.

"David got me this?"

"Well, I did, but…" She shrugged. "It was David's idea. He thought it would be good to stay connected. I don't know if you've ever had a phone before…"

"Not one like this," I told her. My phone had been able to fold in half once I was finished making calls on it. I don't think you could fold this one in half. It was flat and shiny…and as thin as a pancake.

"You had a phone without internet, I assume."

I frowned. "I was able to call and text."

"You can do that on this one, too, and so much more. You can watch TV and movies. You can Google whatever you want…" She cleared her throat, tucking a piece of hair behind her ear.

"Thanks, Pam."

"You're welcome, Jules." There was a lengthy silence, and then Pam called into the lounge room. "Kids! Come get it."

Tanner and James came rushing into the kitchen. They clambered onto their chairs and shoved their spoons into their bowls.

"Careful," Pam said. "The soup's hot."

The soup *was* hot. And it was earthy and creamy, like it had been prepared by an experienced chef. But I still preferred Angela's.

It didn't make any sense. Angela's soup tasted like the inside of a can—like watery pumpkins and stale potatoes. But it also felt like Fremantle. It felt like our little brown house at the end of the street, like Angela sneaking in a meal with me before working at the hospital, like the two of us laughing about how bland the soup was. I always hated when she had to work night shifts as a cleaner. My babysitter up until the age of twelve had been a grandmotherly woman, and every meal she made somehow ended up tasting vaguely of onions.

Maybe I was just used to Angela's uninspired cooking. Or maybe some things were just better the way we remembered them, not the way they actually were.

Chapter 8

The next few weeks carried on mostly the same. But at least the media attention died down. We quickly worked out that not having adults with me was the best way to deter them. They could only hassle the adults in my new life with all their questions, not me.

I started riding my bike to places, including school, and Elijah cut back to seeing me every other day. Chelsea called me every night to listen to me breathe. Pam continued to cook gourmet meals that somehow tasted wrong, no matter what she put in them. People continued to stare at me, and Jasmine continued to ignore me.

Most people ignored me at school, actually. It was strange: I was a celebrity in the media but a social pariah in the classroom. Okay, it wasn't *that* bad. Most people were nicely awkward around me, seeming to smile forcibly whenever I caught their eyes. But that was as deep as any of the interactions ever got, almost like they were afraid to engage in conversation with me. After all, what do you say to someone who looks exactly like your classmate who just died? Someone who spent the last seventeen years of their life under a false identity?

The only people who actually had the guts to talk to me were Chelsea and Gavin, although I had serious reservations about Gav's intentions. All he'd done since I met him was tell me how close he and Jack had been, but I wondered if his definition of close was similar to Uncle Ray's. I wondered if maybe he was trying to get close to me for *other* reasons.

One day, after school, he offered me a joint while we were in the car park. There were no reporters around, but something still soured in my gut.

"What is that?"

He chuckled. "You're kidding, right? It's weed, Jules. You smoke it."

"Isn't it illegal?"

He shrugged. "Everybody does it."

I fumbled for an excuse. "I don't think I should be smoking before my job interview."

"Interview where?" he asked.

"Beacon Heights Nursing Home."

"Jesus," he said. "Forget Chris Hemsworth. You really are trying to be Jack."

"I'm not trying—"

"You're living in his home, taking his job, stealing his girlfriend—"

"I'm *not* stealing Chelsea," I said. I glanced over my shoulder, hoping no one had heard me. Of course, there were about three people intently listening to our conversation.

"That's not what she's saying. According to her, you two are one closed-mouth kiss away from a fully-fledged relationship." He stuck the joint in his mouth. It stuck to his bottom lip as he talked. "She's Christian, so don't expect anything more than that."

"I don't want anything more than that." Honestly, I didn't *really* know what more there was than that.

He grinned. "Oh, but you do want to kiss her! The truth always comes out, Julesy Boy."

I didn't know what was worse: Gav calling me *Julesy Boy* or that stubborn cowlick he always had. He always looked like he'd just showered in oil.

"Don't tell Chelsea you're working at Beacon," Gav told me.

I started unchaining my bike. "Oh, yeah? Why's that?"

"Because that feisty chick works there."

I looked at him. "Jasmine?"

"Yeah… They don't like each other."

"Why not?"

He shrugged. "Chelsea was jealous, probably. Jack worked there with Jasmine twice a week, and that was on top of seeing each other at school. That's a lot of time to spend with one person. Beacon probably has a *lot* of empty storage cupboards."

I stared past Gav's head. I tried to picture Jack and Jasmine in a storage cupboard together, tried to picture them touching. *Kissing.* It looked a lot like Jasmine kissing me.

"Jack never said anything, but surely something had to have been going on. There was too much tension between those two. And also, why else would he want to work at a retirement home?" He cackled. "I could think of nothing worse."

I got on my bike. Now I couldn't stop picturing Jasmine and I kissing in one of Beacon's storage cupboards. "It's a good way to earn money," I said.

"There are other ways," Gav told me, relighting his joint.

I frowned at him. "Other ways…"

He nodded. "You don't have to slave away in a fossil factory, or put up with little Miss Morè…"

"I really don't mind."

"Whatever. Give me a call when you realise Beacon sucks."

"Sure," I said, pulling on my helmet. Honestly, I wasn't really listening anymore. I was still thinking about Jasmine kissing Jack/me in a supply cupboard. Thinking about the way it would look, the way it would feel.

Bloody *Gav.*

An older woman with short red hair greeted me in the foyer of Beacon. Her name tag said Barb. She reminded me of a human version of Big Bird from Sesame Street, but this familiarity didn't do much to calm my nerves. My body was in fight or flight right now—like I was about to wrestle a bear instead of having a chat with a potential employer. She seemed completely harmless, but of course that didn't matter. My brain still associated her with a news reporter or doctor trying to psychoanalyse me.

…Or a bear.

"Wow," she said. Her green eyes started to well behind her glasses. "Julian. You just… You really…"

"I get that a lot."

"Remarkable," she whispered. She was shaking her head, clutching her clipboard to her chest. "It truly is remarkable. This whole story…"

I laughed awkwardly. "That's one word for it."

"And how lucky we are, that we get to have you here at Beacon. That the residents get to have you."

I looked past Barb, at the double glass doors that led into the aged care sector of the facility. The walls were a deep taupe colour, and there was an old man with a walker staring at me with his mouth open. I couldn't tell if he recognised me or if he was just staring at his own reflection.

I nodded at the man. "You sure it's not going to be confusing for them?"

"Oh, don't mind Bill. The man thinks he's still a cardiothoracic surgeon. He's probably wondering if you're his next patient." Barb smiled a sad kind of smile. "Most of the residents here suffer from mild to moderate cases of dementia. Some cases are more severe, like Bill, but they don't pose a risk to themselves or to staff. Those that are high risk are in a separate ward downstairs."

"High risk?"

"They're the ones that will mistake you for an old boyfriend, try to kiss you or give you a good whack. They may think you're their son, or their father, or God knows what." Barb shook her head. "Jack got his fair share of smooches from Ms Cameron. Kept thinking he was her husband."

"Right," I said, biting my lip.

"You'll mostly be up here, so don't get scared away. The residents here on Level Four are just beautiful. They may just like to chat to you from time to time, or need to be reminded of where they are and what they're doing here." She gestured for me to follow her, and we headed deeper inside the facility. Bill's vacant gaze didn't leave me the entire time we were walking.

"Do they know…? I mean, are they aware that I'm…?"

"Oh, yes, we informed them of Jack's passing. We had to. Many of the residents became quite attached to Jack during his time here. I think a part of him really loved them, too."

"Jack!" someone said, and I flinched.

There was an old woman with short grey hair hurrying over to me. She was wearing a long pink skirt and a light brown sweater, and she looked a little bit like my my babysitter from years ago.

"*Pip,*" Barb said. "We've talked about this. Jack has passed on. This is Jack's brother, Julian."

"Oh, I could have been sure it was you!" Pip said. She put a hand on my shoulder and squeezed tightly. "Sorry, yes, I remember now. Julian… How are you, dear?"

"I'm just taking Julian for an interview now, Pip. Why don't you go watch a movie with Ally and Peter?"

"Oh, lovely," Pip said. "A movie sounds wonderful." She squeezed my arm again and smiled up at me. She had thick black glasses that made her eyes seem bigger than they were. "You're welcome to join us, Julian."

"Oh, that's okay. I'm a little busy right now." I stared down at her hand on my arm. "Um, but maybe after my interview is over."

"Perfect," she said. "I'll let the others know."

I watched her walk away, my chest aching as she joined a circle of other residents in front of a large flat screen TV. A person in a bright blue uniform was helping people sit down—a person with a white rose in her hair. The ache in my chest softened into light.

"You're a natural," Barb said. "A lot of the job is just comforting them, being an ear to talk to. A lot of what they say won't make sense, but just pretend it does for their sake. Pip is one of our more moderate cases."

"She's lovely…" I muttered. I was staring at Jasmine as I said it. She had walked over to Pip and was giving her a long hug.

"That's one of our trainees, Jasmine. The residents just adore her."

I nodded. "She goes to my school."

"Oh, of course she does! Well, I'll skip the introduction then. You two have probably already gotten to know each other quite well."

Not at all, I thought.

Bill muttered something to Jasmine, and she threw her head back in laughter. He had a smile on his face now, too—the same old man that had just been staring at me with drool running down his chin.

"She really livens up the place," Barb said.

I kept staring at Jasmine. I felt like Bill staring through the glass doors, like my mouth might be hanging open a little. I didn't know what to do with what I was seeing. Her gentle hands, the sparkle in her eyes, the little dip in her cheek from when she smiled at Pip...

But then she looked at me. Her gaze trailed from me, to Barb, to the clipboard in her hands that she probably used for job interviews, and the sparkle in her eyes was suddenly smothered by darkness.

"You have *got* to be kidding me," she said.

Chapter 9

I left Beacon with a strong suspicion that I had the job, and an even stronger suspicion that Jasmine wanted to fight me. She was following me into the underground car park, arms flailing at her sides.

"What is your problem?" she asked me.

I turned to face her. "What do you mean?"

"Who got you the interview, huh? How did you even know about this place?"

I stared at the building. "Pam told me about it."

"Bullshit," Jasmine said. "Look, I don't know what you're playing at—"

"Neither do I."

"—But you better cut it out. I'm not going to be a part of this sick game of yours."

I stared at her. Her hair was pulled back into a bun tonight. The ends of her fringe brushed against her eyelashes. "What part of this is sick to you?" I asked.

"I don't know…maybe the fact that Jack used to work here. And now here *you* are." She clenched her jaw. "You don't think it's weird enough seeing you at school every day?"

"Oh, I'm sorry. Is this weird for you?"

"Yes—"

"Well, shit, Jasmine, how do you think it feels for me?"

She narrowed her eyes. "No one is forcing you to take a job here."

"I need to earn money. I can't just depend on Pam for the rest of my life."

"Well, get a different job," she said. "This one's mine."

"Oh, so I should turn down a job just because it makes you uncomfortable?"

"It should make *you* uncomfortable!"

"Everything makes me uncomfortable!"

Jasmine shrank back a little, her eyes widening.

I sighed, running a hand over my face. "Do you think I like this new life, Jasmine? A month ago, I was living in Fremantle, fucking around on my Xbox. Now I'm interviewing for the job that was previously held by my dead twin. Do you think this is fun for me?"

She kept staring at me. I don't think we'd ever looked at each other for this long.

"I can't stand it," I told her. "Any of it… That house. Pam. The fact that I have a little brother and sister I don't know. The fact that no one cries, no one even acknowledges the fact our lives have all been turned upside down. No one says *anything*."

"Welcome to being a Rosemary," Jasmine muttered. "Nobody talks."

"Do you honestly think that I like this new life? Knowing that my mum—?" I pinched the bridge of my nose. "That the woman who raised me is sitting in a jail cell? That everywhere I go, someone has some predetermined idea of who I am, and there's nothing I can do about it? Seriously, Jasmine, do you think I *enjoy* having Chelsea breathe in my ear every single night before

I fall asleep?"

Her eyes widened again. She shuddered, like that last part was unimaginable.

"Not to mention that the media is just waiting for the moment I turn eighteen, and they can finally print my face, even though everyone *knows* my face—" I huffed, squeezing the bridge of my nose. "It sucks, Jasmine."

Jasmine stayed silent, a deep frown between her eyebrows.

"So, yeah, I want this job. Not because Jack had it. Not because I want to feel close to him, or because I know anything about administration, or how to talk to people who have no idea what I'm saying. I want this job because…I want to get away someday, Jasmine. I *have* to get away."

She was watching me in this quiet way—a way that made me want to cry. If I did cry, here, now, I'd never forgive myself.

"So…" Jasmine said, and she glanced back at the facility, "this had nothing to do with me?"

"Did you *want* it to have something to do with you?"

She looked at me again, her gaze razor sharp. "No."

"Good. Well, it didn't."

She nodded. The two of us just stood there for a moment. The longer she spent out here with me, the more I was convinced this whole conversation was a dream.

"What was the deal with you and him, anyway?" I asked her. "Did he break your heart or something?" I thought about what Gav had said, about Beacon having a lot of empty storage cupboards.

"God no. I never went anywhere near your brother." She scrunched her nose up. "Not like that… We just worked together. That's all."

"Well, you seem to have had a real problem with him." *You seem to have a real problem with me.*

"I saw the way he treated other people," she said finally, and that sentence had my mind whirring. "It wasn't always very nice."

No one had ever talked about Jack negatively before. Sure, Gav had alluded to him cheating on Chelsea, but no one had ever said outright that he treated anyone badly.

"How do you mean?" I asked.

"That's not for me to say," Jasmine said. "Everyone is entitled to their own opinions. Let's just leave it at that."

"Okay," I said, but I didn't want to leave it at that. I wanted to know everything about my brother—every good thing, every rotten thing. I wanted to know *him.* I knew that nobody was perfect, but after the way he'd been lionised at his funeral, I'd started to believe he was. In a strange way, it was almost… relieving to know that he wasn't. That I no longer had to live up to an impossible standard.

Jasmine sighed, tucking a piece of hair behind her ear. "I have to get back to work. Pip is probably wondering where her room is. She forgets every night."

I nodded, thinking that was probably the saddest thing I'd ever heard. I wanted to tell Jasmine all the nice things that Barb had said about her, all the nice things that I had thought in my head since I'd met her. But I just smiled at her. I watched her walk back to the elevators in her bright blue polo, and I kept these thoughts as unsent letters in my head. *Jasmine: You are kind, even if you've convinced yourself you're not.*

I had just unchained my bike when I felt a hand on my bicep. I froze, then threw out an arm as I was spun around.

"It's you," the man said. He looked no older than thirty, and was dressed in a black, hooded jumper despite it being summer.

I shook my head, staring at the ground.

"You're that Rosemary Boy," he said, leaning closer. His hoodie had grease stains on it, and he smelled like cigarette smoke and alcohol—a grizzly mix of scents that reminded me of Ray.

I went back to unchaining my bike, trying to hide myself from his leering face. "That's not my name," I told him.

"I saw you in the papers," he said. "Am I gonna have paparazzi jumping out and taking my photo?"

"Maybe," I said, and the notion seemed to excite him. "…If you stand too close."

For some reason, I thought about Jasmine, who had only just disappeared into the elevators. If I called loud enough, maybe she'd hear me from upstairs, maybe she'd come running. Then I realised that was the last thing I wanted. I didn't want Jasmine and her white rose to be anywhere near this gapped-toothed, grease-stained weirdo.

"You know, you could make a lot of money," he told me. "Lots of people want to talk to you."

Yeah, well, I don't want to talk to them. "I don't want any money."

"That's crazy," Black Hoodie said. "If you're gonna go through tragedy, you may as well capitalise on it. There are media outlets that would pay thousands just to get a few words from you."

I nodded. "So, you're a journalist?"

This made him laugh. "Mate, do I look like a journalist?"

I shrugged my shoulders. Honestly, I really didn't know what they looked like. Any member of the media existed as a faceless entity in my mind. A dark, mechanical force.

"I'm just here visiting my ma. Last person I expected to run into was Mr Media Darling—Mr Rosemary Boy himself."

"I'm not that interesting. I promise you." I tried to wheel my bike away, but Black Hoodie held the handlebars.

"Just a second, now."

"Please, let go," I said.

Black Hoodie chuckled. "Relax, I'm not gonna hurt you or nothin'."

"Okay," I said. My heart was beating so fast I thought I was going to have a heart attack. There was no one else in this car park, and the doors that Jasmine had just disappeared into needed a key card to open. There was nowhere to run. "I can't talk to the media," I told him. "They can't talk to me… There's a gag order."

"So, here's what you do. You let me interview you, like one of them world-class journalists, and I'll hoard that clip for the next year and then sell it to the media. We'll split the profits."

"I don't think my mum would be too happy about that."

"I'll talk to her, don't you worry." Black Hoodie smiled at me, but the thought of him being near Pam made me feel even worse. "It's a smart move," he said. "Could really set you up for the future. Then you won't have to slave away in this miserable place. The world's just one giant matrix, mate. No one's taught you how to break free of it yet, but that's what people like me are for."

I just stared down at my bike. What he was saying made sense, but why did it feel like something thick and icy had wormed through my stomach?

"If it makes you feel any better, I knew your brother."

I looked at Black Hoodie. "You did?"

"He was a good kid. I can tell you about him, if you like. You can ask me anything. Come over to my place for a beer. I'll look out for you."

I tightened my grip on my handlebars. Now that I was no longer looking at him, he'd morphed into Ray in my mind. *Jack and I used to go shooting all the time out in Blackwater—*

"Jack would have taken this deal," he said next. "He was a real savvy kid. Just like you seem to be. Such a shame what happened to him."

He finally left after that. He left and I stayed frozen to the spot, holding my stomach, holding my tears—trying to keep everything inside. I wanted to go home. Not to Pam's house or her delicious fucking soup. I wanted Fremantle. I wanted my mother.

I tried to hop on my bike, but my hands were shaking so badly that I couldn't keep the wheels in alignment. My chest was so tight I couldn't think straight—I could only focus on the phantom metal pipe lodged beneath my collarbones.

"Jules?"

I don't know how long I'd been standing there. We were underground, so it was hard to have any concept of time, but people were now leaving the facility. Visiting hours must have ended.

I glanced up. Chelsea was walking over to me, her arms folded. She was wearing a fuzzy purple singlet and a white skirt. It was the first time I'd seen her not wearing either a funeral outfit or our lifeless school uniform.

"What are you doing here?" I asked her.

She pointed behind her. "I was visiting my grandfather. What are you doing here?"

"Job interview."

"In the car park?"

"No. It was inside…"

She frowned at me. "Are you okay?"

I nodded. My eyes were full of tears, and I was half straddling my bike, but sure, I was okay.

"Do you need a lift home?" she asked me.

"I've got my bike."

"Can you ride it?"

I nodded again.

She stood there for a minute or two, as if waiting for me to prove it to her. My limbs were completely frozen, like my body had shut down.

"Jules, are you having an anxiety attack?"

"I don't know," I whispered. "What's that?"

"Well, there's this bucket analogy in psychology. You ever heard of it?"

I shook my head.

"Most of us have holes in our buckets, so when we get stressed, and the water starts to fill up, it leaks out slowly, and we eventually calm down. But some people don't have enough holes in their buckets, so the water just keeps overflowing with nowhere to go."

"I'm overflowing?"

"Maybe," she said. A few more minutes passed and then she asked me, "Do you want a lift home?"

Chelsea drove a white Toyota Camry. It smelled like old newspapers. My seatbelt had been jammed, so she'd had to lean over to put it on for me. She smelled like some kind of liquorice perfume and strawberry shampoo.

We'd had a tough time getting my bike in the back. We'd had to lay down her backseats and I'm pretty sure I'd tracked dirt all through her boot, but she didn't seem to mind. She just kept speaking to me in this soft, lulling voice. *It's going to be okay, Jules.*

On the drive back to my house, I watched a man walk across the street before his kid—before the little icon had turned green. Maybe the man wasn't related to him. Maybe my mind was just seeing something that wasn't there, filling in the dots. But the kid nearly walked right out onto the road—right into traffic. In my mind, I screamed at him to stop.

The icon flashed from red to green. The kid safely crossed the road. Chelsea drove forward before I could confirm whether they actually even knew each other.

I started to cry. It was the first time I'd cried in front of somebody since I'd left Fremantle. It was the first time I'd realised how skewed my worldview had become. Nothing was the same anymore. A kid crossing the road was no longer just a kid crossing the road.

Ordinary things were now painful to look at.

"I get really nervous driving now," Chelsea said, filling in the silence. "I mean, everyone's nervous when they first learn to drive, at least for the first few months. But I was just starting to get the hang of things. I wasn't thinking about it so hard."

I looked at her. "And now?"

"Now it's different." She tightened her hands around the steering wheel. "Feels like maybe we're never meant to *stop* thinking about it so hard."

I sniffed, staring down at my hands. For some reason, it felt safe to cry in front of Chelsea. Maybe because she'd done nothing *but* cry in front of me.

"Angela never taught me to drive. I asked her plenty of times, but she was always too busy with work. She said there was no point since I didn't need to go anywhere. She also said it was dangerous…"

Not for the first time, I wondered just how much of Angela's *excuses* were actually steeped in truth. Was she trying to shelter me, or was she trying to keep me safe? Or was it some complicated hybrid of the two?

"You can call me, you know."

I looked at Chelsea again. "What?"

"It's got to be scary, riding around in this new world. Especially at night. I can drive you to work, and to school, if you ever need it… Wherever you need to go."

"You don't have to do that, Chelsea."

"I know," she said softly. She turned down the air conditioning, and her voice lowered with it. "…I want to."

"Why?" I asked her, but I already knew. *Because of Jack.*

"Because I think we could really get along…"

Because of Jack.

I stared at the road ahead. It was still puzzling to me, how some people turned out to be like that man in the hoodie, and other people turned out to be like Chelsea. What bridged the gap between these two subsets of people? The two of us ended up parking down the end of the street, and I texted Pam to let her know I was hanging out with Chelsea for a while. We listened to music mostly, and it was nice not to have to make conversation with someone. To just let myself cry and not have to worry about saying the right things.

When I finally went home, it was around 9 p.m. The light was still on in the kitchen, like Pam had left it on for me. I walked up the patio steps to my strange little off-white house. I was so on edge I didn't even notice the door opening. A tallish figure stepped out into the darkness and my hackles rose.

It was Ray. He was staring at me with glassy eyes and a tired smile. He put a hand on my shoulder. "Bit late to be getting home, isn't it, champ?"

I shrugged. "Bit late to be leaving, isn't it?"

He laughed. "You got me there. When the two of us get drinkin' and talkin', time seems to slip away." He tilted his head. I could see him squinting in the glow of the patio lights. "You all right?"

I nodded. "I'm fine."

"It'll end, all this attention. You'll be yesterday's news in no time. But if you want to capitalise on it…well, I could help you there."

I tried to walk past him, but he stopped me with his body— just like that man had. I curled my hands into fists.

"Hey—you been on the grog?"

"No."

He squeezed my shoulder. "I wouldn't tell Pammy."

"I've never even drunk alcohol." I didn't mean to sound pissed off. Maybe I did.

"Okay, champ. I'll let you go. Hey, we've got to go out sometime, yeah? Go kick a ball or something?"

"Sure," I said. I just wanted him to go away.

He stared at me for a few seconds. But then he did go away. He stumbled down to his car and got behind the wheel even though his whiskey breath was still lingering in the doorway.

I walked inside the house. It was dark, except for a few dim lights in the kitchen. Pam and her damn aromatherapy candles. She was sitting at the dining table with tissues all around her, and the kids were nowhere to be seen. I briefly wondered what Ray and Pam had been talking about for so long that *time had slipped away*. Probably his ten-point *Rosemary Boy* marketing plan.

"Jules," she said.

"Pam."

"You're just getting home?"

I stared at her. None of this felt real. "Yes."

We didn't say anything for a long time. I thought of telling her about Black Hoodie, but it didn't seem like the time.

"Are you being safe?" she asked me. She started to cry.

I nodded. "Yeah. Of course."

"You need to be careful, Jules. There's a lot of...there's a lot of shit out there."

I looked at my hands. I wished I'd hit that guy tonight. I wished I'd made him hurt the way I was hurting.

I wasn't the kind of guy who hit people. Maybe Jack had been that guy. Maybe he'd had guts. Maybe I was just a watered-down version of him.

"I couldn't protect him from it," Pam whispered. It was the first time we'd spoken of Jack's death. "I wanted to, so badly. When he got his licence, I thought it meant he could be free. But he was always driving too fast…"

We were completely still. Visions of Jack's car losing control and ploughing into that tree flashed through my brain, as vividly as if I'd been there, as if I'd been the one who was driving. I wondered if that was a weird twin thing—telegraphing memories into each other's brains, even after death.

Pam just looked at me. There was just the darkness and the candles and the flicker of something tender, something unspoken. I wondered what Ray had said to her. I wondered if he had sparked all of this.

"You have to tell me, okay?" She looked at me with glazed, drunken eyes. "You have to tell me if it all gets too much."

"I'm fine, Pam."

She nodded. She took a sip from her mug that I knew had vodka in it. Maybe it made her feel better drinking from a mug, more motherlike.

"Are you okay?" I asked her. I should have just gone to bed.

She closed her eyes briefly. And she smiled. When she looked at me again, her eyes were so glassy I wondered whether she could even see me.

"I'm fine, Jules."

Chapter 10

Usually on a weekend, I'd wake up and watch TV with Angela. Morning shows with cringey advertisements or daytime movies that we'd both already seen. She'd make a coffee and I'd make cereal and we'd keep watching until the sun was high in the sky.

It didn't seem like much at the time, but nothing ever does until it's gone.

Since I didn't have anything to do, I did…nothing. All day. Now that I had access to the internet, I was curious whether there were any similar stories to mine. I'd scoured through someone called *Dr Phil* on something called *YouTube*, in a bid to find a comparable story there, but I'd turned up nothing. Even on Google, there were stories about babies being kidnapped from hospitals—some of them even twins, but there were no stories about children having to live with their biological family in place of their dead sibling. I was alone. All alone in a narrative not even Dr Phil would touch.

When I did get the courage to finally Google Jack's name, I wished with everything in me that I hadn't. I was soon convinced that social media, and the internet in general, was a sickness of some kind. A self-inflicted kind of sickness that began as an innocent sneeze—a single Google search—and slowly plateaued into hours of full-body chills. By the time you realised how sick you were, it was too late. The virus had already seeped into your bloodstream and was beginning to take over your motor functions. *Keep scrolling. Keep clicking. Keep digging.*

Snippet after endless snippet…

Jack Rosemary, Linked to Infamous Twin Kidnapping, Dies in Crash

Jack Rosemary, widely known for the unsolved 1999 kidnapping of his newborn twin Nicholas Rosemary, has been tragically killed in a car accident.

Rosemary Twin Saga Continues with New Tragedy: Jack Rosemary Dead at Seventeen

The tragic story of the Rosemary twins has taken another dark turn with the death of Jack Rosemary in a car accident, leaving behind a trail of heartbreak.

Rosemary Privacy: A Double-Edged Sword?

Pam Rosemary's decision to maintain her family's privacy in the years following the 1999 kidnapping of her newborn twin son has been both a source of respect and speculation.

Rosemary Boy Found Alive: Media Frenzy After Jack Rosemary's Death Leads to Discovery of Missing Twin

The seventeen-year-long search for "Rosemary Boy" has ended with his discovery, just days after the death of his twin brother Jack Rosemary brought renewed attention to the case.

I clicked on too many snippets, and everything I read only made me feel worse. There were people casting blame at everyone— not just Angela. There were articles theorising about Jack's death, and whether he'd crashed his car on purpose. There were social media posts pointing fingers at Pam for 'going cold' after the kidnapping and tapering off media appearances once she met and married David. There were countless slanderous stories about Angela, or Donna, as I'd recently discovered was her real name.

QUEENSLAND TRIBUNE

The Double Life of Donna Jones

INVESTIGATIVE REPORTER — TARA GALI   FEBRUARY 27, 2017

FIFTY-three-year-old Donna Jones harboured a deep, unspoken obsession with motherhood. Having had a stillborn son at 21, and subsequently unable to have children after requiring a hysterectomy to treat ovarian cancer while still in her early twenties, Jones' psychological state deteriorated. Her desperation for a child drove her to commit an unthinkable act.

While on long-service leave from her nursing role at Southside General Hospital, a then thirty-five-year-old Jones calmly donned her uniform and walked unchallenged—seemingly even unnoticed—into the maternity ward at Central North General Hospital where the Rosemary twins were being kept. There were no CCTV cameras anywhere in the hospital back in 1999, and all staff on duty were subsequently thoroughly investigated and cleared. Jones' plan was meticulously calculated: she took advantage of the busy hospital environment to execute her crime and had legally changed her name just two weeks prior to Angela Edwards.

Immediately after the kidnapping, she drove 4,350 kilometres across Australia over five days, settling in Fremantle in Western Australia where no one would suspect her dark past. As "Angela", she presented herself as a loving and protective mother. To the outside world, she was a model parent, never letting anyone get too close or ask too many questions.

The discovery of "Rosemary Boy" has brought mixed emotions to his birth mother Pam and her family—a bittersweet reunion overshadowed by years of pain and uncertainty. As the search for her missing twin dragged on without success, Pam subsequently met and married her real estate agent husband, David. They retreated from the spotlight and had two children together.

For the kidnapped boy, now a teenager, the truth about his origins would have shattered everything he thought he knew about his life. The road to healing will undoubtedly be long and uncertain for everyone involved.

After reading that article, I made a pact with myself not to Google or click on any other Angela or *Donna* headlines. I still couldn't believe that was her real name. The police and Eloise had mentioned it to me several times, but I'd just refused to acknowledge it. When you know someone as one thing your whole life, it's hard to suddenly believe something different. It's hard to see that person with anything other than the rose-tinted glasses you were wearing in their presence. It's hard to hate someone you love.

After that, I went onto Chelsea's social media profiles. I looked at all the photos of her and Jack, and couldn't help but think how good they looked together. How good *she and I* looked together. It was weird, almost like seeing myself in a relationship. Seeing myself in love.

Jasmine's profiles were all private, so I couldn't see anything about her—only her profile picture, which seemed to be the same across the board. A photo of the back of her head, with her white rose resting elegantly in the centre. She appeared to be half turning, and her long, wavy hair was billowing in the wind.

Jack's profiles were all still active, but I almost wished they weren't. The comment sections were strange places to be: digital voids where people could deposit their sympathies and strangers could satisfy their strange, parasocial relationship with my brother.

RIP Jack Rosemary

What a tragic end. I followed your story from the beginning.

The only upside to all of this was that my name wasn't published anywhere aside from a few Reddit articles—but that seemed to be a lawless social news forum where people could post whatever they wanted anonymously, with absolutely no consequences.

r/AskReddit • 6h ago
animorph_donut

Why is no one posting that kidnapped twin's name anywhere? I can't find a single article calling him anything other than 'Rosemary Boy'. I want to see what he looks like.

VelvetNebula · 3h ago

He looks exactly like the twin who died. Like Jack. Duh.

CaseCrackerRosemary23 · 4h ago

My cousin in the police says there's a gag order so the media can't post anything, as much as they want to. Gotta wait until the kid's 18.

PixelatedDreamer5563 · 18m ago

That makes sense. I'm so nosy tho lol.

Banana-in-pyjamas3 · 10m ago

he's literally a child. Grow up.

PixelatedDreamer5563 · 6m ago

17 is hardly a child tho, come on.

Banana-in-pyjamas3 · 5m ago

true I guess it's just a bit of a grey area. He'll be 18 soon, but until then u needa respect his privacy. Anyway what do I care lmao. He'll be rich the moment he sells his story so kind of a happy ending imo. The dude below seems to think his name is julian. Dunno if he's legit but

User_223847599 · 5h ago

I have a very good source (close friend of one of the kid's old neighbours) that tells me his name is Julian. So he'd probably be going by Julian Rosemary now. Or perhaps Julian Edwards (that was the fake surname of the crazy nurse who took him). Went by Angela Edwards but her real name is like Donna Jones or something like that. Honestly that just sounds fake too. Who knows with this story! #RosemaryCase #UnravelRosemary

CaseCrackerRosemary23 · 4h ago

I have also heard his name is Julian. I won't confirm my sources.

Isawsomething-once22 · 4m ago

ur suck a hack lol nobody asked @CaseCrackerRosemary23

PixelatedDreamer5563 · 1m ago

can u imagine how whacked in the head 'julian' must be?? poor kid. imagine growing up with a psycho and then essentially being shipped back to ur bio family and expected to take over ur dead twin's legacy?? so fucked for everyone involved. there's no way his real mother looks at him and doesn't see jack.

After that, I had to go to the bathroom and dry heave into the sink for a couple of minutes. As I hovered over the basin, I could see my reflection in the metal tap—a distorted vision of grief and *Jack*.

When I came back to bed, I vowed to stay away from the internet for good. That left me with very little to do, which was strange seeing I'd spent my entire life living without it. Now, suddenly, it was all there was. This beautiful, terrifying nebula of dubious information and uninformed opinions.

I stared at my old Nokia flip phone. It was lying face down on Jack's sheets, and I'd been avoiding it as much as possible the last few weeks. It had no internet access, but the mounting number of missed calls and text messages still made me squeamish when I picked it up. I knew I should have replied to them—they were from friends back home, after all—but I just couldn't bring myself to do it. Talking to them would only remind me of my old life. It would only pick at the wound.

I picked up my new iPhone 7. Pam had taken the liberty of transferring a few of Jack's close friends' numbers, as well as giving them mine. Gav, Hux, Mindy, Chelsea…

Unfortunately, she'd neglected to add Jasmine's. I was ashamed to say I'd scrolled right to the letter J upon unlocking it. There was just one J contact, someone named Joel, and I doubted I'd ever have reason to call him, whoever he was.

The phone started ringing, and I nearly dropped it in my lap. It had a strange ringtone, like some kind of rhythmic marimba sound. For some reason, hearing it made my heart ramp up a few extra beats.

Gav was calling.

I picked up on the fifth ring. Some god-awful music blared over the receiver, and I jerked the phone away from my ear. "*Julesy Boy*," I heard distantly.

I rubbed my eye. "I can't hear you."

"Sorry, mate. Hux is on DJ. What's up?"

"…You called me."

"Fuck, must have been a butt dial. Pam gave me your number last week—anyway, I'm a little busy right now. How about you come and hang out?"

"It sounds like you're having a party."

Someone shouted in the background, and Gav told him to *get fucked.* "What gave it away? You know, you really should be at this party, Jules. Jack used to come to all our parties. He loved them."

I'm not Jack, I thought for the hundredth time that evening.

"I totally would have invited you to this party, but it was last minute. I'm inviting you now, though."

"Can't," I told him. "I've got a lot to do tonight."

"Like what? Staring at walls? Dodging social media? The internet? This party—*Fuck you, Hux!*—will be the perfect distraction from all of the other shit going in your life. Trust me."

"But I've never been to a party—"

"I'm texting you the address. No better way to lose your party virginity than at a Lewis party. *See you soon, Julesy Boy!*"

The line went silent. A few seconds later, the phone pinged loud enough to make me jump again. Why were these fancy new phones so *loud*?

Gav's address was staring up at me. Somewhere in Marsden, which meant it was close to our school. I locked my phone. *Nope.*

Absolutely nothing good could come from attending a high school party. Angela had told me they were full of drugs, and alcohol, and all of those terrible, dangerous things that I definitely did not want to try.

I lay there for what felt like hours. It was somewhere around 9:30 p.m., and Pam hadn't come to check on me in a while. She must have been hungover from last night. Either that, or she could feel my stress permeating the rest of the house. I could almost see it seeping under the door, souring the air.

"Screw it," I mumbled.

Chapter 11

Gav's house was nicer than I expected it to be. In a perfect world, I'd be the one living in a nice house, and Gav would be the one salvaging the broken puzzle pieces of his life. But no one ever wants to steal a kid like Gav.

I walked up to the front door and was overwhelmed by the scenes unravelling: a boy and a girl having a slurred, emotional, *private* conversation right on the doorstep; four guys trying to land tiny balls in full cups of alcohol; a girl vomiting up purple stuff in the garden.

There was another overwhelming sight, and she was standing directly in front of me.

"Jasmine."

She turned around, seemingly in slow motion. The rose in her hair was a sweep of white in the darkness. She frowned at me. "Well, if it isn't Rosemary Boy."

"I don't like that nickname."

"Sorry. *Julesy Boy.*"

"I don't like that either."

For some reason, I liked it far too much when she said that.

I moved closer to her, and she seemed to breathe in a little deeper. I tried not to think about that too much. Was she afraid, or was it something else? Did I smell nice? Jasmine smelled nice. But she always smelled nice. Like vanilla and grass and… Jasmine. The flower *and* the person.

"What are you doing here?" she asked me.

I glanced over at the makeshift table. It was fashioned from eight empty cartons of XXXX Gold, and there were ten red cups lined up in diamonds on either side. "I came to challenge Jeremy and the guys. At…whatever this is."

"Beer pong," she muttered. "Also, pretty sure that guy's name is Joel."

Oh, that's *Joel.*

"You should play with us," I told her.

"Not my thing." She shrugged, rubbing her arms. She was wearing a plain grey t-shirt and cargo pants. She didn't look like she was dressed for a party—at least, she wasn't really dressed like any of the girls here. But Jasmine never looked like she was dressed for anything. Except war, maybe…

"It's not really my thing either," I said.

"What is your thing?"

"I gucss I'm still figuring that out."

She stared at me, squinting a little. I'll always wonder what she was going to say to that, before Gav came barrelling in between us like Foghorn Leghorn.

"*Julleessyyy Boyyy!*"

He half-hugged, half-tackled me into a marble pillar. "Man, I'm so glad you made it." Gav did a double take, noticing Jasmine in front of me. "What the bloody hell are you doing here? Hux told you that you're not invited."

"I came to tell you to keep it down," Jasmine said. "It's almost eleven, and my mum has to work in the morning."

"We don't have school tomorrow?"

"Her other job, moron."

"She has another job besides being a teacher? On a *Saturday*? Damn, that's rough."

Jasmine sighed. "Keep the noise down, and maybe I won't call the police."

Gav laughed in her face. "Honey, my parents run this town. I can assure you that no one will care about this party. In fact, Inspector Fitzpatrick might come 'round for a few beers after he knocks off."

Jasmine smiled sweetly—the kind that wasn't really sweet at all. "Fine, then I'll call your mother." And with that, she turned around and disappeared into a crowd of people—presumably back toward her house. I tried to track her to see what house she walked into, but she was too damn quick.

I followed Gav into the house, ignoring the pungent cocktail of smells that had just invaded my senses: vomit, body odour, smoke.

"Welcome to my humble abode," Gav said, guiding me toward the stairs. There were two people making out on the third step, and Gav shoved at the guy with his foot. "Take it to the bedroom! No jizz on the carpet!" He looked at me over his shoulder. "Can I get you anything? Beer?"

"I'm fine, thanks."

"I'll get you a beer."

Gav rounded the corner at the top of the stairs and then disappeared into one of the rooms. It was like a maze in this place; every hallway led to an even grander part of the house, and a discovery of new rooms that seemingly had no purpose. There were photos of a pudgy Gav dotting almost every wall, and below them, shiny golden trophies signifying even the most basic of achievements. *Most Likely to Enter the Business Sector*

– Gavin Lewis Junior: Age 12. Apparently, the word 'Junior' next to his name meant that he was named after his father. I could barely tolerate the thought of one Gavin Lewis, much less two.

I followed Gav into what looked like the den—but then again, there were three other rooms that had looked exactly like it. There was a large flat screen TV that took up almost an entire wall, and a totally useless fireplace in the centre of the room. We were in *Brisbane*, for Christ's sake.

Gav took a seat on a long, suede leather couch. He gestured for me to sit beside him, and then seemed to think better of it. He motioned for me to sit on the opposite side of the marble coffee table—on a wooden stool.

"What can I do for you, Jules?"

"Well, I—"

Gav bent down suddenly, and I realised the underneath of the couch doubled as a cooler. He grabbed out a beer for himself, and one for me.

"*Gav*," I said, my insides turning inside out. "I don't think I'm allowed to drink this."

"Don't tell me this is your first beer, Jules."

"It's my first beer."

"Well, shit—congratulations! I feel honoured to be the first person to crack open a cold one with you." He took a long swig from his bottle. "They should write about *me* in the papers. *Gavin Lewis Gives Rosemary Boy His First Taste of Freedom.*"

I tried to open it, but the lid wouldn't twist off the cap. "*Ow—*"

"Oh, shit," Gav mumbled. "Give it here. You need a bottle opener." He took the bottle from my hands, and then lifted the top off with a small metal device. "Jeez, you really were sheltered, weren't you? It's like teaching a baby how to walk."

He handed it back to me, but I just held it for a moment. The smell was already nauseating, like Ray's breath.

"So, what's it like being in the big city? Logan must seem like The Big Smoke compared to where you're from."

I shrugged. "It's fine."

"The girls are all talking about you, you know."

Something hot pooled in my gut. "Like who?"

"Well, basically any girl that thought Jack was a looker now thinks you are as well. Go figure." He took another sip of his beer. "Honestly, it's kind of unfair."

I just kept staring at him, and he laughed.

"Oh, you want names? Okay. Um… Well, Chelsea, for one. She'd accept a proposal from you tomorrow, I'm sure. Then you've got Mindy, and a few of the girls from Jack's advanced English class, and then the ones he played touch footy with. Honestly, though, I'd stick with Chelsea. She's a good girl, Chelsea. Brainy. Loyal. All that crap. Is she a bit cooked in the head right now after the whole Jack thing? Yes. Would I still take advantage of that? Absolutely—"

"What do you mean, *take advantage*?"

Gav just stared at me blankly. "Jules," he said. "You're kidding, right?"

I chose that moment to take a sip of my beer, but I almost spat it back into the bottle. God, why was every dude obsessed with this? It tasted like room temperature piss.

"Jules, you have kissed a girl, right?"

"Yeah," I told him. "…Once."

"*Once!*"

I cringed. Gav had shouted so loud that other people were now crowding around the door. They peered into the room, and I felt like I needed to hide my beer bottle. Pam and Elijah would probably kill me if this got into the media somehow. *Rosemary Boy Drinks His First Beer!*

"My god, Jules. What a blushing little virgin you are."

"*Gav*," I growled.

"Well, who do you want to pop your cherry? It'll be easy, trust me. Some girls are into the virgin thing. Not all of 'em, but some. Mindy would get a kick out of it. Chelsea would probably think it's romantic as shit."

"I don't want to have sex with Mindy. Or Chelsea…"

Gav frowned. "You gay?"

"No—"

"Because, look, I'm cool with that. I'm sure I could put the call out for some nice dude at Sparks…"

"Gav, please don't tell people I'm gay."

"Why? There's nothing wrong with that—"

"I know, but I'm *not* gay."

"But you've kissed one girl in your entire life. The maths isn't adding up, Jules."

"I just haven't…" I took another sip of my beer. For some reason, it was getting easier to stomach. "…I haven't met anyone."

"Oh, you're a romantic," Gav said.

"I just…" *I don't know what to do.*

"Your kidnapper didn't give you sex ed?"

I kept drinking my beer, hoping it would soothe the heat of my skin. God, I hoped no one was listening to us. Angela had gone over the basics, but I'd learned most of what I knew from that girl across the street. Sometimes we'd watch movies together when her mum wasn't home, and sometimes those movies would get…interesting.

"Okay," Gav said, holding up his hands. "Baby steps. I get it." He pointed at me with the hand holding his beer. "You're blushing, though. Look at you! At least we know it's on your mind. The question is *who*. Who's getting Julian Rosemary—?"

"Edwards-Rosemary," I corrected. That was the official compromise, according to my last phone call with Elijah. A way to bridge both identities in the most time-efficient way, at least on paper.

"Who's getting Julian Edwards-Rosemary all hot and bothered? It's not Mindy. Or Chelsea…" Gav's eyebrows lifted. "Oh, wait a minute."

I chugged the rest of my beer. Somehow, I'd gone from hating the stuff to drinking an entire bottle within minutes. Gav handed me another, and he didn't take his gaze off my face the entire time. There was a sick smile slinking across his mouth, and in that moment, I wished I could blur my face like they did in all the articles. *Rosemary Boy Blushes Over Girl!*

"It's Jasmine, isn't it?"

"No," I told him.

"Ah, that's what gets you going. A little spunk, a little Jasmine Morè—"

"Stop talking about her."

"You're quite protective of her, you know that? Jack was the same way, and I could never understand it. Always had a soft spot."

"I don't have a soft spot," I said.

"You do, though." Gav took a swig of his beer. "You know how I know?"

I shook my head. I opened my beer myself this time, and I felt an odd sense of achievement. That little metal thing was like magic—beer opening magic.

"Because I notice things. Things that nobody else notices. Like how you seek her out in a crowd. The way you jumped at the chance to work with a bunch of senile old geezers for minimum wage. The way you looked at her when she was standing outside just now." He pulled out a pack of cigarettes from his pocket. He placed one in his mouth, and cursed under his breath when he couldn't light it properly. "Actually, come to think of it, you're making it pretty bloody obvious, Julesy Boy. You might want to tone it down."

"I'm not—there's nothing going on with Jasmine and me."

"Oh, I don't doubt that. She's a hard nut to crack. But you want it to happen. I mean, Jesus, the way you blushed like a bloody five-year-old when I mentioned her name—"

"Stop talking. Please…"

Gav finally lit his cigarette, and he stared at me with wide eyes. "Oh, Clinton, my Clinton. You love her."

I took a sip of my beer. "Who's Clinton?"

"It's my catchphrase. I think it's gonna catch on."

"Whatever," I said. "I don't…I don't love her."

Gav glanced out the door, blowing smoke out of his nose just as he started to scowl. He looked like an enraged bull, or an overboiled tea kettle. "Oi, you motherfucker! I'm going to come out there and shove this lamp up your arse if you don't stop scabbing my beers!"

"*Whoa.*" I pinched the bridge of my nose. The room was spinning suddenly. "*Shit*, my head feels weird."

"Feels good, doesn't it?"

I stared at Gav. His face was starting to blur, and the room was feeling too small. Like I was in a fishbowl. "Gav, what's happening to me?"

"You're drunk, Jules. Off two beers."

"This feels really weird."

"Fun though, right?"

I nodded, and Gav handed me another beer. We stopped talking after a while, or maybe I just stopped listening. I lay on the floor and drank two more beers, and somehow Gav ended up lying down next to me.

"Man, it's crazy to me that you're this innocent," he said. "If only you knew how loose the people are in Perth. My cousin lives out there and he's having orgies every second day. He says there's really nothing to do out there besides drink and bang."

"I don't want to bang Jasmine," I told him. I'd never heard anyone use the word *bang*, but I assumed it meant had sex with.

"What do you want to do, then?"

"I just want to talk to her."

Gav hummed. He seemed nicer right now. More likeable.

"I want her to talk to me." I stared up at the ceiling. Gav's fan wasn't on a minute ago, but I could've sworn it was moving now. "I want her to look at me. At *me*, and not…him."

"Maybe you should grow a moustache."

"You think that would work?"

"It might. Or you may just end up looking like a used car salesman."

I laughed. It was a deep belly laugh that I hadn't felt in a long time. It made Gav jerk his head toward me.

"Shit. You laugh like him," he said.

"I do?"

"Just then, you did. I swear, it sounded like he was right next to me."

We looked at each other. His eyes scanned over my face like he'd gone somewhere else for a moment, like he was remembering something. It was the first time I'd witnessed any kind of sadness in Gav since I'd met him. The first time I'd recognised even a hint of grief.

That's when I realised he really had cared about Jack. He just handled his grief by not thinking about him, rather than making himself sad or angry.

"I need to find Jasmine," I said. "I need to tell her all of this."

Gav nodded, blinking his eyes. "You go, Jules. Go get her!"

I tried to stand up and almost fell through the table. I steadied myself on the glass countertop. My reflection was strange and rippled. I didn't look like myself. I looked like…

"Jacky Boy would be proud!" Gav yelled.

I stumbled past him, out into the hallway and past half the footy team playing beer pong in the hallway. Seemingly hours later, I collided with the staircase railing. I hugged the cool, polished wood, my head peering over the side. *Jeez*, I was high up. I was at least nine storeys high.

"Jules," I heard someone saying. "Jules!"

I followed the voice. Within these walls, amidst the warped sounds of the party, it sounded like my mother. *Like Angela*. My real mother. The mother I wasn't allowed to claim—only in the quiet, darkened corners of my mind.

"Jules!"

I staggered down the steps, my mind racing, that voice so alive and real in my heart. "Mum?" I mumbled.

"Jules!"

I made it to the bottom of the stairs, and I stumbled forward…

Right into Chelsea's waiting arms.

Chapter 12

Chelsea smelled like lolly perfume and the same port wine that Angela used to drink. She soothed her hands over my shoulder blades. "Shh," she said. "It's okay."

I went completely still in her arms, letting her take my weight. I half expected her to fall over, but she stayed as sturdy as the marble pillars holding up Gav's house. "I don't feel good," I told her.

"I know," she whispered, stroking my hair.

"No, I mean—"

"It's okay to cry, Jules. Let it out."

I pulled back, and Chelsea kept her hands locked around my neck. "I don't want to cry."

"I know you don't *want* to, Jules. But sometimes you *need* to."

I glanced around us. Everyone was staring, and suddenly she was this strange, sickly extension of me and my anxiety. I could almost hear the rumour mill swirling, and that was just what everyone at school would say. *Did you hear about Jules and Chelsea?*

There was also the rest of the world to worry about. *Rosemary Boy Dates Dead Brother's Girlfriend!*

"Do you know what I need, Chelsea?" I didn't like the sobering edge to my voice. I could feel it lurching inside of me—the real me, untethered from my inhibition.

Her eyes softened. "Tell me, Jules." She was wearing red lipstick and blue eyeshadow, and in the dim lights of the hallway, she looked like a sad clown.

"I need you to leave me alone."

Her entire body went taut against mine.

"What?" she asked, her bottom lip trembling.

"It's drawing too much attention, having you hanging all over me. I don't need it, and I don't want it. The media is going to have a field day once I turn eighteen and they see me hanging around with you."

"What the hell?" someone said. It wasn't Chelsea; it was a slightly deeper voice.

Jasmine.

She came and plucked me off the stairs by my collar. Beside her, Chelsea was starting to cry, but my head was lolling around too much to care.

"Ignore him," Jasmine told her.

Chelsea sniffled. She gave me one last longing look before turning around, and then she was gone. A group of girls now stood between us like a protective shield.

Jasmine grabbed my face with both of her hands, almost slapping me with the action. "I was gone for an hour," she said. Her eyes were bright and pissed off. "What happened to you?"

"Gav," I said, smiling even though I didn't want to. It was like I'd lost all motor function, like I was just a pile of goo trickling through Jasmine's fingertips.

"What did he give you?"

"Beer."

"*Beer?*"

"Quite a few beers."

She was still holding my face. "You've never drunk before, have you?"

I shook my head.

"Well, it can make you do things that you wouldn't normally do, Jules. Things you regret, like being mean to Chelsea."

"I wasn't mean…" I said, hiccupping. "Wait, was I?"

"Extremely."

I stared at her. At her pretty, pretty face. She was still holding me, like a warm anchor in the darkness. I wrapped a hand around her wrist. "Do you think I'm mean?"

She swallowed. Carefully, she removed her hands from my face, and I felt like I was going to fall over without their foundation. "You need to go home," she said.

"I can't go home."

"Why not?"

"Because David's dumb brother will probably be there, and he'll be drinking and making Pam sad—"

"Okay," she said gently. "Okay."

"I just don't want to go home, Jasmine. I really, really, really don't want to go home."

She was silent for a long moment, studying me. I saw her eyes soften for maybe the first time. "Come on. We're getting out of here."

"I can't go—"

"I'm not taking you home," she snapped, wrapping my arm around her shoulders.

"Oh."

We stumbled out into Gav's front yard. I felt like a wounded soldier being carted away from battle. People were catcalling us, and for some reason I was catcalling them back.

"Jules and Jasmine!" somebody yelled.

"*Jules and Jasmine*!" I yelled back.

"Shut *up*," Jasmine grumbled.

"I'm sorry," I told her. But I wasn't really sorry. It had a nice ring to it. *Jules and Jasmine.* She had to appreciate the alliteration, at the very least.

We finally made it across Gav's lawn, which seemed to be the length of two football fields. Once we stepped over that threshold—once we'd made it through that labyrinth of empty beer bottles and raucous partygoers, everything became quiet.

It was just Jasmine and me.

"Where are you walking?" she asked me.

"To your house."

"How do you know where I live?"

"You told Gav, in class… You told him it was three houses down, but I don't know whether you meant this way or that way."

Jasmine stopped, and I nearly toppled over onto the grass.

"You remembered that?"

I turned around to face her. The party was still raging on behind her like a bad dream, but I couldn't really hear it anymore. It was like she was standing in front of a television set with muffled volume.

"I remember he was mean to you, and I didn't like it." I shook my head. "A lot of people are mean to you, and I don't like that either. You're a bit mean to me, but that's okay. Your mum's really nice, so that means you must be nice, too. Somewhere…" I gestured to her heart.

"Jules. Stop talking."

"I mean it. She's a really nice lady, Ms Morè—"

"Jules—"

It was coming out of me before I could stop it. Word vomit—and *actual* vomit.

Right over Jasmine's pretty white shoes.

I sat on Jasmine's bed like a scolded child.

"Let me clean them," I told her.

"Sit there and don't move," she barked back.

I nodded, smoothing my hands over her peach-coloured bed sheets. Her room was not how I pictured it to be. If you met Jasmine, you'd picture a room of skulls and heavy metal records. You wouldn't picture peach sheets, fluffy rugs and an old dusty typewriter on her bedside table.

When I looked back at her, she was glaring at me from the bathroom. She placed her shoes into a yellow garbage bag and then sealed it off in the sink.

"I, uh, really like your room," I told her. "You…you've really put a lot of yourself into it."

She exited the bathroom, still glaring at me.

I read the page in her typewriter. *"It was a queer, sultry summer, the summer they electrocuted the Rosenbergs, and I didn't know what I was doing in New York."*

"I didn't write that," she told me, sounding almost embarrassed.

"I know," I said. "I know Sylvia Plath."

She raised an eyebrow at me, wiping her hands with a Wet Wipe.

"Well, actually my mum knows her—*Angela* knows her."

She kept staring at me, still wiping her hands. Eventually, she motioned for me to hold out *my* hands, and she started wiping mine too. Now I really felt like a child.

Her voice was quiet when she spoke. "You can say *mum* around me."

"What?"

"Your mum. Angela… You don't have to pretend."

I swallowed. Jasmine was cleaning my hands with such gentle precision, and I wondered if this is how it felt to be eighty years old, like one of the residents at Beacon. Is this how it felt to be taken care of?

It felt…nice. I hadn't even realised all the grass and dirt and vomit that had seeped under my fingernails, and now it was being gently scrubbed away. Maybe I should have been embarrassed, but I wasn't. There was something in the way she took care of people that left no room for shame. She gave dignity to those who were struggling, and that was a rare thing to find in a person. An important thing.

"What are you thinking?" she asked me.

I shrugged. "You're really good at what you do."

"Cleaning hands?"

"Taking care of people."

She paused for a moment. Without her ministrations, we were simply holding hands. I curled my fingers around hers.

"Don't," she told me.

"Why not?"

She didn't move. She kept staring down at our hands, and I could see tears in her eyes.

"What?" I asked her, moving to cup her face.

She slapped my hand away. Suddenly, I was holding nothing. Nothing but that filthy Wet Wipe. Shame pooled in my stomach.

"I don't want to do this," she said. She moved over to the other side of the room, and in the absence of her touch, I felt everything that had been pushed away. An avalanche of self-hatred.

"Do what?"

"Take care of you. I'm not the right person for it."

I sat there for a long time not knowing what to say. I stared at a stain on Jasmine's cream carpet, at her frilly white socks.

"I feel like...I feel like a fucking child," I whispered.

"You are a child."

There was no malice in her voice, no anger. She just sounded... resigned.

"I just want all of this to be over."

The words hung in the air, and my chest burned with how pathetic they sounded. I pressed my knuckles into my eyes and lay back on Jasmine's bed.

"Jules."

"I'm sorry. I don't know what's happening. I don't know what this stuff is doing to me."

"It's just alcohol," Jasmine said. "Jack could never handle his drinks either."

"Did you take care of him too?"

She didn't answer, and I pressed my knuckles harder into my eyes.

"It doesn't last long," she told me. "A couple of hours maybe. I think you're over the worst of it."

I stared at Jasmine's ceiling. "I think the worst of it is yet to come, actually."

"You can stay here as long as you need to," she said, sitting on the edge of her bed. She started running her hands through her hair, and I was left wondering far too deeply about her night-time routine.

"What about Ms Morè?"

"She leaves for work early in the morning. She won't know."

"What does she do? Besides teaching."

"She works part time as a cultural support worker on the weekends. I told Gav she works another job for the money, but that's not what it's about."

"She wants to help people," I said. "Like you do."

Jasmine scoffed. "Mum does far more than I do."

"Is that what you want to do? Help people like she does?"

"I want to work within our communities, but I don't want to be a teacher. I want…" she pursed her lips, like she was unsure whether to tell me or not. I let my eyes flutter closed, trying to show her just how intoxicated I was.

"I won't rem—ember," I promised her, hiccupping on the last word. "I'll keep your secret."

"The Rosemarys are good at keeping secrets."

I opened my eyes. I was about to ask her what she meant by that, but then she was lying down next to me, and all thoughts were drawn to her body and the smell of vanilla.

"I want to tell stories," she whispered.

"Like Sylvia Plath."

"I guess so. Although, I'd like a slightly less tragic fate."

"You want to write stories?" I asked her. "Books? Movies?"

"All of them. All of the stories. About everything. About everyone. Things I've experienced. Things I haven't. And if anyone asks why, I'll say, 'Why not?'"

"Why not?" I said, staring at the glow of her lamp, the way it outlined her nose.

"I want to write about humans. I want to write about what it means to be alive. I want to imagine what it's like to be everyone. That's the only way…" She sighed, shaking her head. "The only way we can even *begin* to understand each other."

"Even people like Gav?"

She looked at me. "Especially people like Gav."

Her words hung in the air. I stared at her ceiling, at the shadow of her fan.

She yawned. "People can be really ugly sometimes. But…we can all be ugly."

I thought about what I said to Chelsea earlier. I thought about ignoring her calls.

"I'm sorry," she said quietly. "That I was ugly to you."

Her hand was right next to mine. I brushed her knuckles with my fingers, and I heard a small hitch in her breathing.

"Why are you telling me this?" I asked her.

She turned her body to face mine. We were still touching hands.

"Because you won't remember it tomorrow. Alcohol makes you forget things."

"I hope I don't forget all of it," I said, and Jasmine rolled her eyes.

"You're starting to sound like a book character."

I shrugged. "Read enough of them."

Our faces were so close, and I wondered whether she was planning to sleep right here. Right next to me… I'd never slept in the same bed as a girl before. Where did you put your legs? How did you breathe?

"Please don't tell Pam," I begged her. "About the alcohol. Or the…vomit. Especially not the vomit. Don't tell anyone about that."

"I won't, Jules. But you owe me some fresh sneakers."

"I could sell you my statement instead. My words go for a lot these days…"

"Who would want to talk to you?"

"I'm *Rosemary Boy.*"

"Sounds like a superhero, doesn't it?"

"Well, I did die and come back to life."

She flinched slightly, just like she always did whenever I mentioned Jack's death. Even with all the progress we'd made tonight—the apologising, the *hand touching*, she still flinched. Every damn time.

"Don't tell Pam," I begged again, my eyes falling closed. "Please…don't tell Pam. I don't think she could handle it if I were like her."

"Like her?"

"Sad." The word was out of my mouth before I could even think about it. I was oscillating between states of consciousness, between broken states of mind.

Jasmine didn't answer me, but she kept touching my hand, and that felt like an answer in itself. In a lot of ways, it felt like hope—like a white rose blooming amidst all the muck and darkness of the world.

Chapter 13

I woke up with my hand stretching across an empty bed. I was drooling into a pillow, and my heart racketed in my chest when I realised it was a satin pillow—and *peach.*

This isn't my room. This isn't even Jack's *room.*

This is…

"Good morning."

I flinched, knocking into the bedframe. "*Ow,*" I muttered, rubbing my elbow. "What the—what happened?"

Jasmine just stared at me. Her hands were wrapped around a coffee mug, and she was sitting at the end of the bed like a particularly serious garden gnome. "Well, if you ask me, it looks like you may have just pissed your pants."

"I didn't—what? What am I…why am I here?"

She took a sip of her coffee. "Well, you were silly enough to go to one of Gavin's parties. Then you were reckless enough to accept alcohol from him."

I shook my head, staring out Jasmine's window. "How did I end up here?"

"Well, when I found you, you were dangling off the edge of a staircase and being mean to Chelsea. For absolutely no reason, I might add."

My stomach soured. I was torn between wishing I could remember the last twenty-four hours and wishing I never would. I wanted to erase it all…to scrub the past clean like Jasmine's sneakers.

"Shit," I muttered. "Did I…?"

"Vomit all over my sneakers? Yes, you did." Her hand tightened around her coffee mug. My stomach tightened along with it.

"Did—did we hold hands last night?"

"Don't be ridiculous."

"We did. I remember… You were rubbing my thumbnail in your sleep."

She shook her head. The mid-morning sun streamed onto her hair, making it look more brown than black. She was wearing that white rose again. "I think you're deluded, Rosemary Boy."

"Do you always wear that?"

She touched the rose. "It was my dad's. He always wore it in his suit jacket."

"Artificial?"

She snorted. "*Obviously.* I know some people wear real flowers as boutonnieres, but he just couldn't bear for it to die. He wanted something that could stay pure forever."

I wanted so badly to ask her about her dad. It was the first time she'd mentioned him, and I noticed that Ms Morè didn't wear a wedding ring. Maybe they were unmarried. Maybe he was on a work trip, like David, or maybe he was dead, like my dad.

Wherever he was, it wasn't any of my business.

But I wanted it to be.

Jasmine looked at me, and there was this weird moment between us, this weird moment where maybe we were having the same thought. Did she want to be closer to me, despite herself? Did she want my problems to be her problems too?

"How do you feel?" she asked me.

"Embarrassed, mostly. Aren't I meant to be hungover or something?"

"That's one of the perks of being seventeen. You can sleep it off pretty well. Also, you did vomit most of it up…"

"It was weird, being drunk. I started to think that maybe I liked Gav."

She shuddered. "What else did you think?"

I stared at her. *I thought that I liked you. I thought that maybe I liked you a lot.*

"Just normal, drunken thoughts."

"How would you know what normal is?"

"I'm learning."

"Just don't try to be too normal," she told me. "I think that's where a lot of people go wrong. They try to be like everybody else."

"I don't think I'll ever be like everybody else," I told her.

"Good," she said.

I cleared my throat. "So, are we, like, hanging out now?"

"If that's what you call giving you a place to hide and sleep off your drunkenness."

"I'd like a place to hide."

Jasmine hummed. She took another sip of her coffee, and my gaze was drawn to the bare skin of her arms. She was wearing a black singlet and a pair of cream shorts. There was so much skin…

"You should go," she said finally.

"Where would you like me to go?"

She stared at me over the rim of her mug. "You can't hide forever, Jules."

There was a grey car parked outside Pam's house. Outside *my* house.

I took a moment to gather myself—straddling my bike, helmet unfastened—and simply stared up at the house. It was eerily quiet, more so than usual. There was no murmur of cartoons, no startled giggles from Tanner, no sizzle of bacon on a fry pan.

There was just…nothing.

My stomach churned, but I wasn't sure if it was remnants of the alcohol, or the memory of vomiting on Jasmine's sneakers. I stared at my reflection in the window of the car, and I realised it wasn't either of those things.

It was something else. Something I couldn't put my finger on…

"She's a beauty, ain't she?"

I jumped, scraping my shin on my bike pedal. "*Fuck*," I muttered.

"Quite the mouth on you! Jack was the same. We got that out of him. We'll get it out of you."

I glanced over the hood of the car. David was aerating Pam's lawn—dressed in a pair of jeans and a white singlet. It was the first time I'd witnessed him in anything other than a suit.

"Good to see you again, Jules."

I shook his hand, and his grip was firm and smooth. Where Ray was all rough edges and grit, this man was refined. Polished.

Still, there was something about him that was so reminiscent of Ray. Maybe it was his energy, the way he seemed to loom over you even though he was standing completely upright.

He frowned at me. "You stay out last night?"

"Uh, yeah, sorry, I know I should have called—"

"You should've."

"I just, I wasn't really in any state to come home."

He nodded, seeming to analyse this information. His gaze trailed over my wrinkled clothes, and I braced myself for the inevitable drug/alcohol lecture, but it didn't come. "Just be careful with the media, okay? Don't be doing anything other than drinking. Even then, make sure it's indoors and around people you trust. There are lots of eyes on you at the moment, Jules. A lot of people wanting to take advantage, waiting for you to trip up."

"I'll be smart."

"Good man." He frowned at my bike, testing the tyres with his foot. "Hey, where'd you stay last night?"

"Uh, at Gavin's house."

"Gavin Lewis?"

I nodded.

"He's a good kid, Gavin." He scratched his beard. "I know he and Jack were close."

I nodded again. There it was—everything I needed to know about David in two sentences.

"Well, as long as you're keeping safe. I don't need to go throwing my weight around. You're seventeen. You're old enough. You've also been my step kid for all of three minutes."

"Thanks."

"You got a good head on your shoulders, Jules?"

"I'd like to think so."

"Good," he said. He glanced at the house, and then back at me. "Because you know, your mother, she worries a lot. I swear, Jack had her vibrating out of her skin half the time. He was a very lost kid, that one. It's terrible what happened to him." He tilted his head, his gaze seeming to linger on my face. "But now you're here, and you can make things right."

"I hope so." I was still hovering over my bike, and I tightened my grip around the handlebars.

"You hope so?"

"I mean, yeah, I think… It'll be good."

David stared at me for a beat longer, and then he smiled, lightly tapping my arm. "That's good to hear, Jules. Head inside and go help your mother clean up."

"I can't stay long. I've got a counselling session at two."

"Counselling?" David scoffed, shaking his head. "God, they had Pam into that for months before she met me. I get why she fell for it. I mean, her family are all broken. You probably met some of them at the funeral."

"A few," I said, but I couldn't really remember. Everyone had morphed into one giant Rosemary blob. I wasn't sure who were my real relatives, and who were *Uncle Rays* who were just trying to manipulate me.

"She has no contact with them. They're a bunch of drunks and gamblers. They tried to come after her settlement money, and she had to cut them off. I'm surprised she even let them come to the funeral. I told her she was stupid for that. They just stressed her out the whole day."

I wanted to say that it was probably her son's *funeral* that stressed her out, not her family. But I just kicked at a spot of dirt on the footpath.

"They were never close to her," he continued. "Never supported her. Not even when she got pregnant. There she was, barely twenty-one, no money, pregnant with twins. She had no one, really, until she met me. Jack was only a couple of months old, and the media was all over them like a rash. Her relatives only showed up after the settlement money came through a couple of years later."

I wondered how lonely all that must have been for Pam, how terrifying. It must have been nice to meet someone who could take care of her and her baby.

He went on. "Anyway, they had her in all these different therapies. Trauma therapy. Grief therapy. *Breath* therapy." He shook his head. "I swear, all that crap was just making it worse. A bunch of strangers getting inside her head. Perpetuating that dark mindset."

"Elijah says it's standard…"

"No standard in a situation like this. It's unprecedented. Astonishing, truly, just how many people had to fuck up their jobs for what happened to happen. Now the government's in damage control. Everyone's flapping around with their dicks out trying to figure out the best way to prevent any future lawsuits."

I sat down on my bike. "I guess I'd never really thought about it like that."

David rolled his eyes, like he was expecting me to say that. "Besides, all these New Age counsellors are just keen to get perfectly healthy people in a room and invent trauma that isn't really there." He leaned an arm against his car. "The plain and simple truth? A woman wanted a child, she snuck you out of that hospital and raised you as her own. Didn't do a bad job, by the looks, but it wasn't right. You weren't her child, and now you're reunited with your biological mother and everything's the way it should be. Justice will be served, and you'll live the life you were meant to live. Time to get on with it, don't you think? No point getting into a room and crying about it with some government-appointed stranger."

I fiddled with the bell on my bike. It was so rusted I doubted it worked. "Yeah. I guess you've got a point."

"But, hey, if it makes you feel better…"

"I think it's mandatory."

"Well, you're eighteen next month, and then no one can tell you what to do—not even me." David winked, slapping a hand on my shoulder. "Let's head inside. We can talk about all the counselling bullshit another time."

"Yeah, sure. Sounds good."

I hopped off my bike and then waited for David to lead the way, but he just stood there, staring at me. He stared at me as I put my bike away, and then he kept staring until I'd entered the house. He was smiling at me, so I suppose he was just being friendly. *Refined, polished, friendly.*

I suppose some people just had that way about them. That way of looking at you that gnawed right through your bones.

Chapter 14

By the time I made it to Park Ridge, I was over twenty minutes late, and I was so sweaty that my clothes were dripping onto the floor. It was the first of my scheduled weekly sessions with Yong, the counsellor Eloise had told me about on the way to Perth airport. That seemed a lifetime ago now. And in a way, it kind of was.

His receptionist merely stared at me and my dripping clothes.

"Julian Edwards-Rosemary," I said.

She smiled a small, tight smile. "I know."

I frowned. Did she know who I was because it was written somewhere? Or did she know because she'd watched literally any news channel over the last five weeks?

She sighed and changed the channel on the waiting room TV. *Definitely the latter.*

I sat down on one of the plush leather waiting chairs. For whatever reason, I was expecting to see a text from Jasmine when I unlocked my phone. It was completely irrational, seeing as she didn't have my number, and that she wouldn't text me even if she *did* have my number.

What's even more irrational was that I was even expecting a text from Chelsea… That I was anticipating it. A slew of angry missed calls, some form of digital abuse or defamation. But there was nothing. Not a single notification from anybody.

I opened my old Nokia after that, which I still kept in my bag, always fully-charged. There was no point, seeing as I didn't use it anymore. I suppose it was strictly sentimental—the only remaining thread between me and my old life.

I opened up my text history with Angela. The last message was sent over a month ago, by me.

Sunday, January 15th at 4:58 am

I love you. It's going to be ok.

I imagine that she would have responded, had she been able to. Had she not been in a holding cell in Canning Vale with no access to a mobile phone. Had she not been legally prohibited from all methods of contacting me.

"Jules?"

I flinched. Yong was standing in front of me, backlit by the warm lighting of the hallway. He was wearing a tan button-up shirt and he had a smile that instantly made him look five years younger.

I followed him into his office. It was a safe room with safe furniture and safe artworks—nothing too visceral or rousing, nothing that could potentially offset or influence a client's fragile state of mind.

Yong was the first counsellor I'd seen in Brisbane, but I'd already been grilled by several psychologists before leaving Perth. This meant that I was already familiar with the mental health specialist/client dance: we sat, facing each other, like awkward dates. He got out his pen and notepad and I was expected to disregard them like props. He milled around, asking me benign questions about my day, and then he launched into the meatier stuff:

"How are you feeling, Jules?"

I thought of David. I thought of Pam drinking vodka out of that ceramic coffee mug. I thought of Jasmine's hand in mine, and the tears streaming down Chelsea's face. I thought of that hooded man in the car park, and *Gav*, and the look on his face when he handed me that beer. I thought of the night beyond that point, the lucid colours of it, the way it morphed and disappeared beyond the recesses of my mind.

"I feel fine."

"You look a bit stressed."

I heard David's voice in the back of my mind. *Time to get on with it, don't you think?*

"I think that's normal, given the circumstances." I shrugged. "I'll get over it. It'll just take time."

Yong frowned. He put his pen down, opening himself up to me. "Sure, Jules. That's one way to look at it. The other way is to observe what happened and your current situation with the nuance that it deserves, and with empathy for all those that have been affected. First and foremost, empathy for yourself."

"So…you'd rather I just cry about it and never get better?"

"Well, I don't think there's anything wrong with crying, if that's what your body needs to do to process and begin to regulate—"

"What if I don't want to cry?"

This seemed to give him pause. "What do you want to do, Jules?"

"I don't know. Normal seventeen-year-old stuff. Go to parties. Have sex. Drink?"

Yong hummed. I'd just said a slew of edgy buzzwords, and he looked like he was trying his best not to look concerned.

"There's no normal behaviour for a seventeen-year-old, Jules. Especially not for someone who's experienced trauma. And while some of those things might seem appealing to you in the present moment, they shouldn't be something you do just because you want to be viewed as *normal.*"

"I'll never be normal. I know that." *I'll never be anything other than fucking Rosemary Boy.* I shrugged again, picking at the peeled leather on my seat. "That's okay."

"You are, and you will always be more than what the media calls you. A great American critic named Susan Sontag once said, *A thing is a thing, not what is said of that thing.*" He smiled at me. "See? Even the critics know that what they say is ultimately meaningless. The good ones, at least." He tapped his pen against his empty page. "*Opinion is the medium between knowledge and ignorance.*"

"Another critic?"

"Plato."

"Right," I said. "Yeah, that's…that's true, I guess. But what about the rest of them? The people that think they know everything?"

"Well, we get earplugs."

I smiled. "Right."

Yong smiled too, but it faded as quickly as it appeared. The room dissolved into awkward silence, and now it really did feel like a bad date.

"How is everything at home?"

"Fine," I said.

"It must be quite the adjustment. Not only because of the surreal circumstances, but because you're now living with an entirely different family unit. You have siblings now, and a father figure in David—"

"But David's not my father," I said.

"No, but he could serve as a role model. It's important for young men to have positive male role models in their lives. Given your sheltered life back in Perth, and Angela's employment of a female home school teacher and babysitter… You seem to have been lacking in this throughout your development."

I wanted to disagree with him. I wanted to tell him that Mum—Angela—had done just fine with me. I wanted to tell him all the terrible things that David had said about his profession. But I just nodded. Maybe he was right. Maybe there *were* things I could learn from David, even if I didn't necessarily like him.

"I heard you had an interview at Beacon Heights Nursing Home," Yong said next. "How did that go?"

"It was fine," I told him. I rubbed the back of my neck, unsure if I should tell him this next part. I still hadn't told anyone, and the memories seemed to be getting heavier with each day that passed. "Actually, there was this guy there…" I muttered. "…In the car park. He kept asking me to give him a statement, and it kind of freaked me out."

"A journalist? They shouldn't be talking to you—"

"He wasn't a journalist. He was just a guy, looking to make money."

"I'm sorry that happened to you, Jules. Unfortunately, there are a lot of immoral people in this world that will try and cash in on other people's misfortune. They're the lowest of the low."

"He didn't do anything bad," I told him.

"He ambushed you, and he shouldn't have done that. If it happens again, we can get the police involved and have him arrested for harassment."

I nodded, playing with a loose thread on my pants.

"When you say that it freaked you out, how did it make you feel exactly?"

"I just…I couldn't really move for a while afterwards. My chest was so tight…"

"It sounds like you were having an anxiety attack. This is very common when dealing with situations that feel unsafe, or when your body perceives a threat. Sometimes our bodies are right, but sometimes this feeling can strike us seemingly out of nowhere. Regardless, it can feel completely debilitating."

I licked my lips. "I was supposed to ride home, but I couldn't, and then Chelsea…"

"Chelsea…Douglas? Jack's former girlfriend?"

"She drove me home. She was…really nice to me, actually. She offered to drive me around instead of me riding my bike."

"You don't seem particularly happy about that."

"It was really nice at the time, but…" I scratched the back of my head. "I don't know, I kept thinking about it… And I just kept thinking, *why*?"

"Why is this stranger showing kindness to me?"

"Well, that's the thing. She's not a stranger. She was really close with Pam and the kids. She was really close with…"

"Just because this young lady knew Jack, doesn't mean that she now knows you. It's a complex situation, but you may find that some people may feel more familiar around you than you do with them. They may feel a fondness toward you…" He made a note in his pad. "They may also endow you with traits or values that don't actually align with you."

I remained silent, and Yong continued making notes.

"Then there's the inverse," he said, finally gazing up at me. "Some people may feel they want to distance themselves from you and their memories of Jack. You may serve as a reminder of something unsavoury, or some people may simply find it too hard to cope with such a vivid association. None of this is your fault."

I thought about Jasmine, and how angry she'd been that I'd taken the job at Beacon. "But what if I don't want these people to distance themselves from me?"

"Unfortunately, Jules, we don't control how others feel. Just like how you can't control the fondness Chelsea feels for you, you can't control the alienation you feel from her." Yong rubbed his chin. "Perhaps it could help you to accept a ride from her. It could be an exercise in trust."

"You think this is about trust?"

"You've been betrayed, Jules—very deeply, and by someone very close to you. These wounds will heal over, but they will leave tender scars."

"I just don't want them writing articles about us. I don't want people to think I'm going after Jack's girlfriend…" I took a deep breath, staring out the window. "Also, I think she kind of hates me now…"

Yong just smiled at me. "Most of the time, Jules, the way we think others perceive us is a lot worse than the way they actually do."

I thought about Jasmine again. I thought about her cleaning

my hands.

"Do we have to keep doing these sessions?" I asked him. "After I turn eighteen?"

"We can stop these sessions whenever you like, Jules. But I would like to see you again, especially with the gag order being lifted soon." Yong set down his pen again, closing his notepad. "We don't even have to talk, if you don't want to. We can just sit here."

"Yeah, I don't…I don't think I want to talk anymore. At least, not about that stuff."

"We can talk about anything that you like, Jules."

"Okay," I said. But I didn't really know what to talk about anymore. I couldn't remember the last time I had a normal conversation with someone that wasn't fraught with the undercurrent of everything that had happened to me.

I looked down at my phone. There was one new text: just Pam, asking me if I wanted a lift home from counselling.

"Bad news?" Yong asked me.

"Uh, no," I said. "Just…thought it might have been someone else."

"You might want to set your phone to airplane mode for a while. At least until after your birthday, and this next wave of hysteria blows over."

I looked at him. "Airplane mode?"

For the next month, I went to school, went to work, and existed mostly in a quiet state of survival mode. I found myself wanting to do something. I wanted to do a lot of things, actually. I wanted to figure my life out in my spare time, what I needed to fix it. But all I could seem to do was sleep, or make a sandwich, or lie on the floor and stare at the ceiling. Days and days of doing things I don't remember. I remember how it felt, though. This dull pain…

The only times this pain didn't seem so overwhelming was when Jasmine was around. She seemed to quiet something inside of me. She didn't even have to be doing anything. I'd just see her from across the schoolyard and I'd get this feeling. I'd never had that feeling leaving Yong's office, and I started to wonder if maybe David was right. Maybe letting strangers get inside your head wasn't as good an idea as everyone was telling me it was.

Then again, *Jasmine* was a stranger…

But she didn't feel like one. That's the thing.

Ever since I met her, a part of me felt like I knew her.

One afternoon, after a session with Yong, I decided that it would be our last. Not because he was a bad guy, or because I thought he was making me feel worse, but because I couldn't tolerate letting any more strangers inside my head.

"You've made the right decision," David told me, but Pam didn't look so convinced. He waited until she was out of earshot before he said, "By the way, when you turn eighteen next week, a lot of things are gonna start to change. The media's gonna start contacting you directly. It's gonna get a hell of a lot more intense. I could handle the negotiations on your behalf. It's what I do for a living." He smiled at me, loosening his tie. He always wore a suit to work, even in the summer. "This situation right here is no different to selling a house. We sell to the highest bidder."

We were sitting at the kitchen table. I could smell the alcohol in Pam's empty coffee cup. "Pam said she doesn't want us talking to the media," I said.

David scoffed. "If we started taking Pam's advice, we'd never stop crying."

I stared at the cracks in the wooden table. I didn't like what he'd just said, or the way he'd said it, but maybe he was right. Maybe that's what Yong had been referring to when he was talking about the importance of a male role model. Someone to make all the decisions. Someone to take control. One thing I'd noticed was that a lot of guys state their opinion as fact, and women don't tend to do that as much. It made me wonder whether guys viewed women as being beneath them. Maybe it was just guys like David.

His voice changed—softened a little. "Look, I know what Pam says, but you let me work on her, okay? In the meantime, start thinking about what you'd like to say. This could be a very lucrative opportunity for our family. You're a part of our family now, Jules. Don't forget that." He clapped a hand on my shoulder. "Just think about it."

I wanted to question him, then. About why he'd taken down all the photos of Jack from the hallway. About why he cared more about money than honouring his wife's wishes. About why he'd never once asked me what *I* wanted.

But I just smiled, and I said, "I'll think about it."

David polished off the rest of his drink—beer, I think. Something called *Guinness*. It was blacker than any drink I'd ever seen. Blacker than the pupils of David's eyes when he stared me down in that way.

I started to go up to my room.

"Make sure the kids are in bed, will you? Tanner loves to

fuck about at this time of night. Tries to keep that bloody night light turned on that Pam got her. Turn it off. She'll stop cryin' once she falls asleep. James is in there with her, and she's too old for a fucking night light."

"Uh, sure," I said. I headed out of the kitchen and down the hallway. I could see a dim light permeating from beneath the kids' door, and that's the first time a night light ever made me feel sick.

I took a deep breath and entered their room. As soon as I did, it was like someone had just ripped the cord out of an old television set. All the light and sound disappeared, leaving only a dark, lifeless rectangle.

I swallowed. My mouth had been dry all night. "Y-you guys sleeping?" I whispered. It felt like a dumb question. If they really were sleeping—which they *weren't*—then they weren't about to pipe up and answer me.

Neither of them moved. I'd almost believed they'd disappeared from the room, except that I could hear the faint rustling of fabric. I wondered if one of them was trying to hide under their sheets.

I heard a small, boyish whisper. "It's Jules."

I waited a moment, then I said, "Yeah. It's just me."

The room was plunged into silence again. I walked in a little further, quietly shutting the door behind me. I used the torch on my new phone to shine a bit of light. It immediately met James and Tanner's eyes—both sharing the same bed—and their faces startled like disturbed possums. I quickly shone the torch on the ground instead, and there was just enough light for me to make out their faces. I hoped there was enough for them to see mine, and that they knew I wasn't a threat.

A threat. The words racked through me like a cold wind.

"It's okay," I told them. "You're not in trouble. I just came in here…" *to see if you guys were asleep.* "…to see if you guys needed anything."

I heard a small exhale. It was too dark to see who it came from, but I think it was Tanner.

They didn't answer me. I had a strong suspicion that this question had never been asked at that time of night. *Maybe it had never been asked.*

"You guys are okay?" I whispered.

James nodded.

"Okay," I whispered. "Okay. That's good." A few beats passed, and I spoke so quietly I wasn't sure if they could hear me: "Wait until you hear your dad go to bed, and then turn your light back on. I'll make sure it's turned off before he gets up."

They were frozen again. Finally, James whispered, "Promise?"

"I promise," I said. And I swear, I'd never been more serious about anything. Afterwards, I waited until the unmistakable sound of David's footsteps trudged past the door, and then I nodded at James. After a moment's hesitation, he reached under his bed for the cord to the night light. Soon, the room was bathed in a soft, yellowish glow.

I closed the door, and that's how it became my routine: getting up at 5 a.m.—right before I knew David's alarm sounded at 5:15 a.m. I'd get up and groggily wander down the stairs. I'd always try to get to sleep again after that, but I never could. The sight of Tanner and James curled around each other—artificial light fusing into natural sunrays—was enough to obliterate my heart into a million pieces.

Chapter 15

I always thought turning eighteen would cure something inside me. Unfortunately, for most of April 5th, I found myself feeling dismally, painfully the same. It probably wasn't helped by the fact that I'd always celebrated my birthday on the 4th of May, when Angela had told me it was.

I woke up. I spent about thirty minutes staring mindlessly out the window. I brushed my teeth and vomited yellow stomach bile. I checked my phone, but there were no notifications because of *airplane mode*, which was essentially a way of quietening all the noise. Like taking a trip to nowhere and then returning whenever you felt strong enough to face reality. It was almost 7 a.m., and I still didn't feel strong enough to leave my room.

When I finally ventured downstairs, I was struck by the smell of bacon and pancakes—no, *bacon* pancakes…with maple syrup.

Pam grimaced, as if only now realising her mistake. "Happy birthday, honey. These were, uh, these were your brother's favourite." She shrugged, setting the plate down like some kind of morbid birthday cake. The only thing missing was the candles, and the fact that I wasn't dead.

"Thank you, Pam. Looks delicious."

"Your mum's one hell of a cook." David dug into his pancakes, polishing off the entire plate within minutes. Clearly, the morbidity of today hadn't done much to curb his appetite.

In a weird way, David's detachment was comforting. While everyone else was walking on eggshells, he was ploughing through them like a truck driver. There was simply no room for awkward silence when everything about him was so *loud*: his voice, his car, his footsteps, his chewing.

Well, that was until the kids were around.

Tanner's placid voice drifted in from the living room. "Mummy, can we sing 'Happy Birthday' to Jack?"

My stomach soured, and David nearly choked on his juice.

"Uh, honey," Pam said, reaching for Tanner's hand, "you know that this is Jules, right? We talked about this."

"I know."

"You want to sing to Jack anyway?"

Tanner nodded. Beside her, James was holding onto her elbow. They were still in their matching SpongeBob pyjamas, hair dishevelled, eyes wide and lost. Distantly, I knew that they were my siblings, but most of the time they just looked like sad little hobbits.

"Maybe, maybe we could sing to both of them?" Pam said softly.

David grunted. "That's a little bit morbid, don't you think? A little...*off*?"

Ah, so there was the line. Making Jack's favourite saturated breakfast: *Delicious, nutritious*. Singing him 'Happy Birthday': *Morbid... Off.*

"It's okay," I told Pam. "You guys can sing whatever you want."

Pam's eyes widened. In that moment, she looked just like an older version of Tanner. "Are you sure?" she whispered.

David turned to me, his eyebrows raised.

"Yeah. I mean…it's just a song, and…you know, it's his birthday too."

Pam squeezed my knee beneath the table. She held both mine and Tanner's hands as they started to sing, and David just shook his head, helping himself to another stack of pancakes.

Happy birthday to you
Happy birthday to you
Happy birthday dear Jack and Jules
Happy birthday to you

Luckily, we had begun our first term break, so I didn't have to worry about going to school that day. Pam also dropped me to work that afternoon as a protective measure. We weren't sure whether the reporters were going to start ambushing me again given their newfound freedom, but we didn't want to take the risk. She'd also phoned Barb at Beacon to inform her of the situation, but I'd assured them both that I was still happy to go to work. Maybe it wasn't exactly *work* that I was happy to go to, but…something else.

Pam dropped me off right outside the doors of Beacon, and my eyes did a cautionary sweep of the car park. There were no men in hoodies, no *Chelseas*—just an old couple being escorted back to the home by one of their carers.

"Call me if you need me," Pam said softly.

I nodded.

"The upside of working in a retirement home is that these people have much bigger issues to deal with. I doubt they'd be concerned with or even up to date with current affairs. Also, they probably aren't cognisant enough to be able to *read* the news—"

"It's okay, Pam."

She reached across the car and squeezed my hand. "I hear you, some mornings. I hear you coughing in your bathroom."

"It's just a thing I do."

"It'll pass, Jules. It'll all pass."

It'll pass.

The carer with the elderly couple buzzed me into the elevator, and we took the lift up to level four. My heart was beating so fast I thought I was going to pass out. Elevator lifts are naturally awkward, but this was interminable.

The old woman crooned at me. "You look very familiar."

I kept my gaze locked on my shoes.

"Doesn't he look familiar, Neville?"

I closed my eyes, and the headline JULIAN EDWARDS-ROSEMARY flashed across my corneas. *Rosemary Boy Finally Revealed!*

I wondered what photos they used as the elevator finally stopped. I let the couple move ahead—at a glacial pace, considering they were both using walkers—and I just stood there for a moment, mentally preparing myself. My first shift at work. My first outing as an adult. My first outing as me—the real me, demystified in the public eye.

Jasmine was helping Pip again in the foyer. When I entered, she just smiled at me briefly, and that was it. There was no staring, no talking, no well wishes of any kind.

But that was *fine*.

I wasn't expecting her to wish me a happy birthday, just like

I wasn't expecting one of the phone calls I received this morning to be from Melaleuca Women's Prison—and not an endless slew of distant family members I'd only met once. *Hi. Yes, I remember you. Thank you. Yes. I'm doing well. I'm very happy. Yes, I got your present. It looks/smells/fits just right.*

I wasn't expecting her to remember... But it still sucked, because knowing something isn't going to happen doesn't stop you from wanting it. It doesn't stop you from torturing yourself with the fantasy, and it doesn't save you from the silent, crushing weight of reality.

I sat down at my desk. Barb had run me through most of the job at my trial, but I still felt like an imposter—like someone pretending to be a receptionist, pretending to be *Jack*. According to her, my two afternoon shifts a week would run like this: arrive after school at 4 p.m. Let Pip give me a big squeeze if I found her roaming the corridors, bid good day to *Doctor Bill* and give him his *schedule* for the day (it was just a stack of papers Jack had compiled with fake patient names), check emails, create the daily PowerPoints that would be broadcasted on the residents' televisions screens for the next week, clean the coffee machines, and then watch Netflix until 8 p.m. as soon as Barb and the other big bosses went home for the day. The duty nurses left in charge never paid any attention to what I was doing, and the carers were usually busy attending to resident call bells that always seemed to be ringing. That meant the last couple of hours were free for me to do whatever I wanted.

"Excuse me, sir," someone said to my left. He was a tall, gangly man with a walker. "I would like some documents printed, if it's not too much hassle, and it shouldn't be, considering what I paid just to have a one-bedroom balcony-view apartment. A balcony I can't even enjoy without *supervision*, I might add. A half a million dollars! Can you believe that?" He looked at Jasmine, who'd appeared at his shoulder.

She smiled at him—a genuine smile. "Well, Reg, the good thing is that when you finally cark it, you can leave it to people you love in your will."

My stomach soured. *What the—?*

"Oh, yes," he said, grinning with tarnished teeth. "The sweet release of death and all my material possessions." He looked at me. "And who might you be, young man? I have to say, you look a tad familiar."

Reg gave Jasmine a knowing look, a wily smile on his face. I decided to try a joke.

"I'm Julian," I said. "Jack's living half."

A dark, startled laugh erupted from Reg's belly. "There he is! A man with *humour*. Trust me, young man, that is the only thing that will save you in a world such as this. We must be able to laugh at our troubles so as not to be *overwhelmed* by them. Just take me, for instance: eighty-nine with a mind as sharp as a tack and a body that can barely withstand a stiff wind. Take Miss Morè to my left: exceptionally overqualified in every facet but confined to the Château d'If until she can earn enough pennies to leave this stale town in her dust. And you, young man, kidnapped at birth and then returned to the grocer like a bruised banana."

More carers appeared behind Reg. It was nearly five, which meant that the next round of staff members were beginning their shifts. They each signed in at the desk, grabbing their name tags. Usually, it just meant they all took turns staring at me.

"Mr Burns," someone said, presumably to Reg. "What are you doing causing trouble at reception?"

"Getting my affairs in order, Mr Kaupa. I have given Mr Rosemary here the indispensable task of printing my last will and testament."

"Are you sure he can be trusted?" he asked Reg. It seemed they all had this strange, sarcastic way of communicating with him.

"Well, he *seems* like a well-adjusted, capable young man." Reg glanced at Jasmine. "Thoughts, Ms Morè?"

"The jury's still out on that one. Also, it's Edwards-Rosemary."

"Of course," Reg said. "How could I forget?"

Jasmine glanced at the boy who'd just signed in, avoiding all eye contact with me. "Norman needs help in 402."

"Yes, Boss."

He and Jasmine disappeared down the hallway, and I watched them leave with a strange ache in my chest. They seemed close-ish, judging by their body language: the way their shoulders hovered mere centimetres apart. Was I jealous? Of what, exactly? Their friendship? Their physical proximity? The fact that they were both small and unassuming, and I was a sensational headline trying to assimilate into Brisbane society? And why had Jasmine cared about correcting my name?

"Brrr," Reg said, shivering. "What did you do to her?"

I turned to look at him. He was leaning casually against his walker, almost like it was a fashion accessory more than anything. There was something about Reg that I was jealous of too, though I couldn't put my finger on it. His lack of concern despite the piling concerns in his life? The way he seemed almost amused by his frailty, like the very thought of getting old was some cosmic joke he'd beaten to the punchline?

"I didn't do anything," I told him, plugging in his hard drive. "She just…doesn't like me."

"Ms Morè wouldn't dislike anyone without a reason," Reg said. "She's far too intelligent for that. Mindless hatred is for extremists and internet trolls." He pushed his glasses higher on his nose. "Yes, I know about internet trolls."

"I don't know, it feels a bit like mindless hatred to me."

"Well, then maybe it's a different feeling."

I frowned, sending his file to the printer. "What?"

"*I beg your pardon*," Reg said, "is a far more respectable way of saying you don't understand. I know you grew up a little differently, but perhaps I can teach you some decorum."

I sighed internally. "I, um, beg your pardon?"

"Well, I'm merely suggesting that there is another intense feeling, you know."

"What's that?" I asked him.

Reg just smiled at me, like this conversation was amusing to him. Life seemed to be amusing to him, and it pissed me off. Why wasn't he miserable?

"What?" I demanded. *Screw him and his respectability.*

"Love, young man."

Heat surged through my stomach. *Oh.*

"Well, that's just ridiculous," I said.

"Yes, it is," Reg agreed. "Being in love is just about the most ridiculous condition a person can find themselves in."

"Jasmine is not in love with me."

"Hmm. Love might be a bit of a strong word, at least for the moment. Would you say that you fancy her?"

I chewed on the end of my pen. "No, but I wish people would stop assuming I do."

"And *I* wish people would stop asking me if I want to move to a room on the third floor." Reg sighed, picking up his document that was sitting in the printer. "Sometimes, Mr Edwards-Rosemary, other people can see things that we're not ready to see."

Reg took out a pen from somewhere in his vest. It was silver and gold and embossed with the letters RB. He signed the document in smooth, sweeping lines.

Reginald Burns

"And there it is: the summation of a life half-lived, signed by the perpetrator himself."

"Half-lived?"

Reg didn't answer me. He just used his walker to turn himself around, whistling quietly beneath his breath. He moved at a glacial pace back toward his room, and it was only then that I realised his walker was *not* an accessory. That walker was the legs with which he moved around this dreary place, and there was nothing enviable about that at all.

"Mr Edwards-Rosemary," he said. He was paused halfway across the foyer, his body facing straight ahead.

"Uh…yes, Reg?"

"I used to know someone with a birthday on the 5th of April." Reg turned his face slightly, but he still didn't look at me. "Happy birthday."

A slow smile crept across my face. "Thanks."

"Jasmine did remind me, so I can't take full credit."

"She did?"

"Indeed."

Something loosened around my heart, and the smile on my face only widened. Thank God there was no one around—no one except Bill. He was busy going through his 'patient' files, and his atrophied brain meant that he was never present for a conversation even when he looked like he was. There was something deeply comforting about his presence. I didn't have to worry about him recognising me, or asking me invasive questions about my personal life. The two of us could just…be.

Reg slowly proceeded back toward his room, and soon it was just me, and those words, and Bill, asking me if I could sterilise his instruments for his surgery.

"Already done," I said, handing him a glue stick.

Just as I was powering down my computer for the night, I noticed a tab open in the top left corner of the screen. It must have been from the daytime receptionist, and I was about to close it for her when I realised that it was a news site.

I tried to exit the tab, but it was too late. The word caught the corner of my eye—a word I'd seen a million times—my own name. My body sank into a dark, bottomless abyss. My name was the headline, as well as a photograph of me from Jack's funeral. I was leaving the church, half-covering my face with one hand, and clutching Jack's memorial pamphlet in the other.

RIVER CITY TIMES

Julian Edwards-Rosemary Adjusts to New Life After 17 Years in Captivity; Kidnapper Awaits Extradition

BY LAN ZHANG   **APRIL 5, 2017**

JULIAN Edwards-Rosemary, who was recently reunited with his biological mother after being kidnapped and held captive for 17 years, is gradually adjusting to his new life. The now 18-year-old, who was taken as newborn twin Nicholas Rosemary and raised under the false identity of Julian Edwards, has spent the past few weeks reconnecting with Pamela Rosemary, his stepfather, David Leman, and his two half-siblings born more than a decade after his kidnapping.

The media have been restricted from revealing Julian's real name until now due to a gag order, which was lifted upon his 18th birthday. His kidnapper, Angela Edwards, formerly known as Donna Jones, is currently in a Perth prison awaiting extradition to Queensland. Edwards was apprehended in January following news reports publicising the sudden death of Julian's identical twin, Jack. Reports say those in Julian's life were quick to make the connection, including his former home-school teacher and several concerned neighbours. An anonymous tip was made to police and Edwards promptly turned herself in.

"Jules."

I didn't look up.

"Jules. It's time to go home. I don't think you have a key card yet, so Barb told me to let you out—"

Tears were blurring my vision. It was awful. It was like that moment in the car park all over again, except I wasn't straddling my bike, and I wasn't being harassed by a goon in a dirty hoodie.

I was being harassed by *words*. On a *computer*.

"Jules, what's the matter—?"

The person moved to look at the monitor, and I only just realised that it was Jasmine. I scrambled to exit the article, but I wasn't fast enough.

"Oh," she said softly.

I stared down at the keyboard. The pressure in my chest was building. *But some people don't have enough holes in their buckets, so the water just keeps overflowing with nowhere to go.*

"Do you want to go up to the roof?"

I glanced up at Jasmine. "Are we allowed?"

"Absolutely not."

"Oh." I looked down at the keyboard again. *Damn.*

I picked up my phone, about to call Pam to pick me up, but Jasmine was already halfway to the elevator.

"Well," she said. "Are you coming or not?"

Chapter 16

It occurred to me, in that moment, that I'd never been on a roof before.

I'd also *certainly* never been on a roof with a girl.

I stared over the edge of the building. There was a black metal railing, but I still didn't like looking down. It was much nicer to look directly ahead at all the sparkling buildings filled with people safe inside their apartment complexes. Cuddled up on couches. Their television screens flickering like tiny light bulbs.

"It's beautiful," I said. I glanced at Jasmine, who was standing silently behind me. "You don't think?"

"It's just Logan City."

"But look at all the buildings," I told her. "I've never seen the tops of them before."

She shrugged. "I'm up here all the time. I guess I just don't really look at them that often."

"What do you look at?"

"I mostly just come here to listen to music. I stay sitting in that corner."

"But you can't see any of this from over there."

I looked back at the buildings. I could still feel Jasmine's gaze on me.

A few moments later, I heard Jasmine pulling up two stools. She sat them right near the metal railing, so we could still watch the city.

"It'll stop, you know. The articles. The media… They'll move onto something else. It's what always happens."

I nodded, staring into one of the apartment complexes across from Beacon. There was an old shirtless man parading around his living room. He didn't have to worry about being photographed. He could just exist, and it was nobody's business.

I'd never wanted to trade places with an old shirtless man so badly.

"I know it's irrational," I said. "But I'm scared of them saying I'm dating Chelsea. I'm scared of them saying I got drunk. I'm scared of them saying I'm a bad person."

"You're not a bad person."

I looked at her. "How would you know?"

"You can tell these things, most of the time. Sometimes people fool you, but it's rare."

I glanced back at the building. The shirtless man was dancing now. "Mostly, though, I'm afraid of what they're going to say about Angela. I'm afraid of what I'm going to find out about her."

"Hey," Jasmine said. "Come here."

"What?"

She got off her stool suddenly, and she climbed over the metal railing. There was a small landing just before the edge of the building, enough space for two people to sit.

"Jasmine, what are you—?"

"It's not as scary as it looks, I promise."

I swallowed. My anxiety had permeated through my entire body. I could now feel it throbbing in my fingertips, in my toes. "This isn't helping, you know."

"Not yet," she said. "You're thinking too much."

I took a deep breath. Slowly, I hooked one leg over the metal railing, and then the other. "Oh, God…" I mumbled. "I can see the headlines now: *Rosemary Boy Plummets to His Death.*"

"Don't be silly," she told me. "They'd use your real name for that headline."

I glared at her, but for some reason, it actually made me laugh. Maybe it was the adrenaline—the fact that I was gripping onto a metal pole for dear life. "How do you even have access to this roof?"

"When Barb was activating my key card, she accidentally made it all-access. I just never said anything."

"You could get fired," I told her. Wind was rushing my ears, and my heart was dancing like that shirtless old man.

"Maybe," she said. "Or maybe not. I'd rather take my chances." She pulled on my pant leg. "Sit *down.*"

I carefully lowered myself into a sitting position.

"Wow. This is a lot better," I said.

"Right?"

"You can see the shirtless guy a lot more clearly from here."

"We're like eye-level."

I tried looking down again, but it made my blood feel like lead. "I don't think I'm good with heights," I said.

"You don't say."

Each passing car seemed to lurch through my stomach. I closed my eyes, trying to quell the nausea in my gut.

"Hey," Jasmine said. "If you look at these buildings, and you squint just right, you could be anywhere in the world."

I tried it. The city mostly just looked like a giant stained window.

"Where would you want to be?" she asked me.

"Fremantle."

Jasmine was silent. Our legs were dangling over the side of the building, and I wanted to see how close they were but I also didn't want to look down.

"It's so weird," I told her. "I spent my whole life thinking I was adopted. I used to fantasise about my real parents all the time. I used to wonder about their names and what they looked like, and whether they looked like me. Now I know—well, I know Pam… And I feel even lonelier than before. My dad died before I was born, and he was just someone she met on a holiday. I haven't even seen a photo of him."

Jasmine hummed. "Sometimes the fantasy's more comforting than the reality."

"I thought Angela was a good person,' I said. "I thought she was the best person I'd ever met. You said that sometimes people have you fooled, but what if she didn't fool me? What if she was bad, and I loved her anyway?"

"Well, she was right about social media. The concept of sharing photos and experiences is nice. But it's turned into millions of people screaming at each other without sound."

"I miss her so much, Jasmine. All the time. Every day…" My eyes started to burn. Maybe I could convince myself it was the wind. "And I'm so *afraid* of finding out evil things about her, because it makes me wonder whether loving her makes me evil too."

"Maybe this is wrong of me to say, but I don't think the truth has to change what you had with her." She was quiet for a moment, and then she sighed. "That's yours, Jules. That's yours no matter what anyone says."

I rubbed my eyes. It was the nicest thing she had ever said to me. I started to wonder if maybe it was the nicest thing anyone had ever said to me—not because of how it sounded, but because of what it meant.

"Why do people have to say things?" I asked her. "Why do they have to talk about other people at all?"

"I think it's biological."

"Like, we're wired to be this way?"

"My mum says it's because we're wired to take the path of least resistance. She says that sometimes it's easier to find meaning in other people's lives than it is to find meaning in our own."

My right leg brushed against hers. It was like rubbing my skin against a livewire. I almost pulled back, but then I imagined falling over the side of the building. It felt only slightly safer to stay still. To risk the wrath of Jasmine…

But she didn't move either. We stayed there for a long time, just watching the skyline. I started to feel like this was a very important moment in my life. I'd never had that feeling before. I'd never anticipated missing a moment before it was gone.

I can't remember who shifted a leg away first, but soon we were getting to our feet. Jasmine reached out a hand to steady me, and I thought about kissing her. I thought about closing the distance and pressing my lips against hers very gently, the way I'd done with the girl across the street. But she seemed too far away, and I really didn't want to fall to my death.

Instead, we just helped each other back over the metal railing. Once we were safely on the other side, we walked back to the elevator doors in silence.

Jasmine swiped her key card, and she pressed the number four. We stood in silence for a few moments, and then, right before we were about to get in, she said, "Happy birthday, Jules," in a voice so quiet I couldn't be sure I'd heard it.

I smiled to myself. It wasn't until we got back to reception that I realised all the bad feelings in my body were gone. That rooftop and fresh air had been like a salve. Or maybe it had been something else.

After the two-week term break, the world returned to normal. Well, my version of normal. There were a couple of reporters waiting for Pam and me when she dropped me off, but it was easier to ignore them after my conversation with Jasmine. It was easier to understand why they were prying for information about my life—about *me*.

"Julian, do you have a moment?"

"No, he has school." Pam beeped her horn at them.

I shoved in my earphones. That was Pam's tip: *put in your earphones and block out the world.* So that's what I did; I put on The Lumineers and I drowned out their questions. Questions like, *How are you feeling? Do you want to talk to us now that the gag order has been lifted? What can you tell us about your new life?*

Despite David's best attempts, Pam still wasn't budging on talking to the media, which meant that *I* wasn't budging. Honestly, a part of me was relieved that she was so steadfast in her decision, because it meant that I didn't have to be. I could live in complete silence and use *Pam's wishes* as a protective shield against any peer pressure. I wondered if that was the reason she was refusing to talk—to protect me—or if it was something else.

Another part of me that was too afraid to ask.

One good thing is that they still couldn't take my photo, but only because I was wearing this uniform, and it's a violation of the Privacy Act to photograph students in uniform without school or parental consent. They could write about me, but they couldn't photograph me—at least, not here—and that was deeply comforting. That was when my transition to 'normal school' started to feel a little less daunting. It was almost like a safe haven, like the rooftop of Beacon.

For the most part…

Classes were still uncomfortable—especially English class with Ms Morè, because everyone seemed to be extra disobedient in that class. Jasmine and Ms Morè were always trading strange looks, and Gav and Bradley making mean remarks about Jasmine that only *I* seemed to hear, and I was always clenching my fists beneath the desk to abstain from doing something about it. Chelsea also sat directly beside me, and that was rather unfortunate seeing as we hadn't spoken since that night… That night when I'd told her to *leave me alone*.

When the bell finally rang roughly eighty-nine minutes later, I couldn't leave the classroom quick enough.

"Jules? Could you hang back a second?"

I sighed. The rest of the class funnelled out either side of me, including Gav, who slapped me on the shoulder.

When it was just the two of us, Ms Morè leaned against the back of her desk. "So, how are you going? I hear David's back from his business trip."

"He is. He's um…yeah, he's nice enough."

"Step-parents can be tough. Especially when you're just getting to know your *biological* parent."

"Yeah, it's pretty weird," I muttered. "I mostly just feel like I'm staying at a friend's house, only the friend is never home."

"If you ever need to talk, Jules…"

"Well, I have a counsellor. Actually, I *had* a counsellor. I think I'm going to give it up now that I'm eighteen."

Ms Morè frowned. "Oh? Why's that?"

"Well, I just don't know how much good it's doing. David says that the government is just trying to cover their arses."

"David said that?" Ms Morè nodded, staring out the window. "Okay. You do realise that's just one person's opinion though, right? Opinions are like arseholes, Jules. Everybody has one."

I huffed out a laugh. "Are you meant to say stuff like that?"

She shrugged again. "It's just *my* opinion. It's also my opinion that you should be listening to a variety of trusted adults in your life and forming your own opinions."

"I don't really think I have many of those," I said.

I wasn't really sure what I was referring to: trusted adults, or my own opinions.

"There's a man named Coach Finlay," Ms Morè said. "He teaches touch football at a local club. I think you'd really take a liking to him."

"I think I met him already…at the wake. He was Jack's coach, right?"

Ms Morè looked sheepish for a moment. "I promise I'm not trying to saddle you with every former role model in Jack's life. I know it may seem like it, but there was a reason Jack liked these people, why he trusted them. And I guess, I know how much it would mean to them…to know that you're okay."

I nodded, even though the thought sounded about as appetising as Jack's favourite breakfast. *Bacon pancakes.* Maybe it would be nice to spend time with these people, but there was a good chance that they'd see right through me, and then what? What would it mean to these people to know that I *wasn't* okay?

"You're an adult now," Ms Morè said. "That means you can listen…or not listen…to anyone you want." She placed a hand on my shoulder, tilting her head. "Happy birthday for the fifth, by the way."

"Thanks," I muttered. "I didn't think…I didn't think anyone remembered."

"On the contrary: I think most people remembered, but they were too terrified to say anything."

Right. So, I wasn't *unpopular*; I was just terrifying.

Ms Morè dismissed me after that, but not before giving me the address for Coach Finlay's football club, and not before giving me another one of those *looks*—like she was physically holding back everything she wanted to say to me. Real things. Things that would probably sever the tentative line between high school English teacher and concerned parental figure.

When I walked out of the classroom, it was directly into someone's back—someone small and vanilla-scented.

Jasmine frowned at me. "What was she talking to you about?"

"Were you waiting out here this whole time? Waiting for me to run into you?"

"Well, I didn't expect you to physically run into me."

"I didn't expect you to be waiting right outside the door." I glanced behind me. "Were you eavesdropping?"

"Definitely not. I was waiting to talk to my mother."

"Well, she's free now." I moved aside for Jasmine to pass, but she stayed where she was.

We stared at each other for a long, heated moment. Neither of us moved.

"Well?" I said.

"I think I'll just talk to her later."

I played with the strap of my bag. My capacity for understanding women was small—especially small, given my circumstances. But it sure did seem like Jasmine wanted to hang out with me. "Did you want to do something? Have lunch together?"

"No."

Oh. Never mind.

"Well, I guess I'll just go and have lunch by myself then."

"Okay."

"You're kind of hot and cold, you know that?" *Like the Katy Perry song.* At last, I understood what all those pop songs were talking about.

She rolled her eyes, turning on her heel. She made it halfway down the corridor before I finally caught up to her.

"Do you have a problem with me talking to your mum?"

"She's just always getting involved in things."

"Well, she is my teacher."

She stopped suddenly, and I had to turn around to face her. There was a stubborn crease between her eyebrows, and I wanted to smooth it away. I wanted to take away all her bad feelings like she'd taken away mine. "She just…she was always talking to Jack, and she would never tell me what she was talking about, and now she's talking to you." Jasmine shrugged. For some reason, I got the feeling that even *she* didn't know what was wrong.

"I think she's just trying to help."

"That's my mother." She rolled her eyes. "Always trying to help."

"The other night was really nice," I said, trying to change the subject. "On the roof…"

Jasmine just stared at me, and I tried in vain to find the rest of my sentence.

"I just…I thought that maybe you and I could be friends," I told her. "But now…I don't know. It seems like that door is closed."

"Yeah, well, life is a series of closing doors."

"Did you just quote *BoJack Horseman*?"

"Did I?" She stared past my head. "I've never seen that show… I just read a lot of quotes."

"You should watch it. It's like…" *It's like the only thing that's kept me going the last month.* "It's good, and dark, and funny." *Like you.*

"Maybe," she said. She was still staring at something past my head, and I realised then that someone was approaching us. "Later, Jules."

She turned around, and I didn't follow her this time. She disappeared down that grey tunnel of a corridor, and those bad feelings from yesterday started creeping back into my heart.

"Jeez, that looked heated."

I flinched. Brad Huxtable was standing behind me, *very pointedly* checking out Jasmine's legs. I clenched my jaw, stepping into his line of vision.

Hux tilted his head. "So, you guys are…?"

"No," I said.

"Really? Damn. I thought I was picking up on some mad sexual tension there. Maybe I was just projecting."

"Yeah, definitely," I said, momentarily blinded by Hux's teeth. Were those veneers? "Wait—*what*?"

Hux laughed. "I don't know, she's kind of hot, right? I'd always thought she was pretty—you know, her personality aside."

I shrugged. "If that's what you're into."

"I think it might be." He rubbed the stubble on his chin. How the hell did he have stubble? Why hadn't the principal made him shave it? Why were his teeth *so* white?

"You're…into Jasmine?"

"That's okay, right?"

That sick feeling inside me only got worse. "Of course. Why would I care?"

"I just know that Jack was kind of weird about her. Never went for her himself, but also didn't seem to like the idea of anyone else having her. Pretty selfish, if you ask me." His eyes widened. "Shit—don't tell anyone I said that, all right? I don't want anyone to think I was badmouthing him."

"It's not like I knew him."

Hux laughed slowly, like he wasn't sure whether it was a joke. "Man, you're funny, Jules. Like…dark kinda funny. It's cool."

"Thanks," I said, but I wasn't really listening anymore. I was too busy trying to see my own reflection in Hux's veneers, too busy trying to see him from Jasmine's point of view. Was he, like…was he *hot*?

"Jack was a cool guy," Hux said, and my gaze snapped back up to his eyes. Jesus, even they were fucking mesmerising. Like brown rock pools.

"You, Jack, and Gav were pretty close, huh?"

"Kind of. Jack wasn't really that close to anyone."

I frowned at him. Here Gav was, telling me they were best friends. And now Hux was telling me he was a loner.

"I still liked Jack a lot. When I heard what happened, I…" He rubbed his head. That's when I realised how uncomfortable he looked. How *sincere*. "I can't get in my car without thinking about him."

I stared at the ground between our feet. I didn't like knowing Jack was best friends with people like Gav, but somehow it seemed better than thinking he wasn't close to anyone.

"Hey, you should come to my birthday party," Hux said.

"Your birthday?"

"Yeah, it's in June. Everyone's going to be there. Maybe even Miss Morè if she cuts back on the attitude."

I could feel the blood in my veins—hot, pulsing. "I really don't think she would come to one of your parties."

"We'll see," Hux said. "I'll see you 'round, Jules. Party's on the eighteenth. Put it in your calendar!"

Hux had just about disappeared from my line of sight when he stopped suddenly. He popped his head around the last locker. "Oh, and shit, man… Happy birthday for a couple of weeks ago!"

"Thanks," I said.

"We'll have to have a party for you soon…you know, when it's not so morbid."

I nodded, my stomach tightening into a knot. "Sounds good."

"Kind of sucks that you have to share that as well as everything else."

I tried another joke: "At least I get all the presents."

Hux just laughed, looking startled once again by my *dark kinda funny*. I didn't even know what I was saying anymore, who I was trying to be.

The knot was getting tighter though, and all I could think about was bacon pancakes with maple syrup, and that look on Ms Morè's face, and Hux's teeth, and the sound of Pam and the kids singing 'Happy Birthday' in innocent disharmony.

Happy birthday to you
Happy birthday to you
Happy birthday dear Rosemary Boy
Happy birthday to you

Chapter 17

"Are you cleaning the coffee machine or making faces at it?"

I froze, my hand deep in the machine's drip tray. "Uh…both?"

I didn't have to turn around to know that it was Reg standing behind me. I recognised his deep, regal tone, and the unmistakable squeak of his walker. He'd been complaining to the carers (and to me, incessantly) about his faulty back wheel for the last six weeks. We were almost at the end of term two, and I could hardly believe that I'd lasted almost a full semester at Sparks High—at *real school*.

Reg tsked. "Well, you've been scowling at that machine for over forty minutes now, and unless you'd like to tell that machine how you're really feeling, I would like you to wrap it up so that I can make a cup of coffee."

"Right. Sorry." I reconnected the drip tray, and then I stepped aside so that Reg and his walker could fit in front of the bench. It meant that I was now caged between his walker and the wall.

"Watch how I make it," he instructed. "Maybe then you won't continue to serve up dishwater coffee to the vulnerable."

"Okay."

He kept his gaze on the machine, pressing his bifocals higher on his nose. It seemed like he didn't know where to start.

"You just press flat white," I told him, pointing to the interface.

"I know *that*," he said, brushing my hand away.

The coffee began to brew, and he hummed, sounding content. Reg was one of the few residents that were permitted to make their own coffees; the rest of them had to drink coffees made by me. I did not make them very well, according to Reg.

"Your relationship with Miss Morè doesn't appear to be improving," he muttered.

I shrugged. "It's the same, at least."

"I'd argue that something has changed. Worsened, even."

I frowned at him. "What makes you say that?"

"Well, she's started putting makeup on once she leaves work. Not *before* work, but after work. That tells me that she's going on dates with another young lad, and that she doesn't care if you see her looking like a dull Debbie—"

"So?"

"Well, that's obviously got to hurt."

I scoffed, staring at the coffee machine. "It doesn't hurt."

Reg was leaning so close to me now; it was hard not to look at him. His gaze trailed over my body, and he *tsked*. "I've got a degenerative eye disease and even I can see it."

I shook my head, grabbing his walker.

"The coffee isn't done—"

"Yeah, well, I am." I tried to move his walker, but the wheels were jammed. *Shit.* Maybe one of the back ones really was faulty. Finally, I freed myself, and I'd almost made it across the dining hall when I heard Reg's voice ring out.

"You can't run from your problems, Mr Rosemary. You can't run from your own hurt!"

I stopped. Everyone warned me about the senile residents of this facility, but they weren't the problem. The Pips and the Bills were saints. It was the Regs—the ones who had lived full lives, who had garnered decades of wisdom and still had the mental faculties to spout it—that were the real troublemakers.

I rounded the corner, leaving Reg and his faulty wheels behind me. I just needed to get out of here for a second, away from Reg and Jasmine and that damned coffee machine that was never clean. I went to my desk and grabbed a bag full of rubbish, and then I headed out one of the back corridors.

The night air was like a salve on my anxious skin, on my raw-bitten lips and watery eyes. I hoisted the garbage bag into the large metal compactor and ignored the assault of smells escaping it—rotten fruit and old meat scraps and sulphides.

I'd barely dumped the bag before I felt someone creeping up behind me. And just like with Reg, I didn't have to turn around to know that it was that guy. Black Hoodie. I recognised his low, bogan voice.

"I was waitin' for you, Jules. Every time I'm at the desk, you're never there."

I slowly turned around. The bag of rubbish had left *juice* on my hands, but that was the least of my worries. "I have to get back inside," I told him.

"I'm a bit upset that you didn't consider my offer, Jules."

It was dark, but I could just see the outline of his face. He was wearing a singlet instead of a hoodie, which made no sense, because I'd say it was colder now than it was a few weeks ago.

"I—I did consider it."

"Well, you never gave me an answer."

My heart was ricocheting in my chest again. My palms were sweaty, or maybe it was just the rubbish juice. Bill was always dumping half-drunk coffees into my reception bin. "I told you…I didn't want to talk to anyone."

"Yeah, when you were seventeen. You're a man, now, Jules. Nothing to be afraid of. You can talk to anyone, say whatever you want."

I rubbed my hands on my pants, gazing longingly at the facility doors. If I made a run for it, now, would Black Hoodie try to stop me? That still seemed like an apt identifier, even though he was wearing a singlet.

"And the *money*," he said. "Since you and your family keep holdin' out, it's only makin' the public want it more. It's only buildin' the anticipation. Or was that your plan? Just keep denyin' the media and their offers so you can cash in even bigger later?" He rubbed a hand over his chin. "It's smart, but there's one problem, Jules. News becomes old news, eventually… Soon, people will give less of a crap about you and your family, and then even less of a crap, and less of a crap. Some other sensational headline will replace yours. They'll find that little girl that's been missin' a decade and *poof*, you'll be a nobody."

Black Hoodie's words were unexpectedly calming. The thought of being a nobody again. When people wouldn't care where I worked, or who I dated, or what mistakes I made, or which deceased teenager I bore an *uncanny resemblance* to.

He moved closer, until I was essentially straddling a piece of the rubbish compactor. I thought about screaming for help, or practising those moves I'd seen in *The Karate Kid*.

"If it's not money you want, then what is it?"

"Nothing—"

"There's nothing you want, nothing you would trade in

exchange for your story?" He shook his head. "Bullshit. Everyone's got a price, Jules. Even a weird kid like you."

Weird kid. I know his words were just words—poorly refined ones, at that. But they still hurt. They reminded me of when the girl across the street had broken up with me. *You're just not like other guys, Jules. And not in a good way.*

"I bet you're missin' that woman," Black Hoodie said. "Angela… It might be wrong to call her your mother, but that's what she is, right? I could take you to Perth to visit her."

My stomach dipped. "You can do that?"

"You're eighteen, Jules. It's a free world, not like the fake one you grew up in. You can do whatever the hell you want. I could arrange your flights, accommodation. I'll book the whole thing, and by the end of it, all you have to do is talk to me. You can't tell anyone though. Otherwise, the deal's off."

At that exact moment, the door to the corridor swung open. You had to swipe a key card to open any door in this place, so everyone's entries and exits were always full of dramatic flair. Right now, under the sudden spotlight that the facility was casting on us, it was like a scene from *Thank God You're Here*. "Thank you—" someone was saying.

Chelsea.

She was standing in the doorway with earphones in her ears, holding a pack of cigarettes. She took one look at me, and then at the guy in front of me.

She frowned, taking out her earphones. "Bobby?"

The man just looked at me—*Bobby.*

"Think about it," Bobby said. "I'll come find you again, and you can let me know."

Bobby disappeared back inside the facility, but not before flashing a polite smile at Chelsea as he passed.

Soon it was just Chelsea and me, and I wasn't sure what was worse. Being isolated on this dock with *Bobby*, or being isolated with her—someone who surely hated my guts.

"How do you know that guy?" I asked her. My heart was still racing in my chest, and I felt like I was breathing through a straw.

"He's Gavin's cousin. I always see him hanging around Gav after school."

Gavin's cousin?

"What was he talking to you about?"

You can't tell anyone though. Otherwise, the deal's off.

"Nothing," I told her. "He just…wanted to talk about Gav."

"You looked scared."

"Well, he's not the most approachable guy."

"I think he's pretty harmless," she said. "Like Gav. He just wants to seem tougher than he is."

We hovered for a moment, not meeting each other's eyes.

"Sorry," I told her. "I'll…uh, let you smoke in peace."

"Oh, I don't actually smoke. I just tell the carers that so they'll let me out here."

I glanced behind me. "You want to be next to the rubbish?"

"No, look." She pointed to somewhere beyond the docks, and if I squinted, I could just make out a body of water in the darkness. "There's a really nice river down there, across the road. Sometimes I come out here to clear my head. Just the sound of sloshing water is…calming."

"I didn't even know that was there."

"It's beautiful during the day. There's a jetty. You can sit right over the edge and let your feet dangle above the water."

"Sounds nice," I told her. My heart was starting to calm down, and the air dissolved into silence again. I rubbed my dirty hands on my pants.

"Smoking's really bad for you," she said next, and then she chucked the packet in the rubbish compactor. "I keep confiscating them from my grandfather."

"Who's your grandfather?"

"His name is Reg."

"Reg? Reg *Burns*?"

"I know," she said, rolling her eyes. "He's a menace."

"No. He's like…the best."

Chelsea's mouth quirked a little. "Yeah, Jack liked him too."

We went quiet again after that. After a few moments, she sighed, and then she went and leaned over the metal railing. I tentatively stood next to her.

"I'm really sorry for how I acted at Gav's party," I said.

"I'm sorry for how I've acted every day since the funeral."

I swallowed. "You don't—you don't have to apologise…"

"I know how you think of me, Jules."

"What?" I asked.

"You think I'm crazy. Some caricature of a grieving girlfriend."

"I don't…" I glanced down at my shoes. Is that what I thought?

"I'm not crazy. I'm not trying to turn you into Jack. I just…" She took a deep breath. "I can't imagine what it's like to be in your position, but you can't imagine what it's like to be in mine."

"No, I can't."

We were silent for a long moment. The orange streetlights were glistening on the water.

"Things with Jack weren't even good when he…" She waved a hand, blinking away tears in her eyes. Until now, I didn't realise she was capable of that—of holding it in. It made me wonder what else she was holding in, just how deep the waters beneath her truly ran. "But, in a way, that made it worse. People don't get second chances after death. But then you came along, and it felt like I did. Like maybe, if I just looked at you a certain way, or breathed in a particular spot on your neck, or called you at just the right time when your voice had just the right amount of exhaustion…" She smiled weakly at me. "But I never can. You're not Jack."

"No, I'm not," I said. "I'm sorry."

"I'm sorry," she said. "I'm sorry I'm not what you want. That I thought the world really gave second chances."

"You don't want me, Chelsea." I shook my head, staring up at the sky. "Nobody does."

"What are you talking about? Everybody wants you."

"Yeah, but they don't really want *me*. They want Jack, or a good story, or a sensational headline." I thought about that goon. *Bobby*. I thought about his offer to take me to Angela. Was it too good to be true? Just like everything else?

"What would make you happy?" Chelsea asked me. "Right now, in this moment?"

"I don't know," I told her. "I just…I want things to get better. But just when they start to, just when it seems like the sky is opening up and something yellow and golden is making its way toward you, there's some fucking storm cloud just waiting in the wings."

"The sun doesn't shine all year, Jules." She rested her chin on her hand. "You've got to enjoy it, though. When the sun does show up, you've got to enjoy it. You just have to…"

I hummed. There was a moment where I thought maybe she was going to kiss me, but she ended up shining something small and bright in my face. It was a mini torch attached to her keys.

I laughed. "Why do you have that?"

"To brighten things up." She turned it off, shoving her keys back in her purse. "Hey, let's go to a party," she said.

"Whose party?"

"Hux's."

I groaned.

"Jasmine's going to be there."

I glanced sideways at Chelsea. There was something in her voice. Something old and hard.

"I know you like her, Jules."

"Yeah, well, she doesn't like me."

"Actually, I think she does. She just doesn't want to."

"People don't make sense to me," I told her. "Why would you not want to like someone?"

"Because some people are scared of getting hurt."

"I would never hurt her."

"Maybe *you* wouldn't," she said. I wanted to ask her what she meant by that, but then the facility doors were swinging open again. For a moment, Chelsea and I were swathed in light.

I squinted. Jasmine was standing in a tight red dress and kitten heels. I only knew the term *kitten heels* from Angela. To be honest, I didn't even know what distinguished a kitten heel from a regular heel, so all heels were kitten heels to me. She must have been dressed up for Hux's party, but she had to put something in the bin.

She *clicked* and *clacked* her way over the compactor. Chelsea and I just stood there, silent. Jasmine gave us both a cursory smile that didn't reach her eyes, and then she was gone. I watched in agony as she disappeared behind the doors. A fire engine blazing back into the facility.

My lungs deflated like a balloon.

"Screw it," I told Chelsea. "Let's go to Hux's party."

Chapter 18

I made Chelsea stop for coffee on the way to Hux's party. It was one of those dumb coffees with all the sugars and syrups and whipped creams, but Chelsea told me it was her favourite, so I was forcing myself to drink it.

"Julian Edwards-Rosemary. As I live and breathe! What the hell are you—?" Gav swiped the cup from my hands. "Is this—is this *coffee*?"

"I needed caffeine," I said, trying to snatch the cup back.

"You can't drink coffee here," Gav told me. He moved the cup out of my reach and then poured it into one of Hux's plants. "Not that you could call this coffee…"

"Gav!"

"Seriously, what were you thinking? This is something Jack would've done."

"Bloody hell, that cost me nearly six dollars—"

"Well, then you got off easy. I could not, in good conscience, let you enter this party drinking a fucking caramel frappe latte macchiato like some wannabe character from a Stephen Chbosky novel. Yes, I've read *The Perks of Being a Wallflower*. Actually, I just pretended to read it for Ms Morè, but I know this is some shit that one of those characters would do, and I can't let that happen." He pointed at me with the hand that was holding my coffee cup, and bits of foam flicked onto my Beacon Heights

Nursing Home shirt. "I just restored your dignity, Julian, and that shit is priceless."

I gritted my teeth together. "Thank you so much, Gav."

"Speaking of money, who is your very expensive date for the evening?"

I glanced behind me at Chelsea, who'd gone a very noticeable shade of scarlet. "*Gav*," I muttered.

"Media alert! *Rosemary Boy and Chelsea Douglas Arrive at Hux's Party—Together*!" He rubbed his chin. "We should find a way to wrangle my name in there somehow. Maybe: *Close Friend Gavin Lewis Always Had a Hunch*."

I froze. "Gav, please don't talk to anyone."

"He's just kidding," Chelsea said, staring pointedly at Gav. "Right, Gavin?"

Gav held up his hands. "Relax, relax. Of course, I'm kidding." He grinned at me, his brown eyes gleaming in the darkness. At least I think they were brown; his pupils were so dilated that it was hard to tell. I braced myself against a sudden wave of nausea, remembering the fact that Bobby was Gav's cousin. Physically, the apple didn't fall far from the tree. Which meant that, *maybe*, like I'd suspected, Gav also had ulterior motives for getting close to me.

Was he also trying to get my story?

I gazed around the party, and most people were staring at me. Were all of *them* trying to get my story too? Did any of them have connections to the media? All this time, I'd been worried about journalists and reporters. I'd neglected to worry about the people physically closest to me—the ones who went to school with me every day, and attended parties, and had families that they went home to each day and undoubtedly regaled them with tales of their sensational new classmate. Families that had friends, friends that had more friends, and more friends, and surely there was a reporter somewhere along the line. Maybe even a television presenter.

Maybe even *Tracy Grimshaw.*

"You look stressed," Gav told me.

"Your cousin visited me tonight," I told him. Surely, since Gav was his family, I was allowed to talk to him about it.

"Bobby? I had a feeling he might. He told me he had a proposition for you. It's a smart move, Jules."

"You don't tell him things about me, do you?"

"Me? Of course not." Gav shook his head, like the notion was offensive. "Here, have a beer. Take a load off."

I took the bottle from Gav. Honestly, I didn't think drinking was a good idea right now. Or *ever.* It didn't seem like the smartest move to make myself incapacitated in an environment like this. Or any environment, for that matter... Why did people willingly make themselves stupider? Why did they want their speech to slur, or to say dumb things they wouldn't normally say, or to vomit on someone's perfectly white sneakers?

I was about to give the beer back to Gav, self-assured in my decision. That was until the front door swung open, and I caught a glimpse of Jasmine talking to Hux over by the kitchen. She was *smiling* at him.

I don't think she'd ever smiled at me. At least, not like that.

"Jules?" Chelsea asked.

For a moment, I just stared at them. Jasmine and Hux. He had his hand on her waist, and suddenly that was all that existed in the universe and all that would ever exist. Just his hand on her waist. So unnecessary. So outlandish. So cosmically *wrong* that it paused time and ripped a hole in space that only I could see, that only I could feel.

Well, then maybe it's a different feeling.

He kissed her, then. He put his mouth on hers in a way that couldn't be unseen, that couldn't be undone. She had chosen him, and I hated her in that moment. I hated her for having that much power over me.

There is another intense feeling, you know.

I unscrewed the lid off my beer with my forearm. (I'd *YouTubed* how to do that.)

"Shit, Rosemary Boy."

I skolled the beer. Well, I almost skolled it. I made it about halfway before it started to fizzle out of my nose, and I almost vomited it back up.

"Jules," Chelsea was saying. "Maybe you should slow down…"

I just shook my head, glancing at Gav. "Got another one?"

I was lying sideways on an armchair. Apparently, three beers were enough to have me feeling happy. Stupid and happy. *And floating… Down… Down…*

Chelsea and I were sitting together on a plush leather lounge. The room was completely empty, which seemed miraculous given the number of raucous partygoers that were currently occupying this residence.

"I don't understand," I muttered. "When two people like each other, why can't they just…be together?"

"It's more complicated than that, Jules."

"Why?"

"I don't know. It just is."

I took a sip of my beer, staring at Hux's glass cabinet in the distance. Why did he and Gav have so many trophies?

"Were you and Jack?" I asked her. "Complicated?"

She shrugged. She was wearing a white dress that hugged her collarbones like the curves of a heart. She was beautiful, but in a totally different way to Jasmine. Chelsea was beautiful in a way that could be clearly observed, and without emotion—like one of Angela's porcelain teacups. Jasmine…Jasmine was the kind of pretty that made you long for something.

"I think every relationship is complicated," she said finally. "There's this giant puzzle at the nursing home. I don't know if you've seen it."

"The communal one? Yeah, I can never seem to add to it."

"It's so hard," she said. "Grandad gave me this analogy, that two people coming together…it's like puzzle pieces. It's really hard to find the right piece. And sometimes people convince themselves they've found the right fit, but it's not quite right. Just close enough."

I looked at her. Was she saying that she and Jack were *just close enough*?

"Also, I think he was cheating on me."

I almost choked on my beer. "You knew about that?"

"I'm not as stupid as everyone thinks I am, Jules."

"Why did you stay with him?" I asked her.

"Because I knew he was struggling. And he wasn't a bad

person, deep down, even though he tried to tell me he was." She started tearing up. "I know he lied a lot. I know he probably cheated on me. But I loved him. I loved the parts of him that were real. I don't know which parts they were exactly, but I know they were there."

"He was struggling?"

She wiped her tears. "I think so, yeah."

"But he looked so happy."

"I think a part of him always felt like something was missing." She looked at me. "He used to talk about you, you know."

"He did?"

"Yeah. He used to say it felt like there was a part of him somewhere, and he didn't know where to look for it."

I drank more of my beer. I didn't like this conversation. For some reason, it made me feel *guilty*. Guilty that Jack had to grow up this way, knowing he had a twin. Knowing that he was meant to have a best friend. I'd been wrestling with this information for four months. He'd been wrestling with it his whole life.

I rubbed at the label on my beer. "I feel closer to him, you know. When I'm with you."

Chelsea raised an eyebrow. "Yeah?"

"You seemed to know him. In a way no one else did."

"Well, it may seem obvious, but I feel closer to him when I'm with you."

"Is it the face?"

She laughed. When she did, she ended up leaning closer to me. Our heads were lolled over the back of Hux's couch, and her lips were so shiny. There were these dangly silver earrings in her ears, and I could almost see myself in them. I could almost see...

"It kind of sucks," I said softly. "He leaves all this behind, and I just have to pick it all up. We had the same start. We came from the same place. How could we have travelled so far from each other? We never even…" I shook my head. "We never even *met*. How crazy is that."

"You did, once," she told me. "You were together for nine months."

"And now what? He's just gone. And I don't think I've ever really thought about that. About what I've lost. Because I couldn't see it to begin with. It never felt…real."

Chelsea hummed softly. It sounded like she was falling asleep. "That's the thing about twins. You're born together, but you die alone."

"I was born two minutes before him, actually."

She giggled. It was the first time I'd ever heard her giggle, and I think a guy could fall in love with a sound like that. Chelsea was the kind of girl you married. She was the girl next door, the white-winged dove, the prom queen I'd seen in all those '80s movies—but also the girl standing in the corner of the room, waiting to be asked to dance. She was so far from a caricature that I ever wondered how I let myself think that way.

Maybe I just saw her the way I wanted to see her.

And maybe I only saw Jasmine the way I wanted to see her, too.

There was another long silence, punctured only by the sound of Chelsea's long, lilting yawn. After a few more minutes, I was pretty sure she was asleep, but I couldn't be sure. I decided to keep talking anyway.

"I…I feel really lonely, Chelsea."

There was a small pause, and then she said, "I know."

"I think I should go home."

"No," she said. "Stay."

Somehow, she was even closer to my face now. Her eyes blinked open, and then she closed the distance, and suddenly we were kissing. Where there was nothing, there were now soft, sticky lips against mine. She took the air from my open mouth, and I let her have it. Her air tasted like strawberry and port wine, and I was pretty sure I was wearing lipstick now.

It was…nice.

Until the door opened, and just like back at Beacon, Jasmine was standing there like a beautiful red stop sign. Only, *unlike* back at Beacon, Chelsea and I were not standing inoffensively against a railing. We were sitting offensively against each other.

"So—sorry," Jasmine said. But she just stood there for a moment, watching us. Chelsea's hand was lightly wrapped in my Beacon Heights shirt, my hands were fisted in my lap, and I had this weird, almost suffocating feeling that I'd just done something wrong.

Jasmine left the room, and I wanted to follow her. It made no sense. She didn't like me, and she'd just been kissing Brad Huxtable, and Chelsea was nice—much nicer than Jasmine— and *Jasmine didn't like me*.

Chelsea appeared to be wide awake now, and the distance between our faces felt like cities apart. Whatever intoxicated spell we'd just been under had suddenly evaporated, and now we were just sitting there. For some reason, it felt like we weren't Chelsea and Jules anymore.

We were Jack's girlfriend and Jack's twin.

"Should we…should we go now?" I asked.

She nodded, already grabbing her purse.

It was almost three in the morning when I finally got back to Pam's. There were no lights on, but I could hear voices coming from the back of the house.

From Pam and David's room…

You stupid bitch. It's all 'cause of you. All of our lives are fucked now 'cause of you.

My entire body seized with dread. I was standing there, mid-step on the staircase, frozen between movements. The horrible, razor-sharp words continued to cut through the darkness.

I wish I'd never become a part of this freak-show family. I got reporters callin' me every damn day offering me big money. But I turn 'em down. I turn 'em all down 'cause you ask me to. 'Cause you can't handle all the attention. Tell 'em why, baby. Tell 'em all the truth. You're an alcoholic and a terrible mother.

My hand coiled around the railing. Fear and rage and adrenaline were all coursing through me, and I was about to charge downstairs—really, I was—but then another voice rang out. A smaller, fragile one.

"Jules?"

I looked behind me. Tanner was standing there at the foot of the staircase, her pink Moshi Monster pyjamas just visible in the glow of the kitchen light.

The sight of her standing there tethered something in me. To her. To this moment.

I picked her up. I don't think I'd even touched her before

tonight. Now, I cradled her frail body in my arms and tucked her head into my chest, and I took her upstairs to my room. "Where's James?" I asked her, just as I opened the door to my room. *Oh.*

James was already in my bed.

He was covering his ears, just like I was doing to Tanner's ear with my free hand.

He looked terrified, and he appeared to be shaking just as violently as Tanner was in my arms. It was just the three of us, yet I swore there was someone else. I felt him standing behind me—a carbon copy of me, but taller, with shorter hair and slightly crooked teeth…

He was there with me, in that moment. I was sure of it.

"It's okay," I told Tanner and James. "It's…it's going to be okay."

Chapter 19

The next morning, an avalanche of memories collapsed on my chest all at once.

I could take you to Perth. You can't tell anyone though. Otherwise, the deal's off.

Because I knew he was struggling.

You stupid bitch. It's all 'cause of you.

I glanced down at my body. Tanner and James were each curled into my sides like little puzzle pieces. I'd never had siblings before, and now I had two that could barely speak a confident sentence. I had a brother and a sister that had emotionally imprinted on me as a result of me looking exactly like their dead big brother—a big brother that they obviously relied on in times like these. When Mummy and Daddy were hurling verbal razors at each other.

Tanner began to stir, and I used the opportunity to gently disentangle myself. It was a Saturday, meaning that I had only a few short hours before I'd need to go into Beacon and work the night shift. How the hell was I meant to leave?

There was a gentle clanging of pans downstairs, and I could smell breakfast cooking as I descended the staircase. *What the hell?*

I'd expected stony silence. For David and Pam to have locked themselves inside their room and for the explosion of last night to sizzle into today. But they were congregating in the kitchen as if it were business as usual, as if this slow Saturday morning was completely out of the ordinary.

"Morning, son." David nodded to me over his paper. "How'd you sleep?"

I stared at him. My muscles were clenching and unclenching beneath my skin, and I wasn't sure whether I wanted to throttle him or scream at him the way he'd screamed at Pam. "Uh, fine, thank you."

"Work today?"

"This afternoon, yeah."

"Good. It'll be good for us to spend the morning together." Paper still in one hand, he reached for his mug of coffee. "You've been sleeping in a lot lately. Having a few late nights."

I ran a hand through my hair. It was matted from Tanner compulsively fisting it in her sleep. "There have been a few, uh, events at school…"

"Parties, you mean?"

The hair rose on the back of my neck, and I hated it. "I guess so."

David took a sip of his coffee, and I used the reprieve to glance over at Pam. She was wearing a cream apron, which was something she only started doing once David returned home. Her hair was assembled like a spooled rope on top of her head, and she looked oddly presentable for someone running on less than four hours sleep.

"*Shit*," I heard her hiss. She started fussing more frantically over whatever she was cooking in that pan.

"What is it?" David asked her.

"It's nothing."

"Is it nothing, or did you ruin breakfast?" David looked over at me and winked. I felt nausea swelling in every direction of my stomach.

"I just…the eggs," Pam said. "The yolks are…um…"

"You split the yolks, huh?" David shook his head, still smirking at me. "Pamela, Pamela, Pamela."

Pamela Pamela Pamela. It was the first time he'd ever said that, but I had the sudden, sinking feeling that it was a regular taunt.

"I think we have some more—"

"Nope, we're out," David said. "Remember? You ruined the last batch on Wednesday morning. We need to get you some cooking lessons, Missy."

"I can go to the store," Pam said, already wiping her hands with a tea towel. "I can—"

"Nonsense," David said, still looking at me. "Jules can go. It's about time he starts pulling his weight around here."

We held each other's gaze for a moment, almost as if we were challenging each other. I wanted so desperately to know what he was thinking, but I wasn't man enough to look at him for longer than a few seconds.

"Uh," I said, "sure."

"Fantastic. Pick up some more beer, too, would ya? You're eighteen now."

"But the media—" Pam said, then seemed to think better of it.

"Can't keep him holed up forever. All he does is work and go to school. Let him be an adult. Buy some fuckin' beers. Let them have their headline: *Rosemary Boy Goes Grocery Shopping.*"

My stomach rolled. "Sure," I said.

"VBs."

"Yep."

David went back to his paper, and Pam went back to cooking… bacon, or whatever part of breakfast she hadn't *ruined*, according to David. The world resumed as normal—or at least, my version of normal.

My version of normal that just kept getting more and more messed up.

When I got to the supermarket, there was a weight pressing down on my heart.

I don't even remember parking my bike and walking into Aldi. One minute, I was in that kitchen with David and Pam, and then I was there, standing beneath bleached lights staring at a wall of poultry.

"Excuse me?"

Shit.

The foot on my heart pressed down. Harder. *Harder.* Was it a reporter? Someone who knew Jack?

I turned around. It was just Brett.

"Oh—Jules."

The pressure in my chest eased somewhat, but only because I knew that I was allowed to swear around him. I wouldn't have to censor my vocabulary like I had to with David.

"It *is* you," he said, his expression softening into a smile. I thought that you were an Aldi employee."

"Well, don't ask me where anything is," I said. "I can't even find the fucking eggs."

Brett nodded, a small frown between his eyebrows. He

seemed to be reading my body language or something, and I was too exhausted to fight his gaze. Could he see the pain in my body? Did he know that *I can't even find the fucking eggs* meant *My fucking life is falling apart?*

"Okay," he said. "Okay… Let's find you some fucking eggs."

My whole body sighed in relief. He turned away from me, and I followed him toward the back of the store. My heart instantly began to calm. The foot on my chest lifted, and I could breathe again.

"Here they are…" Brett said. "Fucking eggs."

"Thanks," I told him, but we both just stood there for a moment. We didn't move.

"How are you doing, Jules?"

"Good," I said. "I'm doing good."

"Really?"

No, I wanted to say. *You ever go into a supermarket and feel like you're missing something? Like…not just a longing, but sincere loneliness.*

"Hey," he said. "Jules, you okay?"

I thought of telling him about Pam and David. I thought about telling him a lot of things. Jasmine. Bobby and his offer. The fact that I kissed Jack's ex-girlfriend last night.

But how do you say all of that to a stranger? How do you say all of that to anybody?

Brett took a step forward. Just half a step. He leaned down and looked directly into my eyes, but it didn't feel predatory like when David did it. It felt…natural.

There was something so familiar about him; I couldn't explain it. Being around him was like being around Santa Claus, or Jesus, or your biological father—like some storybook masculine figure that you always hoped would appear but never did. It was the same feeling I got around Elijah, but now that the government had decided I no longer needed him, there was only Brett who gave me that feeling.

Like he could read my mind, Brett frowned at me. "You still going to counselling?"

I shook my head. There were some people standing too close to us, and I was worried they had a recording device in their groceries.

"I think you should get back into that," he told me. But I was too afraid. If I told Yong, then he might have me taken away from Pam. Then I wouldn't have Angela *or* Pam. I'd go from having two mothers to none. And David had been nice enough at the funeral, so maybe this was out of character for him. Maybe he was just having a bad week at work, or maybe he was finally grieving Jack. Eloise had told me that grief can manifest in many different ways: numbness, sadness, *anger.*

Brett put his hand on my shoulder, squeezing firmly. "You're gonna be okay, Jules."

I swallowed. There was a lump in my throat now the size of an egg, and I wanted him to go away so that I could go somewhere and cry. Somewhere dark and isolated where I knew no one would be watching.

"I'm going to write down my number," he told me, grabbing a pen out of his back pocket. He looked around for something to write on, and eventually settled on the carton of eggs. He scribbled ten digits on the outside of the box and I just watched him, numb.

"Brett?" I asked.

"Yeah, Jules?"

"Um…" I gestured pointlessly with my hand that wasn't holding the eggs.

"You can tell me. What is it? Work? School? Home?" He held my gaze as he said that last word, gravity in his voice.

I stared down at the eggs. I imagined Pam's shaking hands, and Jack's presence, and the entire cursed Rosemary bloodline. What if I told him, and he didn't believe me? What if David found out I told and hurt Pam even worse? What if he hurt me?

"Thank you…" I said. "For the eggs."

Brett looked momentarily confused. "Sure, Jules. My number's there. My phone's always on."

"Okay," I said.

Did he already know? Had Jack told him?

Had it changed anything?

Maybe it didn't matter. Maybe it was enough just to know that there was someone out there. Someone I could call.

Brett nodded at me, and then he left. I was left standing alone in the middle of the dairy section with a carton of eggs and a mobile number, but suddenly I didn't feel so alone anymore.

I really needed to stop taking Beacon's rubbish out at night. It always ended with an ambush of some kind.

"Have you thought about my offer, Jules? It's expiring."

I didn't flinch as badly as I normally would. Maybe because this was *Gav's cousin*, not a reporter—not someone with any link to anyone important whatsoever.

I didn't turn around, lobbing the soaking bag of rubbish into the bin. *Damn it, Bill.*

"Oh, you're ignoring me now."

"I'm not ignoring you," I said. "I'm just thinking."

"Oh, yeah? Penny for your thoughts, Rosemary Boy?"

"I'm thinking that I'm going to find another way to visit Angela. Since I'm eighteen, like you said, and I can do whatever I want." I was too afraid to turn around, too afraid to see the look on his face.

"You think you've gotten savvy, huh?" I heard him spit off the side of the balcony. "Rosemary Boy… Where's the quaking little kid from the car park?"

His comments made me feel mildly smug. "He's learning."

"Don't get too cocky," he said. I felt him getting closer to me. Try as I might, I couldn't stop the way I moved further into the compactor, almost like I was going to jump in with the rubbish. His voice seemed icier tonight. There was a desperation that hadn't been there the last two times. He kept itching his wrists, and the sound was like someone trying to grate plastic.

"You think you can get to Perth, by yourself, without attracting any media attention? You really think you can hop on a flight and walk into that jail without anyone finding out? Without Pam and *David* finding out?"

He seemed to emphasise David's name, and that only made the lead brick in my stomach more painful. Did he know something? Did he know about David's rage?

I swallowed, and I tried to keep my voice from shaking. "I—I'll find a way."

He moved closer again, and I tripped over a metal bar on the ground. I tried to catch myself but ended up slicing my hand on a rusted screw. The pain was so extreme it was momentarily blinding. Like someone had reached inside my palm and yanked out the tendons. I couldn't help it; I screamed in pain.

"*Shit*," he muttered. "Don't tell anyone about this. I didn't do nothin'. You hurt yourself on your own."

I waited a few minutes until I was sure he was gone. Then I took a few moments to inspect the damage. It was dark, but I could see the blood pooling in my palm. Red, and maybe a little bit of coffee, too. A painful mix. It hurt so badly I had to grit my teeth from screaming again.

I hobbled my way over to the doors. It's funny—when something hurts, even your hand, it makes your legs move differently. I was practically limping through the facility doors, and I ended up getting blood on my new key card. There was a smudge of red right across my ID photo.

"What happened?"

I looked up. Chelsea was frozen in front of me.

"I just—" I glanced behind me at the doors. "I was taking out the rubbish."

"How did you slice up your hand?"

"I tripped."

She frowned at me, like she didn't believe me. "You should go to the doctor."

"No," I said. "That's…there'll be too many people there."

"So, you're just going to bleed out onto the floor?"

I stared at my hand. "I could…I don't know, maybe wrap some tissues around it…"

"Let me look at it."

I moved closer to her. Hesitantly, I held out my hand, and she briefly looked into my eyes before touching my palm. I hissed between my teeth.

"I think you'll need stitches," she said. She was still holding my hand, and I realised this was the first time we'd spoken since the kiss.

"I'm sorry," I told her.

She swallowed hard. "You don't need to be sorry."

"We shouldn't have done that."

Her jaw seemed to tighten. She shook her head, letting go of my hand.

"I wanted to talk to you about it, *properly*, but I—"

"Jasmine's in the kitchen," Chelsea muttered. "She'll know what to do. She's good at this first aid stuff."

I cradled my hand to my chest. "I'm sorry," I said again, just because it seemed like I needed to keep saying it. *I'm sorry for kissing you. I'm sorry for leaving again right now. I'm sorry for liking Jasmine.*

I made it to the nearest elevator, and I mashed the button for the third floor. I waited, eyes screwed shut, my hand bleeding onto the carpet.

The elevator door finally opened. There was an old woman named Margaret waiting in a wheelchair by her room.

"Excuse me, young fellow, could you please tell me where I live?"

I didn't stop. "Right in there, Margaret."

"Oh. Thank you."

I charged down the hallway. Carers were staring at me, asking me if I needed help. I felt like Margaret, confused and trying to find my home.

"Jasmine," I said. "I need Jasmine. Where is she?"

They all just stared at me. There were a group of them huddled by this floor's coffee machine, and there was no doubt this scene was going to make for salacious gossip in the breakroom later. I fought the urge to flip them off, just as one of them pointed cautiously to the kitchen.

When I got to the kitchen, it was completely dark, save for the light of the refrigerator, and an automatic dining hall light that had just flicked on.

There she was, black cardigan, earphones in, stealing bites from the residents' leftover desserts. Her eyes widened when she saw me, and she immediately dropped her plastic fork.

"Shit," she said, removing an earphone. "Te Mania said I could have this, so don't go lecturing me about stealing food—" she frowned at me. "What's wrong with you?"

I just stood there, shaking.

She took her other earphone out, her gaze trailing over my body. "Are you okay?" she asked me.

I didn't answer her. Now that I was here, all the adrenaline had left my body. I could feel it all: David's insults, Pam's fear. I could feel my hand, sliced and burning.

"Jules?"

I started to feel woozy, so I looked for a place to sit down. I had just barely made it over to one of the tables when I felt Jasmine's hands on my body. She guided me down into a chair, and then she hovered beside me, silent.

She slowly grabbed my right hand. When she spoke, her voice was only a few shades lighter than her touch. "What happened?"

My entire body went slack in her arms. "I fought the rubbish compactor."

"Looks like you lost."

I started to snatch my hand back, but she held on.

"What really happened?"

I gritted my teeth together. God, I could feel it coming. I could feel it all coming. I felt wrong and claustrophobic all of a sudden, like I was pressed between Bobby and the compactor. Between that wall and Reg's faulty walker.

"Jules," she said slowly, and suddenly I couldn't look her in the eyes anymore. She was kneeling beside me now. There was no escape.

"I can't tell you."

"You can't tell me who hurt you?"

"No," I said, squeezing my eyes closed. I didn't want to tell her, *Gav's cousin*, because at that moment it didn't even feel like the truth. The truth felt closer to something I couldn't say, something that would unravel me if I even tried.

"Was it a resident?"

I couldn't help it, then. I laughed. I laughed, and then tears pricked my eyes, and I realised I wasn't laughing anymore. I was hyperventilating, and the world was closing in, and my hand hurt so badly I wanted to cry.

"Jules. Look at me."

"I can't breathe," I told her. "I can't…I can't breathe."

"I know. Just look at me."

I shook my head. My eyes were screwed shut, and there were tears streaking down my cheeks. I tried to pull my hand back again, but Jasmine wouldn't let go.

She didn't speak for a long time, but when she did, her voice sounded unsteady. "Jules. Look at me."

I rubbed my eyes with my free hand, trying to scrub away my tears.

"Look at me."

Finally, I looked at her. One of the automatic lights must have turned off, because the room was darker now. I could hardly make out Jasmine's face, and I hoped that maybe she couldn't make out *my* face, either.

I could feel her though. I could feel her vice grip on the undamaged parts of my hand, and the way her body seemed to be shaking, holding something in. It felt like we were two avalanches just waiting to be tripped.

I let out a sigh, just as Jasmine began mopping up the blood on my hand with a linen napkin.

"Chelsea said you could fix it," I said, my voice barely above a whisper. *She said you could fix me.*

"Maybe, but I think it would be better if you went to a hospital—"

"*No,*" I told her. "…No."

For a moment, she stopped mopping up the blood. She just sat there on her knees.

"I don't want anyone knowing about this," I said. "I don't want any more attention."

She looked up at me, only briefly. Then she went back to cleaning my hand. "Okay," she said softly.

Somehow, just that word was enough to calm something within me. Or maybe it was her touch. Whatever it was, I felt some of the stress leaking out of me, little by little.

We were silent for a long time. I just watched her work, and I wondered about the last time I saw her. When she was standing in the doorway of Hux's party, with *that look* on her face.

"It hurt me," I said quietly. "When I saw you kissing Hux."

There was a deep frown on her face. "You saw that?"

I nodded.

"Well, you kissed Chelsea."

"Did that hurt you?"

"Were you trying to?"

"No," I told her. "I wasn't meaning for you to find out. I wasn't even meaning to do it, but she was right there, and it just happened, and I felt…guilty."

"Why did you feel guilty?"

"Because I felt like I was betraying Jack. And because…I wanted to be kissing you instead."

Jasmine's hands faltered in their movements.

"Why do you push me away all the time?" I asked her.

"Because," she said, continuing to wipe the blood.

"Because why?"

"Because you're a mess, Jules. You *deserve* to be a mess. You deserve to figure out who you are outside of Jack and all the people who knew him. It's not fair. It's not fair for people to just…project their ideas of him onto you."

"Is that not what you're doing?"

She paused again. "What?"

"Projecting your ideas of him onto me. You clearly didn't like him very much—but you still went to his funeral, which doesn't make much sense. Now it feels like you're trying your hardest not to like *me*."

"I'm not—"

"But you do like me. I know you do."

Jasmine was breathing very fast.

"Are you worried about the media? Are you worried about what they're going to write about you? Because I get it. You don't like people, and you certainly wouldn't like people if they were all suddenly talking about you."

"I don't care about the media. I hear worse things from Gav."

"*And* Hux." I moved my hand away from her. I couldn't have her touching me anymore.

"What?"

"Hux is mean to you, Jasmine. And you go and kiss him anyway. I'm nice to you, and you barely look at me."

"I can do what I want, Jules."

"I know you can. I *just*—"

"You just what?"

"I don't understand girls. I don't understand relationships."

Jasmine swallowed, her gaze darting back to the floor.

"You know how I feel about you," I whispered, leaning forward. "You're smart enough to know that."

"I...I didn't realise you were analysing me."

"Of course I am," I told her. "Every time we're together, and even when we're not... I think about what you're doing, and how you're feeling, and if you ever got around to watching *BoJack Horseman*, and if it made you cry when BoJack begged Diane to tell him that he's good."

There was more I wanted to say. So much more. But all the lights had come back on, and there was a cluster of carers just around the corner, and what did it matter anyway?

I started to walk away, my hand clutched to my chest.

"I did watch it. I didn't cry though…much."

I stopped walking. My hand was throbbing against my heart. "You watched it?"

"I watched it, Jules."

I tried to picture it: Jasmine watching my new favourite TV show of all time. Late at night, the glow of her laptop screen, tears in her eyes.

Slowly, I heard her get to her feet. And when I turned to look at her, her hands were covered in blood—my blood.

I sighed. "I don't want you to date Hux. You don't have to date me, but…you're better than him, Jasmine."

She frowned, wringing the bloody napkin in her hand. When she finally spoke, her voice was barely above a whisper. "What if I want to date you?"

"What?"

She just stood there. "I'm not saying it again."

I stepped closer. "Say it."

"No," she said, and this time *she* took a step toward *me*.

"S—" I started to say, but she cut me off with her mouth.

Chapter 20

She cut me off with her mouth.

She cut me off with her hands on my chest, roughly clutching my navy Beacon Heights polo. She cut off whatever word I was about to say, whatever thought was in my mind, whatever point I was in the process of making.

She cut me off. *With her mouth.*

With the little intake of breath that snaked through her teeth. With the soft but firm press of her lips against mine, like she was putting her daydreams into practice, like she was testing some risky social experiment that she'd been theorising for the last four months. It was rough but soft, passionate but clinical, assured but terrified.

I licked her lip, and she froze.

"Sorry," I panted.

She shook her head, her hands still fisted in my shirt. "Don't apologise."

"Okay. So—"

She kissed me again. It was so forceful that our teeth clunked together, but I only had a moment to focus on the pain before my brain was soaring. *Jasmine. I'm kissing Jasmine.* Jasmine *kissed* me. *Twice!*

Jasmine is *kissing me.*

I let her do her thing. I stayed completely still and let her use me—or *not* use me—for whatever purpose she desired. I'd gladly stand there like a slightly aroused mannequin while she…probed me. While she discovered whatever she needed to discover. With her closed mouth… Her clenched fists… I'd be the best test subject for her to confirm what I already knew.

Her mouth opened slightly, and our lips slid between each other's. She tasted like the dessert she'd just been pilfering, like vanilla and strawberry cheesecake.

"You taste sweet," I whispered.

She frowned at me, like I'd ruined the moment. Then a small smile broke out on her face. We were staring at each other in this drunken haze, like we understood the absurdity of this moment, the absurdity of our feelings. There was an overwhelm of attraction and recognition that seemed almost amusing. As in, *that thing that everyone's always talking about? It's this. It's you and me.*

One of her hands loosened around my polo. In fact, it smoothed over my heart. Then it wound its way up to my head, into my hair, and the drag of her fingernails against my scalp almost sent me crumbling to the floor.

"Well, excuse me—"

Jasmine and I sprang apart.

"I'm not sure what you did to the Level Four coffee machine when you claimed to have *cleaned* it, but it seems you forgot to relink an integral component—mainly, the one that connects the milk to the rest of the system. There isn't enough sugar in the world that can make those wholesale beans drinkable without it."

Reg wheeled his walker right in between us. His faulty wheel screeched across the floor.

"Shit, sorry, Reg." I smirked at Jasmine. "I'll, um, I'll get on that right now."

Reg grumbled, though I could see the amused expression on the side of his face. "By all means, finish up whatever it is you and Miss Morè were chatting about before I interrupted. The coffee can wait until morning."

Reg disappeared around the corner, leaving Jasmine and I standing beneath the tripped lights of the dining hall. They were all on now—every single one, and I could see her in perfect clarity.

Her long dark hair, tied loosely in a chunky braid. Her white rose, almost glowing against the light. Her wispy fringe, overgrown now, the tips of her hair reaching just past her eyebrows.

"So, what do we do now?" I asked her.

"We fix your hand," she told me. "And then you tell me exactly how it happened to you. The real story."

"Jasmine—"

"And you don't lie to me," she said. She grabbed my shirt, her brown eyes boring into mine. "You have to promise me, Jules. You can't lie to me. Not about this. Not about anything. Because if you lie to me, I will never forgive you."

I covered her hands with mine. "Total honesty…from this point on."

She shook her head gently. "You can't lie to me, Jules."

"I won't," I told her.

"You can't."

"*I won't.*"

I kissed her again, and I thought I loved her a little. Maybe everyone thinks they're in love when they kiss somcone for the first time. I wasn't going to discount it. Maybe I was. Maybe I wasn't. I didn't want to think about it too hard. Sometimes love washes over you and stays, sometimes it just washes over you.

"I mean it," she told me. "If you lie to me, I'll *really* ruin your life."

"And I'll let you."

She laughed softly, but there was no humour in it. There was so much pain in her body—I could feel it, compounding with the pain that was already in mine. There was nothing easy about the two of us together; sure, there was an ease of conversation, an ease of merging intellects, an ease of shared values and worldviews. But it was *hard*.

Maybe that's why Jasmine kissed Hux, and maybe that's why I kissed Chelsea. Because it was simply…easier. It's easier to kiss someone you don't like than it is to kiss someone you do. Because when you kiss someone that you do like, there's risk. You're opening yourself up, and you're inviting them in, and you're saying, *Hurt me, if you want. But I really hope that you don't.*

I pulled back, and I held her face in my hands. Her delicate features were dwarfed by my fingers, and she was so small, and so strong, and I knew that I wouldn't hurt her, but I hoped to God that she wouldn't hurt me.

I was in Jasmine's room for the second time. Not much had changed, except her peach bed sheets had been swapped out for lime green ones.

She glanced over at me. The door was shut, and Ms Morè was working late again, so there was really nothing stopping her from closing the distance and sitting right next to me.

She hesitated for a moment, and then she came and joined me on the bed. She had a carry bag with her full of first aid supplies that she'd swiped from Beacon, and my body tensed in anticipation.

"This is gonna hurt," she said.

"I know." I bit down on the inside of my cheek. Truthfully, I wasn't sure what I was more fearful of: the needle in her bag, or the fact that she was going to be touching me. Here. On a bed. After we'd just kissed. After I knew what it felt like to lick my lips against hers—

"Stop moving," she told me.

"Sorry."

I sat completely still while she started cleaning my wound. I thought the worst was over once she'd wiped all the dry blood away, but then she sprayed my hand with some kind of antiseptic.

"*Shit*," I hissed. "What's in that bottle? Fucking poison?"

"Keep it down. You'll wake up the neighbours. You'll wake up *Gav*."

I pursed my lips together. *That* was enough to keep me dead silent.

She pulled out the needle, and I winced. I tried to pull my hand back, but she held on. "Relax," she told me. "Think of Fremantle."

My stomach started to sour, and Jasmine grimaced. "Shit. Think of…think of somewhere else."

"Like where?"

"I don't know. The last time you were happy."

I looked at her. Her eyelashes were shadowed against her cheekbones, and there was a little crease in between her eyebrows as she worked.

"Kissing you," I said.

She huffed, piercing the needle beneath my skin. "That's sad, Jules."

"*Fuck*—" I gritted out. "It's—the truth."

"Kissing me is the last time you were truly happy?"

I shrugged. "There was also…that time you held my hand while we fell asleep."

She kept digging that needle beneath my skin, and it really felt like she was digging a hole to China instead of lightly threading my torn tissue back together. I resisted the urge to clench my hand, to push her away, to *scream*, and instead focused all my energy into thinking of that memory. My undamaged hand in Jasmine's… Peace.

"Is there anything you can think of that doesn't involve me?"

"Not in my immediate memories, no."

"Nothing with Angela?"

I squirmed. "I can't really let myself think about that. I don't… I don't like thinking about those memories."

"So you just…don't think about them? You don't think about her?"

I tilted my head back, staring at the ceiling, trying to focus on anything but the searing white pain in my right hand. "No, I don't… Because every time I do, I feel like I have to question whether or not it was actually real. And it ruins them. So, I'd rather just…file them away. Keep them safe."

"And it's easy? For you to do that?"

I kept staring at the ceiling. "No," I muttered. "No…it's not."

Jasmine was quiet after that, and for a moment, I let them in. I didn't fight the memories back into a vacuum, and I let the colour bleed into the darkness. Angela's pumpkin soup. Sitcoms on a Sunday. The way she carded her hands through my hair when I was sad. The frog-shaped hot water bottle she heated up for me when I was sick. Her teaching me chess on the balcony. Her singing Billie Holiday in the shower. Home school during the day. Saying goodbye to her at night. The fact that I never questioned whether superheroes were real, because I was raised by one.

"Jules?"

I looked back at Jasmine. She'd already finished up the last of her stitches, and she tied the suture with light, practised hands.

"Where did you learn to do that?" I asked her. "To…fix people like this."

She shrugged. "Mum would volunteer at women's shelters back in Jaipur. She'd teach them how to read and write, and she got pretty good at first aid, too. Sometimes she'd take me with her."

"Why'd you leave India?"

"My mum met my stepdad." Jasmine started wrapping a bandage around my hand. "An Australian… He convinced her to move here when I was eight, and then he left us. My mum was too proud to go back home, so we stayed, and she's been killing herself trying to make it work ever since. Back home, she was a university lecturer, but the degree didn't count when we moved here. She could only teach high school."

"That doesn't seem fair."

"A lot of people underestimate her because of that. She's always had to work five times harder to get to where she's going."

"Why'd your stepdad leave?" I asked her. I wanted to ask her about her real dad, about where he was or wasn't, about how those things made her feel. But I was careful. I *had* to be careful—not to push too hard, not to scare her away.

She hesitated. I watched her wrap my hand, gently, methodically. "Because he was a twat," she said finally.

"Makes sense."

She secured the bandage. By this point, the searing pain had tapered to a dull ache. And Jasmine was just holding my hand.

I wrapped my fingers around her palm. *Ow.*

"Idiot," she said. "You'll ruin your stitches."

"Don't care."

She frowned at me, and I wanted to kiss away that stubborn little crease between her eyebrows.

Restrain. Restrain. Restrain.

"Okay," she said. "Your turn to be honest."

I shrugged, rubbing a thumb over her knuckles. "My stepdad's also a twat."

"You know I'm not talking about that." She peered up at me, her eyelashes touching the tips of her fringe. "Who did this to you, Jules?"

"The shoddy stitches? Some girl from work—" She squeezed my hand, and I shouted. "Ow—okay! *Okay.*"

"Total honesty, remember? You can't go back on our deal."

"I don't think we shook on it."

"You want me to shake your hand right now? It won't feel good."

I bit my lip. "It was Gav's cousin."

"Gav's—? What the hell?"

"He didn't actually do it. But he got really close to me, and I fell…trying to move away from him."

"Jules," Jasmine said. Her voice sounded gravely serious. "Why was he getting so close to you? Why was he even talking to you?"

"To try and intimidate me, I think. Turns out the rubbish compactor was more dangerous."

"You've started making jokes, and I don't like it." She shook her head. "Why was he trying to intimidate you?"

I glanced up at her, chewing the inside of my cheek. We were still holding hands. "He was trying to pay me…for my statement. I guess he thought he could sell it to the media and cash in. Then, when I said no, he started trying to bribe me with…other things."

"Other things."

"Like visiting Angela."

Jasmine's lips parted. "Oh," she said softly.

"But I said no, and then…" I nodded down at my hand. "You know the rest."

Jasmine gritted her teeth. "I'm going to ream Gav out on Monday morning. I'm going to go to school and—"

"It's fine," I told her. "Let's just forget about it."

"People can't just keep treating you like this. They can't just…"

"Jasmine. It's *fine*. I'm *fine*."

"Do you mean that?"

Her words hung in the air. We just sat there for a moment, my hand frozen in hers. *I think so. I don't know.*

"If you really want to visit your mum," she said, "there are other ways to do it. You don't need to rely on Gavin or his stupid family."

"Who else can I rely on? I don't exactly have friends here, Jas." There was Reg, but he was ninety-three. There was Chelsea, but as Jack's ex-girlfriend, she experienced almost as much media scrutiny as my family.

"I'm your friend," Jasmine said, without hesitation. It was the first time anyone had told me that since I moved to Brisbane. Maybe it was the first time anyone had ever told me that. It made my body feel lighter.

I raised an eyebrow. "You're going to fly me to Perth?"

"I could convince my mum…maybe."

"I don't think taking one of her students to a prison in another state is going to be very good for her image. She wouldn't be taking me to visit my mum. She'd be taking me to visit a criminal, and that's how it would look to everyone else."

"Well, no one would have to know. We could be careful…"

I looked at her. "You'd come too?"

"If you wanted me to."

I tried to hide the smile that was pulling at my mouth. "Well, actually, I looked into it on the internet," I said. "Visits take six weeks to be approved, so I applied right after Bobby gave me the idea."

"You applied all by yourself?"

"It was a total head spin. I needed to get photo ID with my Edwards-Rosemary name change on it, and then it had to be certified by someone called a Justice of the Peace. I got Yong to sign it right after our last appointment, since, apparently, he is one. I told him Beacon needed it. The prison emailed me last week. My application got approved. But I need to have a prison officer present given the history between Angela and me, and there can't be any media inside or outside the jail."

Jasmine's eyes were all lit up, and she was looking at me

with this expression I'd never seen before. Almost like she was impressed. "In time for next school holidays," she said.

I shrugged. "I was thinking, maybe…yeah. Now I just need to convince someone…or some *people* to fly to Perth with me."

She waved a hand. "We don't need to figure this out tonight, okay? School holidays are still a week away."

I looked at her. "I can stay?"

"It's late. We can sneak you out again in the morning."

Slowly, the realisation dawned on me: I was going to be sharing a room with Jasmine again. Not Jack. Not Hux. *Me.*

"Okay," I muttered, my heart pounding.

I slowly made my way up the bed. Jasmine took off her work uniform while I stared at the wall, and when I looked back, she was wearing only a t-shirt. It was a plain black shirt that looked strangely made for her, even though it came to just above her thighs. As she crawled in next to me, I tried not to think about how badly I wanted to touch her.

"Goodnight," I whispered. My injured hand was lying between us—bandaged and bleeding.

"Goodnight, Jules."

I stared at her body's outline in the darkness. I wanted to reach out and hold her, but it was too dark to see, and I didn't know where that would lead.

Just as my eyes had drifted closed, I felt the tips of her fingers brushing against mine. We interlocked fingers, as much as we could without disturbing my stitches—*again*, and for the rest of that night, a flood of calmness overcame me. An overwhelming sense of peace rolled throughout my body, like a tidal wave with no desire to crash.

There was a moment in my dream, a moment where David came out from behind the vail to yell and hurl intimate objects against walls. I tried to make myself as big as the moon. I tried to cover Pam and Tanner and James as best I could. And then, just as suddenly as he'd appeared, he was gone. There was nobody left to protect, just myself, and Jasmine standing next to me.

The sudden, incessant ringing of my phone sent me crashing into Jasmine. I'd forgotten to turn my morning alarm off, which meant that Jasmine and I had been asleep for precisely three hours before the *rii-iiiing, rii-iiiing, rii-iiiinging* had us scrambling for consciousness. I ended up sprawled across her body as I reached for my phone, and when I finally managed to silence the alarm, it was too late to realise my mistake. I was now straddling Jasmine.

"Good morning," I said, staring down at her.

She huffed out a breath. "Morning."

"Fancy seeing you here."

She rolled her eyes, jutting her hips up to the ceiling. I assumed it was an attempt to move me off her body, but it had a decidedly *different* effect. Mainly, it caused all of the blood to rush to my pelvic region, and the thought of moving off her body rebelled against every primal desire I'd ever had—past and present.

Jasmine's eyes narrowed suddenly, as if she'd just confirmed a suspicion. "You are *not*."

"I'm sorry."

"Seriously? On top of me?"

I licked my lips. She looked so good from this angle—messy hair, open pores, radioactive glare. "Well, I didn't plan to be up here."

"Okay, so move."

"Well, you see, I would, but I think that'll make it worse—"

"Move *off* me."

"Right. Yes. Okay." I rolled off her. For a moment, the two of us were just lying there, staring at the ceiling. Waves of wanting were undulating throughout my body, begging me to get back on top of Jasmine. Begging her to get on top of me. I'd never been so embarrassed in my *life*.

Jasmine pulled herself up into a sitting position, and I took the opportunity to tuck myself into a decidedly less mortifying state. As it turned out, there was no hiding the mountain of hormones in my pants, nor the avalanche of shame that threatened to bring us both down.

"It's fine," Jasmine said.

"If it's any consolation, it's got nothing to do with you. It happens every morning."

She raised an eyebrow at me.

I sat up straighter, and pain sliced through my hand. "*Shit.*"

I felt Jasmine hovering behind me. "Did you forget that you got stitches last night?" She made a *tsking* sound with her teeth. "Here. Let me see."

I turned around on the bed. Jasmine was kneeling, meaning she was a little taller than me for once. I gazed up at her as she took my bloodied hand in her own.

"So, what does this mean?" I asked her.

She frowned. "I'm probably going to have to redo this."

"No. *No*, not the bandage," I said. "You and me…"

Her gaze flickered to mine, and I swallowed. For a moment, I thought she was going to answer me, and then she merely got up to grab her first aid kit. She returned to the bed a few moments later, eyebrows pinched together, seemingly lost in thought.

God, I shouldn't have asked that.

Why did I ask that? I'd never had a girlfriend before. The closest I'd come was the girl across the street, but I'd observed enough to know that this was a social faux pas. When you like somebody, you don't put pressure on things. You present your best self—you don't cry, or beg, or vomit on their pretty white shoes. You smile and you hold fast against all of it: the inner turmoil, the mixed signals, the primal desires. You bear it all with a sunny, laid-back disposition and you never complain, never question, because to question things is to be vulnerable, and vulnerability is…embarrassing.

Jasmine started to unravel my bandage, and I unravelled along with it. I kept imagining the possible responses that could pour from her lips, each as patronising and psychologically damaging as the last:

Jules, you are too messed up for me.

I'm a private person. Do you really think I want to insert myself into the circus that is your life?

Instead, she just looked at me, and she said, "What are you scared of?"

Everything, I wanted to say. But I just shrugged—with the arm that wasn't attached to my injured hand. "It got weird with Chelsea," I said. "And I don't… I don't want it to get weird with you. Because now I feel like I've lost a friend in Chelsea. And I don't want to lose a friend in you. Even if it means losing…all this other stuff." *The kissing. The hand holding.* "I'd lose all of that if it meant I didn't lose you."

Jasmine still didn't answer me. She'd unwrapped the bandage now, and my stitches looked surprisingly unbothered. Maybe that should have been a relief, but right now, my sliced up, possibly infected hand was the least of my worries. It was my sliced up, possibly infected heart.

"I'm just worried this is all too fucked up for you," I said quietly.

I didn't say it, but I know she heard it.

I'm just worried I'm *too fucked up for you.*

Jasmine started cleaning the blood around my stitches. When she finally spoke, it was barely above a whisper. "You don't get it."

"You can't tell me it's not off-putting. You can't seriously tell me that dating someone else's ghost is a good time."

"You're not someone's ghost."

"I am, though." *I kissed Chelsea, and now we don't speak anymore. She doesn't even call.*

"You're not. And stop saying that. You have no idea how much it pisses me off when you do." She shook her head. "I like *you*, Jules. Not Jack. Not anybody else. And when you say things like that, it just… You're diminishing what I feel. It's like you're trying to convince me it's not real. But it *is*. Whether you want it to be or not."

"I do want it to be."

She finished re-bandaging my hand. "Good. Then shut up."

Next, she pulled out her laptop, and then she nestled back into bed.

"What are you doing?" I asked her.

"Let's watch a movie."

"Isn't your mum going to know I'm here?"

Jasmine shrugged. "She didn't come home last night."

"Where'd she go?"

"Beats me. Probably off with some guy."

For a brief moment, I wondered about David, and whether he'd realised I hadn't come home last night. I wondered if Pam would cover for me, or if that would land her in even more trouble. "I really should get going—"

Jasmine looked up at me. Those huge brown eyes. "Why?"

I swallowed. How did I explain it? *My, uh…stepdad is kind of…unpredictable, as it turns out. I'm worried he may be waiting for me to mess up again.*

"What is it, Jules?"

"Nothing," I said.

"Nothing?"

"Just…the twat stepdad. You know how it is."

She frowned at me. "Has he done something?"

"No," I said. Because, really, what had he done? He got drunk and yelled at Pam. But I'd never been around drunk older men before, or confrontation of any kind. Maybe that's just how people had disagreements? Maybe people were just different when they drank alcohol, like I was when I'd been rude to Chelsea? Maybe they were more prone to making terrible mistakes?

I slowly lay down beside Jasmine. Her black hair was splayed out on her green pillowcase. She still wasn't wearing any pants. She logged onto Netflix, and then she selected *The Truman Show*. It's about a man named Truman who was purchased by a corporation as a newborn, and—unbeknownst to him—has spent his entire life living on a television set.

"I've seen this, you know."

"I think you need to see it again."

"Why?"

"Just watch."

We lay there together, and the movie started to play. It was funny; I'd watched it about a year ago, and it had always seemed like a comedy to me. Now it was painfully familiar. It was also…oddly comforting. Soon, all sour thoughts of David had been relegated to the sidelines, like he was merely one of the background actors on the set of *The Truman Show*.

We were quiet for a while, and then Jasmine said, "You have to promise me something, Jules."

"Something," I said.

"You can't trust anyone. Especially not Bobby. The only person you can really trust is yourself."

"I trust you."

"You don't know me well enough yet."

Mike Michaelson: *Christof, let me ask you, why do you think that Truman has never come close to discovering the true nature of his world until now?*

Christof: *We accept the reality of the world with which we're presented. It's as simple as that.*

Hearing those lines made me think about Fremantle. I thought about the people in my life besides Angela. They weren't actors, but they may as well have been.

"It's the same way with people, too," Jasmine told me. "We accept people as they present themselves to us. But only we know our own thoughts."

It reminded me of something Angela had told me when I was

about thirteen or so. *People have to earn your trust, Jules. And even then, you should always keep a little bit for yourself. Keep a room in your heart for you, and never let anyone else inside. That way, no matter what happens, you can always come back to yourself.*

We watched the rest of the film in silence. After a while, Jasmine leaned her head on mine.

Christof: *I know you better than you know yourself.*
Truman: *You never had a camera in my head!*

"That's why Truman gets away in the end," Jasmine told me. "Because he wasn't really theirs. Not deep inside."

In the final scene, I watched a small Truman surveying the expansive backdrop of a cloudy blue sky. We don't know what happened to him after that, or where he ended up. And it isn't our right to know—not anymore. It never was.

The sight brought tears to my eyes, and I tried to hide my face before realising that Jasmine was crying too.

"I dreamt about you last night," I told her, as the credits began to roll. "I thought I was having a nightmare."

She wiped her eyes. "Thanks."

"No, I mean, I thought I was having a nightmare. And then you showed up. You were wearing your hair over your shoulder, like you were the first time I met you."

"I don't know why you remember that."

"Because it was pretty. I thought it was the prettiest thing I'd ever seen."

She smiled a little, but then she tried to hide it behind her hand. "You're not supposed to call girls pretty. It's not a good adjective. Kind of shallow."

"Well, I don't care. You're pretty. Deal with it." I glanced down at my bandage. "But you're smart, too. Obviously. Smarter than me. And funny. And a bit mean."

"Okay, all right," she said. "So, what did I do in this dream, then?"

"Nothing."

"Nothing?"

"Yeah, nothing. You just appeared. I was having a nightmare, and then I was having a dream."

We looked at each other. She was never more beautiful than in the morning.

She exhaled. "I feel like I want to kiss you again and it's freaking me out."

"Me too," I whispered. "Probably slightly less than it's freaking you out. Because, you know, you're pretty."

"You're pretty too, Jules.

No one had ever called me pretty. "No, I'm not."

"Yes, you are. Okay? You are a lot of things. If you're going to believe anything, believe that."

"That I'm pretty?"

"That you're a lot of things." She fisted her hand in my shirt. "You're not just…"

Rosemary Boy.

She pulled me in by my shirt. For a moment, we just hovered there, foreheads pressed against each other's. I'd never felt safer than right there—close enough for nothing to come in between us. Everything I felt for her bubbled to the surface, and everything she felt for me, however small, was there too. It was irrevocable and mine, even if only for a few seconds.

I was Truman and she was the expansive sky, only she wasn't a fake cardboard set.

She was real.

Right as I was about to kiss her, my phone pinged beside us. I groaned.

"Airplane mode," Jasmine whispered.

"Right. I know."

I went to change my settings, but not before replying to Pam's text and letting her know I was safe.

Today 7:43 am

Jules, where are you?
Just at a friend's house.

Pam's dots started moving, which I had now learned meant that she was typing a message to me. The three dots kept appearing and disappearing. Over and over. Finally, they just stopped.

"All good?" Jasmine asked me.

I shrugged, switching my phone to airplane mode. "I guess so."

Jasmine and I spent the rest of the day watching movies in bed. Kissing. Hiding in her cupboard when Ms Morè finally arrived home later that afternoon (that one was just me). Laughing at almost being caught. Laughing at almost being caught from all the *laughing*. I was in bed with her for only an hour, but really it was eight. Time just seemed to move differently with her. I swore I'd blink and spend my whole life with her if I wasn't careful.

By the time the sun started to go down outside, I was tempted to spend another night with her. Another night being *spontaneous*— diverting from what was expected of me by the people beyond these walls, the cyclical life I'd come to know: wake up with the world on my chest. Brush my teeth and vomit into the sink. Brush them again. Go to school. Go to work. Try and get down little bits of food where I could. Go to bed and hope that I'd done enough. Enough to purge all the pain inside of me.

Here, there was no pain. There was just Jasmine and I, and the calm, infinite thing that existed between us.

I'd have to say, before all of the stuff that came later, that it was probably one of the greatest days of my life.

Since it was getting dark, I decided to check my phone. I unselected airplane mode, and moments later, I saw Pam's name on my lock screen. There were three missed messages.

My entire body filled with dread.

Today 3:31 pm

Jules, do you think you could come and take the kids for a walk or something?

Today 6:58 pm

Don't come home. Please stay where you are.

Don't come home.

Chapter 22

I stashed my bike to the side of the house. There were lights on, so I didn't try to be quiet like normal. I didn't take the patio steps with careful precision, careful not to elicit any creaks. In fact, when I heard a plate smashing from the kitchen, followed by a single, garbled scream, I surged up those steps faster than I'd ever done before.

It was a familiar scene, plucked straight from the unconscious nightmares that had plagued my thoughts for the last couple of weeks. Pam, cowering in the corner of the kitchen between the fridge and the glasses pantry, and David—domineering, monstrous—advancing like a predator on its fragile prey.

Pam was as small as I'd ever seen her. "Jules," she said. "Honey—"

"Don't talk to him," David said. "You talk to me."

There was a fire inside me—an anger building so vehemently that I could hardly handle the heat against my bones. *Good.* I wanted the heat. I wanted the fire to burn through me, to light me up. But I kept losing it. As quickly as it built, the fear would extinguish it like a stubborn wind.

"S-stop," I said. *Fuck.* I wish my voice didn't shake. *Weak. Weak. Weak—*

"You want to explain yourself?" David asked. It took a moment for me to realise he wasn't talking to me; he was talking to Pam. It took me even longer to realise he was holding an empty egg carton.

The fire inside me lit up again. Had she broken the eggs again? Had she—

"Whose number is this?" he asked her.

Whoooosshhh. The fire was completely snuffed, just with that—with the realisation that it was not the eggs, or Pam's perceived lack of dexterity in the kitchen. It was *me. I* was responsible for this outburst, for this perverse show of dominance.

The number. Brett's number.

"Whose number is this?" David repeated. He took a step closer to Pam, and I instinctively surged forward.

"It's mine!"

Pam looked at me. So did David. Time stretched interminably before me, as my mind desperately tried to catch up to my admission.

"Er, I mean, it's not mine, but it's—it's my friend's. I ran into them when I bought the eggs."

"Who?" David asked me. He'd turned away from Pam now, toward me, and I felt my body rising and deflating at once.

"C-Coach Finlay."

He narrowed his eyes. "You up to something, Jules? You talking to him about something? Is he trying to get a statement from you? Trying to cash in? I swear to fuckin' God, if you're out here talking to people but not me, I'll fuckin' throw you out of here myself. But not before I take back all the money I've wasted on you already. Your clothes. Your food. Your fucking iPhone. You coulda been holed up in a shithole in Fremantle with some lunatic. Instead, you're here, eating my food, bringing a circus into my life. It's a fucking joke. If anyone should be cashing in on all this bullshit, it's me. Not Brett. Not fucking pussy Brett handing out his number to kids."

Lie, my brain screamed at me. "He…he just gave it to me." *That's not a lie. Lie better.* "I…I don't know why. I think he wants me to join the footy team. I-I said I wasn't any good at sports, but he insisted. He said he could teach me."

David frowned. "What the fuck is that bozo doing handing out his number to little kids?" He swung his attention back toward Pam. "I told you, didn't I? He can't be trusted. He did the same thing with Jack, and look how that ended up—"

"My teacher suggested it," I said. "She reached out to him."

Guilt flooded my body, hot and unforgiving. *Ms Morè. Now you've got Ms Morè involved. Shut up. Shut up!*

"Is this that Indian chick?" David said, and something inside of me shrivelled up and died. He pegged the carton of eggs against the fridge. "They should mind their business. All of them. Stay away from my kids—stop leaving their calling cards on my fuckin' eggs. My own kitchen. I can't even open my own fridge in my own kitchen." He stepped toward Pam again. "You see the problem with this, don't you? Are you really gonna let this happen again? You've got another chance now. You really gonna let this happen again?"

"No," Pam whispered. "N-no, I won't."

"He should get his own family. Get his own wife and kids to take charge of. That's what a real man does. He doesn't go sticking his nose where it doesn't belong. He doesn't leave his fuckin' calling card on another man's groceries. What kind of pussy shit is that? It's pathetic."

I locked eyes with Pam. There was a silent understanding between us. Firstly, Pam was drunk, and so was David. I could see it so clearly now: the near-empty bourbon bottle on the kitchen counter, her red-rimmed eyes, David's slurred speech. This wasn't just testosterone-fuelled, it was alcohol-fuelled. There was no reasoning with David tonight. There was only surviving. He was a raging cyclone I desperately needed to redirect—away from Pam, away from Tanner and James' room.

Tanner and James.

I pictured them huddled under their blankets. Hands over their ears. My heart sank.

"It *is* pathetic," Pam agreed, her gaze still locked on mine.

I nodded. "He must be lonely."

"Always wanted to be a father, I bet. Just couldn't find someone to shack up with and now he's realised it's too late. He's past his prime." David picked up the bourbon bottle. He took a long swig, polishing it off. "What woman wants to get knocked up by someone like that? Someone who teaches kids to throw a fuckin' ball and does admin work for the government? What kind of pussy jobs are those?"

"Let's go to bed," Pam suggested, and there was something in the way she said it. A suggestiveness, an unspoken promise… It made the flickering embers in my body blaze into an unquenchable fire.

I watched her take his hand—this small, broken, fragile man who was almost double her body mass. It took every fibre of my self-control not to insert myself between them, to encircle David in the fire of my rage without also harming Pam.

There was no other way for this to end. If I provoked him, he would hurt us both. He was physically more domineering than both of us, and he was void of any inhibitors thanks to that now-empty bottle of Buffalo Trace Bourbon. His anger would destroy us both. This was the only option…as much as it killed me. I had to let the gazelle gently lead the lion back to its den. While they were in the hallway, I heard David say, "I signed up for Jack. I didn't sign up for him."

"I know," Pam said gently.

Once they were gone, I realised the fire in my body had made its way to my hands. They were red and burning—evidence of how tightly I'd been clenching my fists by my sides. My bandaged hand was bleeding profusely, but the pain was grounding. It was a distraction from just how badly I wanted to charge upstairs and peel David's sweaty body off Pam's, from how badly I wanted to kill him.

I want to kill him.

How would I do it? I'd poison his bourbon. I'd smother him in his sleep. Would I be strong enough? I'd make myself strong enough. *I'll join a gym. I'll get strong. Strong enough to protect Pam.*

I walked over to the fridge. I heard the sound of that plate crashing against the floor. *Crraaccckkk!* It echoed off the walls and reverberated against my chest.

I looked down at the cracks in the tiles, and I wondered what caused them. I wondered how many dishes had met their demise on this very floor—if every chip in its exterior coincided with a chip in Pam's. The egg carton was still on the floor, and for a moment, an overwhelming sense of guilt replaced the curiosity inside me. *My fault. My fault my fault my fault—*

I picked up the egg carton. Brett's number was just barely readable—a few of the digits skewed slightly from the torn cardboard. I shoved it under my arm and ran upstairs.

When I got into my room, the first thing I did was hide the carton in Jack's wardrobe. In my wardrobe. I shucked off my Beacon polo that I'd been wearing since yesterday. I put on a clean t-shirt and then I sat on my bed, hands shaking.

A few moments later, I heard the door open. My heart nearly palpitated out of my chest.

"It's just me," Pam whispered.

All the lights were off in my room. I hadn't bothered to turn them on when I came in. It was pitch black, but I could just make out Pam's yellowish hair beneath the glow of the moon. She came and sat on my bed. She put her arms around me. She even started carding her hands through my hair, but my body was stiff as a board.

"I'm sorry," she was whispering. *I'm sorry. I'm sorry.*

We were both silent for a moment. I could feel her heart racketing against her ribcage. I felt her gaze on my bandaged hand, or maybe I was just imagining it.

I swallowed the lump in my throat. "Does he ever hit you?" I asked her.

She just squeezed me. Next to us, my phone was lighting up in the darkness. Jasmine had put her number in my phone, and she'd already called me six times since I left her house. This was number seven.

Pam put her mouth on my ear. "You can trust Brett."

I frowned in the darkness. "*What—?*"

"Shh," she said. "I can only stay for a moment. Listen to me,

Jules. You can't tell anyone about David. About the way he is. I know you're not seeing your counsellor anymore, and I know David talked you out of it. But you need to talk to someone. You can talk to Brett. Don't trust anybody else. And be careful what you say around David. He says he doesn't talk to the media, but I think he does. Just little stories here and there. Little updates about you and what you're doing. I know you don't read anything, and that's good. You shouldn't, but—" There was a noise outside, and Pam bristled against me. "Be careful what you say to anyone. Even your friends. The media hound them too. Don't tell anyone about this. You can't tell anyone, Jules. David knows things, and he can hurt us all very badly."

Then she floated out of the room as silently as she'd entered. I stayed sitting there, my hands still shaking, my phone still vibrating beside me.

I went into the cupboard. I grabbed out that damn egg carton. With my good hand, I started typing out a text. I almost deleted it, but something inside of me compelled me not to.

I sent the text, and then a few seconds later, I sent another.

Today 9:22 pm

Hey, it's Jules.
Can you come get me?

Brett didn't pull up outside the house. Instead, he parked a couple of streets over and sent me a text.

Today 10:53pm

Here – on Donaldson Road.

I pulled my hood up over my head and set off down the street. It was cold tonight—the coldest night I'd experienced in Brisbane so far. The icy winds sliced through my thin t-shirt, through the blood-soaked bandage on my right hand. It felt like the cyclone of David's emotions was permeating the town.

I climbed into Brett's car. He drove a low slung, royal red 2007 Honda Civic. It was a luxury edition with climate control, making it the perfect shelter from Cyclone David.

My body sighed into Brett's grey leather seats, so much so that I neglected to explain myself, or why I'd texted him out of the blue so late at night. I just sat there, basking in my sudden refuge, in the gentle folk song drifting over Brett's six-stack CD player.

"Uh," I said. "Sorry. For texting you so late…"

"Never apologise, Jules. I'm happy you did."

I glanced over at him. He was wearing a baseball cap, and his usually thick beard had been trimmed back to something neat and manageable.

You can trust Brett.

"Rough night?" he asked me.

I stared down at my hands. Like with Pam, I felt Brett's gaze drawn to my bandage. All I could do was nod.

"You feel like talking about it?"

"Not really."

"That's fair." Brett ran a hand over the growth on his chin. It sounded as scratchy as it looked. "Look, I've got a spare room.

You can always crash there. For as long as you need." A few seconds passed, and then: "Jack used to."

I looked at him. Slowly, sickeningly, things were starting to make sense.

I nodded again. Brett pulled out onto the road and drove toward his place. He lived in a two-bedroom apartment in a suburb called Hillcrest.

As we walked inside, Brett was texting someone on his phone. Presumably Pam.

"Excuse the mess," he said.

By mess, he meant a couple of pairs of shoes lined up next to the arched doorway. He meant a few coffee cups on the porcelain countertops in the kitchen. He meant a grey t-shirt strewn over the back of a white leather couch.

"It's fine," I said, and I nearly tripped over my shoelace when I noticed the wall.

There was a photo of me on there.

Well, not of *me*. Of Jack. But we were identical and so a picture of him was only a bee's dick from being a picture of me. I looked good. Jack looked good. He was dressed in his footy gear. He had an arm around Brett. Not for the first time, I got the feeling that he and Brett were a lot closer than they seemed.

We continued down the hall. It was like walking through a museum—cold and boundary-defying. The walls were swathed in white plaster and, aside from the few family photos, I could have sworn that no one actually lived here—at least not full time.

Brett set me up in the spare room. *Spare* was definitely the right word. There was nothing but a single bed, a built-in wardrobe and an empty desk.

"It's not much," he said. "But…it'll give you some space, at least. To get your thoughts together."

I was sitting on the edge of the bed. The sheets were cold and crunchy, and the entire room smelled vaguely of dust. "Thanks, Brett."

He was hovering by the door, almost looking for reasons to stay. "There are fresh towels in the bathroom. Soap in the cabinets. Just help yourself. Also…" He scratched his head. "I think Jack may have left some shirts in the wardrobe. Maybe a pair of pants. Some jocks."

"O-okay," I said. For some reason, the knowledge of that was like a freight train crashing through my chest.

"Jules. I know you don't want to talk about it." Brett pinched the bridge of his nose, like this conversation was actually painful for him. "But your *hand…*"

"I tripped at work."

"Aren't you a receptionist?"

"Clumsy."

I realised that sounded like a textbook excuse someone rattled off in this kind of situation, but really, it *was* the truth. At least a vague version of it.

"Your mother said she's happy for you to stay here a couple of days. Just take as long as you need. I can go and pick up your bike tomorrow while David's at work. But you may have to catch the bus to school…"

"That's fine," I told him.

"Have you taken the bus?"

"Yeah," I lied. "Loads of times."

Brett nodded again. He gave one last look into the room, like he was searching for something else to keep him there. More conversation starters. Maybe it was just strange for him to see me in this room. Strange for him to see someone that looked so much like Jack, sitting on this bed again, seeking refuge in his house.

Finally, he just shut the door.

I sat there for a few moments, feeling like I wanted to cry. Then I went and had a shower. I let the hot water run over my body, and I used Brett's soap, which was probably *Jack's* soap, and I did cry. A little bit, at least. It's hard to tell how much when you're in the shower.

I got out and went into the wardrobe in search of some fresh clothes. My t-shirt was still relatively clean, so I put it back on and then went digging around for some pants. I couldn't find any, so I went looking in all of the drawers. The last one was jammed, so I had to pull on it harder than the others. When it finally opened, I ended up sprawled on the carpet on my bare arse.

There were pairs of underwear in there. Thank God. There was also a pair of grey track pants, a cheap-looking watch, and a book.

I pulled the book out of the drawer. It was a black, leather-bound book, slightly dusty, like the rest of this room. It had the initials J.R monogrammed in silver.

That's when I realised it wasn't a book at all.

It was a journal.

Jack's journal.

Chapter 23

Jack's journal. My *twin brother's* journal. His words, forever encased in this book. Thoughts never read by anyone else but him. A voice completely foreign to my own. Would it be familiar? Would I recognise myself in these pages? *Should I read them*?

Journals are a place people go to be alone. Did the rules change once someone was dead? I thought about dead authors whose diaries had been posthumously published: *Sylvia Plath, Franz Kafka, Flannery O'Connor.* What are the ethics of reading someone's journal when there were important questions to be answered? A lot of people didn't like the things they read in those journals. In a lot of cases, their controversy almost shrouded their insight. But this wasn't the diary of some tortured, 20th-century writer.

This was the diary of my brother. A seventeen-year-old kid.

And I wasn't planning to *publish* it for millions of scrutinising eyes. I was merely planning to open it. To glance at the first couple of pages…

Right now, it was sitting on the seat across from me, deep in the back pocket of my schoolbag. The bus had been nearly empty when I'd hopped on, but it was quickly filling, and I worried that someone was going to try and sit next to me.

Luckily—or, I suppose, not so luckily—most people were content just to hold onto the straphangers and stare at me. It had started with one person recognising me—holding my gaze just a little too long, their eyes widening—and quickly spiralled into at least a dozen double-takes and hushed conversations.

"Is that him?" a young girl whispered to another boy.

"I think so."

"Should we ask for a selfie?"

"I think that's rude."

There was a beat of silence, and then, "Maybe just take a picture," followed by the unmistakable flash of an iPhone across the aisle.

"*Turn the flash off,* idiot."

I angled my body further toward the window, resisting the urge to cringe. I wondered if maybe I should just get off and walk the rest of the way to school, or if I should finally cave and be one of those arseholes who wear a cap indoors. In the end, I just resigned myself to putting in my earphones and staring out the window. There was no way I was opening Jack's journal here, now. That really *would be* like publishing it for millions of scrutinising eyes.

When we finally got to school, Jasmine was waiting for me just outside the gates.

"Where the hell have you been?"

I kept walking. If I hovered in front of the gates too long, there was a chance someone might come over and talk to me.

"Jules—"

"Not here," I said. "Let's go and talk somewhere else."

We walked to the library. It always made me feel calmer, being around books. Sometimes I'd go to bed with a novel in my hands, and I'd barely read a page. Just the thought of disappearing into its world was enough to make me sleepy, to fill my head with dreams.

We stood near the non-fiction section. Jasmine frowned at me. "Are you wearing Jack's uniform again? I thought you didn't like doing that."

I glanced at myself. "How did you know?"

"It's an old senior shirt."

"It was the only one Brett had in his cupboard."

"Brett? You're staying at Brett's?"

I rubbed my eyes, leaning my shoulder against the wall beside me. "Some shit went down with my family last night. Bad stuff, and…I didn't know who to call."

"So, you called Coach Finlay?"

"What's wrong with that?"

"Nothing," she said. "He just… I don't know, he was always taking such an interest in Jack. An interest that seemed to go way beyond football… And now suddenly he's taking an interest in you. I just don't know why."

"He wants to help me. And for some reason… I trust him." *Because Pam told me I can.*

"Did he?" she asked me. "Help you?"

I nodded. For some reason, I felt like I was going to cry. But I wasn't in the shower, so the tears wouldn't just masquerade as water rolling down my face. There'd be no way to hide them.

Jasmine was quiet for a moment, and then she said, "I was really worried about you."

"I know. I'm sorry."

"You can't just disappear, Jules.

"I know."

"People care about you."

"I know," I said. I heard what she was really saying. *I care about you.* "…I care about people too."

We just looked at each other for a long time. The bell rang for class, but neither of us moved. I thought about what Pam said. *Be careful what you say to anyone. Even your friends. The media hound them too.*

"Does the media… I mean, do they…do they contact you?"

Jasmine's eyes widened. She started scanning the books beside my head, like she suddenly had a keen interest in the studies of bees.

I sighed. "Why didn't you tell me?"

"What difference would it make?" she asked me. "Why would I want to make you feel bad over something you can't control?"

"I don't know. Maybe so that I could stop bringing attention to you."

"You bring attention everywhere you go."

"So maybe I should just stop going places," I said.

"You can't stop living your life, Jules. Just look at Pam. They're going to write about you whether you're going outside or staying home. Whether you're talking or not talking."

I wondered about that. About our society's ability to turn literally anything into a story. It didn't seem like a skill so much as a symptom.

She shrugged. "You can't please everyone."

"No, you can't." Of all the lessons I'd learned since assimilating into my new life, that seemed to be the most important. When I was living my small life back in Fremantle, I never had to worry much about how other people perceived me. Now that I was here, every day was like trying to walk a tightrope above a shark tank.

Jasmine looked into my eyes, like she was trying to find me.

"I'm really scared that I'm going to lose you," I whispered. "That stuff is going to come out about me, about my family…"

"Jules."

"I just don't know what I'm doing, Jas. I don't know what I'm fucking *doing*. I'm living someone's else's life, wearing someone else's clothes. I feel like I'm just waiting to live my real life, because the life I was living before was clearly bullshit, and this life is even more bullshit. It's all just…bullshit. And every time I think I've got it—every time I think I've got one fucking thing figured out—it gets taken away… My whole life I have been fighting to hold onto *something*."

Someone walked past our aisle, and I stiffened. I realised I'd totally forgotten where I was. Forgotten *who* I was.

Jasmine slowly reached out and touched my hand. We interlocked our index fingers, and I felt something unfurl inside me. "It's okay," she told me.

"I'm just…so tired of being Jack."

"You're not Jack."

"I know," I said. "I know I'm not Jack…"

"No, Jules, you're not Jack."

I stared at her. "Don't try to—don't *Good Will Hunting* me, okay."

"I'm not trying to *Good Will Hunting* you."

"Yeah, you are. You're trying to break through to me."

She sighed and scanned the area behind me, like she was trying to make sure the coast was clear. "When I first came to Australia, no one could pronounce my last name," she told me. "Hell, my first year of high school, no one even talked to me because my accent was weird. Then, when they finally did, they called me Jasmine Mor-ee, not Jasmine Mor-ay. When I corrected someone, they told me it was my fault for being Indian. For having a weird name. The only reason they pronounce it correctly now is because my mum is their teacher."

"I like your accent," I told her. I really did. It was the most beautiful hybrid of Indian and Australian. She didn't sound totally like either. Her words were entirely her own.

"Well, I didn't for a long time. Over the years, I went from being completely one thing to half of another. I wasn't just Indian anymore. I was Indian Australian. Part of me just missed my old identity. I missed fitting in."

I tightened my fingers around hers. I was still holding onto her index finger, and now we'd interlocked our thumbs. "When did it change?"

"When I realised that fitting in with no one is better than fitting in with the wrong people. That I didn't need to go back to India, or change who I was. To become one thing or the other thing. I just needed to be myself. The me that I was becoming. And the right people would come, eventually."

I stroked the inside of her palm with my thumb. I wanted to kiss her. I wanted to kiss her more than I'd ever wanted to kiss her before.

"Reg used to tell me that loneliness is the price we pay for real connections," she said, and I swear, all she did was blink. All she did was blink and I was melting at her feet. She had these long, dark eyelashes that seemed to punctuate every glance, so that even *blinking* was a beautiful thing. I started to think maybe everything about her was beautiful. Things I'd never noticed about people… The things that were usually just ordinary were suddenly remarkable.

"Reg is a smart man." I leaned my head against the bookshelf.

"Because he's lived. In a different time, but…the lessons are the same. No matter where we come from, we all live to learn the same things."

"I miss my mum," I told her.

She squeezed my hand. The admission didn't seem to shock or offend her in any way. "I know," she said after a while.

"That doesn't make you judge me?"

She shrugged. "Don't be ashamed of where you came from, Jules. You can't control it any more than the rest of us." She leaned her head against the bookshelf, so we were looking directly into each other's eyes. "I'm a Morè. It's a Marathi name. In India, we have a caste system—it's sort of like the feudal system in England. My family, we're Kshatriya—the warrior caste. We come from warriors.

"You're an Edwards, and a Rosemary," she continued. "You come from two women who wanted you desperately. Who wanted to raise you in their image."

I smiled. It didn't seem so terrible when she put it that way. It didn't seem so confusing.

We kept holding hands, and after a while, I closed the distance between us and pressed my lips against hers. She breathed in sharply, like she hadn't been expecting it, like I hadn't been slowly inching my face closer to hers since the moment she leaned against the bookshelf. I cupped her cheek in one hand, and I pressed my other to the small of her back. Our bodies were flush against each other from head to toe, and she felt so precious in my arms. So rare and yet perfectly tailored to me. Like a puzzle piece.

For a moment, I was totally consumed by my two favourite things: books and Jasmine. And I didn't feel a need to pretend to be anyone or anything. I just surrendered completely to the moment. Everything that had happened. Everything that had made us who we were. It was simple, and peaceful, and I started to think that maybe that's what life is all about. Finding as many of those moments as you can—the moments that seem to put your past into perspective. These moments where everything just makes sense.

"I want to visit my mum."

Brett nearly choked on his chicken soup. It was the only thing I'd been able to stomach over the last few days, so he'd made it for me every night. I highly suspected that he made himself a proper Brett-sized meal after I went to bed, but he never made me feel like less of a person for how little I ate. He just spoon-fed himself little chunks of soup and he only ever went at my pace. With everything. Food, drink, conversation…

He frowned at me. "You want to visit…?"

"Angela."

He nodded, patting at his mouth with a tea towel. "Okay. That's who I thought you meant."

We were quiet for a moment. A part of me felt guilty for bringing it up, especially considering how much Brett had done for me over the past two days. He'd gone over to Pam's and packed bags of clothes for me. He'd picked up my bike so that I no longer had to take the bus to school or work. He'd fed me and made sure I was safe.

But it just wasn't enough.

"I know I can do it, now that I'm eighteen. I just don't know how I'd get there. I don't have experience flying by myself, and I think the media would be too crazy. I want to go under the radar."

Brett just sat there, listening to me.

"I did get an offer from Gav's cousin to come with me," I said. "Gav's a guy from school."

"I know who Gavin Lewis is."

"Yeah, but his cousin—"

"Is a piece of shit."

I nodded.

"I'm not letting you go to Perth with Bobby Lewis. He wouldn't help you out of the goodness of his heart."

"He wants my statement. He wants to sell it to the media."

Brett sighed, closing his eyes briefly. "Look, Jules…"

"I want to go with you, Brett. I'll pay my own way. I've already had my application approved, and I've been saving up my pay each week from the nursing home. I think I've got enough to cover a return ticket for both of us."

Brett stared at me for a long time. He folded his hands together on the table, looking pensive. "You wouldn't have to pay for me," he said.

"I'd really like it if you came. It would really help me out—"

"I'm not turning you down," Brett said. "I just meant that I'd pay for myself."

Something loosened in my chest. "You'd come with me? To

Perth?"

He rubbed his chin. "We just have to be smart," he told me. "The media…"

"They'd be all over it."

And David, I thought. *David would be all over it.*

And then he'd be all over Pam.

Brett tilted his head. "Is there something else that's worrying you about it?"

I stirred my spoon around my soup. Brett had been doing this, albeit subtly, over the last few days. There'd be a small opening, and he'd pry at it with tentative fingers. *You okay, Jules? You want to talk about anything? Anything... Like maybe why you still don't want to go home?*

Ultimately, despite how much I wanted to let him in, I just couldn't do it. I wasn't prepared for the way sharing that information could change my life—could change Pam's life. She was an intensely private person, and this revelation would only cast an even brighter spotlight on her life. It may even threaten her relationship with Tanner and James.

But was that better than them being in danger?

These were the questions I so desperately wanted to ask Brett. Questions I'd never had to ask before, and that felt too big and complicated for me to answer.

"I'd really like it if my friend Jasmine came," I said finally. "And I know… I know how important secrecy is, not just for my sake but for the people that come with me. I know it's a big risk."

"Jasmine?" Brett looked surprised. "As in, Ms Morè's daughter?"

"Yeah," I said. "She said she'd talk to Ms Morè about it, and try to convince her to come too. We know it could potentially damage Ms Morè's reputation if it got out, and I know how hard she's worked to get to where she is… But I think we could be smart about it."

He nodded, a small smile on his lips. "I've known Ms Morè for a couple of years through the high school. She's always struck me as the type of woman who would risk her career to do what she feels is right. She did a lot for Jack, even though it bothered some of the other students."

"They thought she was showing favouritism?"

"She just knew that he needed a bit more help. She's always struck me as a very kind and principled woman…" He trailed off, like he was lost in thought.

I took a sip of my water. For some reason, it was strange to think about Jack and Ms Morè interacting. Maybe it was just strange to think about Jack and *Jasmine's mother* interacting.

"So, you like Jasmine, hey?" Brett eventually asked.

"Yeah, I like her." I stared out the window of the living room. *I don't actually think there's a strong enough word for how I feel about her.*

"What do you like about her?"

I had a spoonful of my soup, just so I didn't have to look at Brett. "I like that…she doesn't judge anything that I say to her. And even though she's hard at first, she's really kind to people. All types of people, too. Old and young… And she's got this way of seeing the world. I swear, it's like she sees everything the way it's meant to be seen."

Brett just sat back in his chair, smiling at me. "Sounds like you're in love."

"I don't know…"

"Don't think about it too hard, Jules. Just feel it."

I wondered if Brett had ever been in love. It seemed like he had, by the way he talked. But it also felt too personal, like the subject of Pam and what was going on at home. We just kept eating our soup.

"I'd have to talk to Ms Morè," Brett said, when we were washing up. "But if they're keen to come, then I'm sure we could arrange that. Maybe over the term break. It's only a couple of days away."

I could barely hold back the smile on my lips. "Okay," I said. "Thanks."

I continued washing the dishes. Brett hovered by the counter. "Look," he said, "I've loved you staying here, Jules, but…"

I swallowed. My hands were frozen beneath the warm water.

"David's back from his business trip next week, so he's going to ask where you are."

I nodded. David had gone to Melbourne the day after I arrived at Brett's, so I was able to prolong my stay. But we both knew this wasn't a permanent solution.

"I'll go back," I told him.

"You don't have to, Jules."

"I do," I said, because *I did*. I couldn't leave Pam and the kids alone, but I also couldn't betray Pam by telling people things that she'd explicitly told me not to. The only option was to go back, and to convince her to leave of her own volition.

Later, after hours of restless turning, I finally decided I wasn't getting any sleep that night. I pulled out my phone, and I decided to do the one thing I'd promised myself I'd never do again.

I Googled the Rosemarys.

Chapter 24

CITYSCOPE NEWS

*Pamela Rosemary's Silence After Years
of Searching for Missing Twin*

BY CHRISTOPHER LANE   **APRIL 2, 2012**

PAMELA Rosemary, once the determined face of the search for her kidnapped twin son, Nicholas, became noticeably silent in the years following the tragedy. In the beginning, Pamela was relentless, appearing on national news outlets and constantly releasing new photos of identical twin Jack to keep her missing son's face in the spotlight. However, around the fifth anniversary of his disappearance, Pamela withdrew from public life, and her once-vocal presence noticeably tapered off.

It has now been almost 13 years since the kidnapping, and Pamela has made great strides to rebuild her life. A year after the tragedy, she married Brisbane real estate agent David Leman and eventually welcomed two more children into their lives—James, now 2, and Tanner, born just last month. The young family has been living quietly in Brisbane, far from the media's glare. While Pamela's retreat from the public eye may be explained by her desire to protect Jack and her new family, her sudden silence has raised questions among those who followed her heartbreaking story.

While it's not uncommon for families of missing children to step back from the public eye as time passes, Pamela's abrupt shift from an active advocate to a reclusive figure has left many speculating. As we approach the thirteen-year-anniversary of Nicholas' disappearance, many wonder whether the emotional toll of the search became too much to bear, or if there were deeper, more personal reasons behind her retreat.

After reading that article, I spent the rest of the night going down a Rosemary rabbit hole. It began with me Googling Pam, and it ended with me sitting on my floor with Jack's journal resting in my lap. It was almost light outside, and part of me wanted so desperately to stop—to just close my eyes and forget all of it. But the sickness had taken hold of me. I was no better than that loser on Reddit, *CaseCrackerRosemary23*.

What that guy wouldn't do to get his hands on this journal… What the *media* wouldn't do. I was certain I could sell this book to any news outlet in the country and have enough money for a house deposit at eighteen years old.

But I just couldn't do it. I couldn't do it to Jack.

I could barely even bring *myself* to read it, but I knew that I had to. If not for me, then for Pam.

After reading over a dozen articles from the last decade, I'd concluded that there was a chance that she was hiding something, or at least not being completely forthcoming about the reasons for her silence. I didn't trust that she had retreated from the spotlight out of a desire to protect her family, but rather, out of fear.

As I finally opened Jack's journal, I realised that my suspicions were justified. Some people never change. Things with David had always been this way.

The pages weren't filled with detailed entries like I'd anticipated. Instead, they were filled with poetry. Love poems.

Sad poems. Poems for every season—and I recognised every single one, because I'd lived these stories myself. I could feel it all: his love, his confusion, his fear, his resignation.

Eggs

I sit in my car.
And there is no smoke to reach for, this time
to replace
the pressure in my chest by
poisoning my lungs.
So I sit, in this despair, the air crisp and clean.
If I told you things, would you understand them?
Would you treat me carefully
like you should?
Like he should?
Like anybody should?
Even if they weren't there
in that kitchen, their self-respect discarded
like a carton of broken eggs.
There are fresh ones in a grocery bag.
Are they broken? Are they fine?
Only weeks later do I realise—
he wanted them
broken.
The lights, the dishes, the endless cartons.
He wanted her
broken.
And now she is.

I closed the book and held it against my chest. The first glimpse of golden white sunlight was filtering into the room, casting shadows onto the floor beside me. For a second, I almost convinced myself it was his shadow.

What should I do? I wanted to ask him. *How do I fix it?*

I opened the book again. I turned to the next unread page. I saw the title of the poem, but it still took me too long to realise who it was about.

Me.

<s>*Nicholas*</s>
Nick

> *Today more than any   Day*
> *I feel the wound   of absence,*
> *Fresh and festering   in my chest.*
> *I want your life   Wherever it is,*
> *In another country   thick with snow,*
> *In the ground   too deep to go.*
> *I want to know you   Because you are me,*
> *I want to gaze inside   a mirror*
> *And see our face   untainted.*
> *I want to know   Oh, how it feels*
> *To know myself   to love myself*
> *To hear your name   just like this*
> *She calls you   Nicholas,*
> *I call you   Nick.*

I stared at the poem for a long time. The words written by my brother. The brother I never knew I had. The brother I never *would* have.

The longer I read it, the more meaning I found. It wasn't just one poem but three. I skimmed a few more pages, and I realised that it was the only one written in this format. I wondered if he'd broken it up on purpose—if each side of the poem represented the two of us. Separately, we still made vague sense, but together we created something even more powerful, even more lucid.

I call you Nick.

I kept rereading that line. I kept imagining being imagined. Answering to a different name in somebody else's mind. It broke my heart to know he died without ever knowing my real identity, that he grew up calling me by a different name.

But it broke it even deeper to know I never called him anything.

I hadn't stopped thinking about Jack's journal all shift. I'd only read a few poems, as it had taken me ages to properly dissect each line and interpret its meaning…

Or maybe that's just what I told myself. Maybe I understood the poems the moment I read them. Maybe I was just too much of a coward to keep reading.

It was around 6 p.m. now. I was watching *BoJack Horseman* on my phone beneath my desk. I wanted to stop, to do something productive, but the only thing that felt safe to me right now was to do nothing.

At least until Bill started falling.

I glanced up. Bill was craning forward in slow motion. Sometimes, if you just waited, he righted himself. He was like an ancient pendulum naturally finding its equilibrium. Other times, his head went a little too far one way, and he needed human intervention. More often than not, that human intervention was me.

"Bill," I called out. "You good?"

He nodded. That was a mistake. It offset his balance just that little bit, and I was out of my seat within seconds, ready to get sued. I ended up bracing his back with my good hand, just as another person rushed to his front. My hand brushed against hers—pale and slender—and she instantly recoiled.

Chelsea.

"You shouldn't be touching the residents," she told me. She looked into Bill's glassy eyes. "Bill, *walker*, remember?"

"Sorry," I said, backing away. "It looked like he was gonna fall."

"You're not qualified. You have to let him fall if nobody's here."

"That's horrible."

I grabbed Bill's walker just as Chelsea began guiding him over to it. "Yeah, well, there's a good chance you'll both get hurt if you try to help."

I frowned, watching her sit Bill down on his walker. "But you're not qualified either."

Chelsea shrugged, not meeting my gaze. I couldn't tell if she was angry at me, exactly. She seemed more...resigned.

"Yeah, but I'm not famous," she said. "I don't have people itching to write an article about me or come after my money."

"I don't have any money."

"You could though, if you wanted it."

"I don't. I don't care about it."

"What do you care about?" she asked me, and then she seemed to think better of it. She locked the wheels of Bill's walker, and then she started walking toward the exit, like this conversation had been a bad idea from the start.

"You kind of are," I told her. "Famous... People write articles about you. I've read them."

Chelsea stopped. She was halfway to the doors, and her ponytail was swishing from side to side. "You've been looking at that stuff?"

"It's hard not to," I said. "It's all just there… All this information."

She turned around to look at me. "Like what?"

I didn't speak. I just kept fussing over Bill, even though Bill was now sitting down, completely safe from…himself. But Chelsea was looking at me. She was looking at me in this way that made me think I wasn't going to get away with lying to her. Not like I did with Brett.

"Is everything okay, Jules?"

No, I wanted to say. *No, it's not.* "Yeah, everything's fine."

She kept looking at me. I wanted to go back to my desk.

"Is it?" she asked.

No, I thought. "Yes."

"Jules."

I shook my head. My vision was blurring, and I felt like Bill, suspended in mid-air. My equilibrium was off, and I wasn't sure if I was going to fall. Chelsea seemed to deliberate for a long time whether she should help me.

Finally, she said, "Let's go outside."

We went out the back exit where the rubbish compactors were. Chelsea grabbed my key card from my pocket and swiped us out. We walked all the way down to the river.

Shame rose to my face. I could feel it, pink and burning, as Chelsea and I sat on the edge of the jetty. As I started to cry, she reached out and held my hand.

"It's going to be okay," she said. It seemed like she was always telling me that.

I looked out at the river. I felt the words bubbling up inside me before I said them, like indigestion.

"David's abusing Pam."

I heard Chelsea's sharp intake of breath. I don't know why it felt safe to tell Chelsea, out of anyone. Maybe because talking to Chelsea always kind of felt like talking to Jack. They had so much shared history… It felt like *we* had the same shared history.

"It's mostly emotional," I said. "At least, I think it is. I think he may have hit her before, but he's careful… You know, with the media and everything."

"I know," Chelsea said quietly. "I mean, I suspected. Jack never said anything, but I could sense the tension whenever I was in that house. David has this…way about him. You feel his presence on you even when you leave, like he's stuck to your clothes."

I sighed. It was such a relief to have Chelsea react with understanding, and not with questions. "Yeah. That's…that's *exactly* what it feels like."

"Have you told anyone else?" she asked me.

"Pam told me not to tell anyone. I'm guessing she and Jack made the same promise, too." I shook my head. "I just don't get it. I don't get why she's protecting David. Why she wants to stay with him."

"That's the wrong question," Chelsea told me. "The question shouldn't be why is Pam staying with David, why is she putting up with it, but rather, why is *he* doing it? What's wrong with *him*?"

I looked at Chelsea, like maybe she had the answer.

"My dad was like David," she told me. "Before my mum left him… Before Grandad put his foot down and got us both out.

Growing up that way sucked, but it taught me a lot about men like my dad. Men like David.

"I think that men like David are mad at the world," she continued. "They're mad and they feel like they have something to prove. They blame everyone else for getting in the way of that. They feel small inside, so they have to shrink everything around them down to size." She'd started playing with a stick in the garden, throwing little pieces into the water. "Grandad always says, *You can tell how small a man feels by how small he makes you feel*."

I thought of one of Jack's poems, one where he referred to *Mr D*. I'd quickly gathered that it was his pseudonym for David. I realised then that he was so afraid to tell the truth, even in his writing.

The Wolf

I'll be so strong,
like you, like the militant wolf
inside you, that would
fall asleep so gently if only
he was sung to.

Would that make you proud of me?

I'll disappear,
like you, like the scared little boy
inside you.
Take the
sharpened edge since it's the only thing
left to cling to.

Would you be proud
of me then,
Mr D?
Would you finally
be proud of me?

That poem had kept me up all night after I'd read it. I felt Jack's frustration, his hopelessness, his desperation emanating from every line. I saw, for the first time, his hatred for David coupled with his desire to be accepted by him. To be loved by him.

I understood, for the first time, Jack's desperation to disappear. Had this been what led him to drive so recklessly that night? Had David pushed him to the edge?

"I don't want to be like David," I told her. "But I'm *mad*, Chelsea. I am. I look around… I look around at people and they all seem to be a part of something. Like they're all just cogs in this machine, and they have their little purpose, and they make up something bigger. But I just can't see it. I can't see this thing that we're all meant to be a part of. I can't see the point." Tears filled my eyes again. I wondered again what it was about Chelsea that made her so easy to talk to. I wondered if she was so at ease with me because of how she'd felt with Jack, and I was just an extension of that. I could feel the familiarity that emanated from her voice, from her gaze.

"I've spent the last four months thinking there was something wrong with the world, and everyone in it… But I've started to realise that maybe it's me," I said. "Maybe there's something wrong with *me*. Maybe…I'm not meant to be here."

"Don't say that."

"I didn't mean—

"I know. But don't." She took a deep breath. "Be sad, Jules. You've had a lot of bad stuff happen to you. But you don't want to be the cause of more bad stuff, do you? Because that's all this talk gets you. It gets you in a hole that's very hard to get out of. So be sad, but don't stay there. Please."

"Okay," I whispered. "I'm sorry."

We sat there in silence for a few moments. I could almost feel the pull of the river tide in my stomach.

"After Jack died, I said a similar thing to Grandad. You know what he said?"

I shook my head.

Chelsea reached into her pocket. She scrolled through her phone, and I realised she was searching for a voicemail. Soon, Reg's deep voice rumbled over the speaker. "*Chelsea... Chelsea... Chelsea...*" He sighed deeply. I'd never heard him sound so lost for words, so distraught. Finally, he said, "*Darling, I know you're hurting, and it feels like no one else could possibly interpret your pain. And I know it's easy to label yourself an outsider— something I've been doing rather comfortably for the last fifty years. But do you know what's really challenging? Living. Feeding the elderly person who can't feed themselves anymore. Making a coffee in the morning and convincing yourself it's going to be the best damn thing you've ever tasted. It's all these little things... All these little things that make up a life. That save it. We're all just saving each other, at the end of the day. We're all just trying to find happiness wherever we can.*"

Chelsea put her phone back in her pocket. I wondered how, almost imperceptibly, she had gone from being that girl at

Jack's wake to the girl sitting here, now. Maybe that's just the trajectory of grief. Maybe a person's wounds only make them more indestructible in the end.

"Jack used to call himself an outsider, too," she said. "I don't think either of us realised what a trap that is."

I started playing with my own stick. I broke off little chunks, throwing them into the river. "Am I…? I mean, am I different to him?"

Chelsea smiled at me. "Yeah, you are."

"How?"

She seemed to think about it for a moment. I got the feeling she was unsure of how honest to be with me. Finally, she just said, "Jack was a really hateful person, Jules."

In a weird way, I think I'd already known this about him. Jasmine had alluded to it, and I could feel it in his poetry.

"I don't think he was always that way," Chelsea said. "A lot of things made him the way he was. David…the media…the kidnapping. I think, had none of that stuff happened, he would have turned out to be a lot like you."

All this time, I'd only been compared to Jack. Now, someone was comparing Jack to me. For the first time since the kidnapping, I think—I felt like a real person.

"I'm sorry," I told her. "I'm sorry that he was so angry. That he probably didn't treat you the way you deserve to be treated."

She was quiet for a long moment. I don't know if she'd ever told anybody the extent of Jack's darkness, or what it was like to be close to it. "He'd fill my head with all of it," she said quietly." His hatred of his life and the world. For a long time, I was just this vacuum for all his pain. And I'd convinced myself that I couldn't be happy without him. That it was us against the world… But when you think that way, and then you lose the person… That kind of loneliness is very hard to come back from.”

“Have you?” I asked her. “Come back from it?”

“I’m getting there.” She shrugged, picking up a new stick. “I don’t know. I loved him, but I guess I see things like that more clearly now. I think…the right people will be there for you, even when you don’t deserve it. The wrong ones will never be there, even when you do.”

“You deserve someone who’s there for you,” I told her.

“So do you,” she said. And then she looked at me. “Is Jasmine? There for you?”

“Yeah, she is.”

“Have you told her about this?”

I shook my head. “I’m scared,” I admitted.

“What are you scared of?”

“Losing her. Losing Pam. Losing everyone.”

“Remember, Jules: the right ones will be there.”

I nodded. I’d started to cry again. “What do I do?” I asked her. I didn’t know what exactly I was asking.

“You look after yourself,” she told me. “As hard as it is. If that means getting away from Pam and David… If that means going your own way, then you do it.”

“I can’t leave her,” I said. “I just…I just got her back.”

“Then you tell someone.”

Chapter 25

As I walked up Jasmine's patio steps, I heard Brett's voice in my head. *What do you like about her?*

I liked the dark freckles in the corners of her eyes. The ones that looked like tiny black stars.

I liked that she made me forget about Jack's journal. About David. About the fact that I'm *Rosemary Boy*.

I liked that she called me in the middle of the night now. I liked that she snuck me upstairs to her room and we laughed so hard we almost woke up her mother. I liked that she was raised by Ms Morè—a strong, gentle woman who had agreed to risk her reputation, and that of her daughter's, to do something that was important to me.

I started to laugh again, and Jasmine put a hand over my mouth to keep me quiet. I couldn't believe that, tomorrow, she was going to fly to Perth with me to see *my* mother.

"Quiet," she scolded me. "Think you can do that?"

I nodded, and Jasmine removed her hand from my mouth.

I liked that, the moment she had touched me, everything in this world made sense again. And all I cared about was her standing in front of me. The white rose in her hair. The pink slippers on her feet. How soft she looked late at night in her own habitat.

I pulled her in closer to me, and I wrapped my arms around her as tightly as I could (as tightly as I could without crushing her to death). After a while, it stopped being a hug, and it started to feel like something else.

It started to feel like me hanging on for dear life.

"Are you okay?" Jasmine asked me.

I shook my head against hers.

"Nervous about seeing Angela?"

I nodded. We were quiet for a long moment.

"Other stuff?" Jasmine asked quietly.

I nodded again. We were still holding each other, and neither of us made any move to separate. I imagined the words coming out of my mouth. I imagined them filling the empty space of Jasmine's room. *I'm afraid of my stepdad. He comes back from Melbourne in two days, and I'd rather go to a prison and visit my kidnapper than spend another day with him. I'm a coward.*

"Hey," Jasmine said. "Talk to me."

I closed my eyes. I began stroking her hair with my uninjured hand, and I wondered whether she could sense how much pain I was in. I wondered if she could pick up on all the parts of me that were bleeding. I didn't even know I was going to say it until I did.

"Jules…"

"I love you," I whispered.

She pulled back to look at me. Her eyebrows were mussed up, and there was a spot of toothpaste in the corner of her mouth. Seeing her like that was always so enchanting, like watching her in high definition.

"You love me," she said.

My heart was pounding. "I do."

Jasmine just stared at me, like she was trying to solve a maths problem in her head. "And you…you know what love is?"

"You give me a pretty good idea," I said.

Honestly, I didn't really know. I just knew that I *missed her*. Every time she wasn't around, I counted down the hours until I could see her again. Every time I was with her, I wished that time would slow down so that we wouldn't have to be apart.

I licked my finger, and without thinking too hard, I rubbed the spot of toothpaste from the corner of Jasmine's mouth. She froze beneath my touch.

"I…" She blinked at me. I knew, in that moment, that she had never said it to anyone before either.

We stayed like that for a while. My thumb on the corner of her mouth, her warm, shaky breath filling my uninjured palm.

"It's okay," I told her. Because it was. I wasn't loving her to be loved in return. I was loving her because it seemed like something madly inevitable, but also like the greatest choice I could ever make.

I pressed my lips against hers, innocently at first. Then I felt her tongue gently prodding at mine, and what was once innocent suddenly became fraught with desire. It was ludicrous, really, how much I longed for her even though she was right in front of me. How much I wanted to touch her, even though she was already in my arms.

We moved over to the bed. *Jasmine's* bed. I liked that she automatically went to the left side, like the right was mine just because I'd slept there twice before. I liked that she seemed to take stock of these little details. She knew that I liked to sleep with two pillows, so she already had two there waiting for me. She knew that I got thirsty in the mornings, so there was already a blue water bottle beside the bed. She knew that I hadn't changed the gauze around my hand in a few days, so she had a first aid kit on her desk, ready to tend to me in the morning.

And in that way, I knew that she loved me, even if she wasn't quite ready to say it. I knew that she loved me because of the way she knew me.

"There's fireworks," she said suddenly. "Outside my window. Look."

"Oh, look at that," I whispered.

"Yeah, I'm not sure why. Maybe there's a game on or something."

I leaned my body back into hers. The fireworks danced in the little rectangle of her window—two separate balls of red and green, exploding and then melding together. Like festive stardust.

"That's you…" she told me. Her breath was a warm rush in my ear. "The pink… I'm the green."

"I thought the pink was red. I was going to say that's *me*."

"You're not red. You're more like…"

"Like what?" I asked her. *What colour am I in your mind?*

I felt her shrug against me. "Like a soft orange."

"Like a sunset," I muttered. I was fully leaning against her now, the back of my head resting in the crook of her shoulder.

"With blue, as well…" she said. "Like a sunset over a body of water."

Her words touched me everywhere.

"You *are* green," I told her. "Earthy. Grounded."

She snaked a hand around my body. For a while, that was how we stayed: holding each other, silent as the pink and green fireworks scattered across the sky.

"Jasmine," I whispered.

"Yes, Jules?"

"I…I really want to kiss you again."

"Kiss me, then."

I turned around. My heart was entwined in hers. Orange and green.

I kissed her. Soon my body was draped over hers, and my thigh was wedged between her legs, and there were so many new things happening that my brain ceased to function. I liked that she dragged her fingers over my scalp when she kissed me. I liked that she tasted like mint toothpaste and her hair smelled like vanilla flowers. I liked that she clearly had no idea what she was doing, but she seemed to have more of an idea than me. I liked that she took the lead. I liked that she grabbed my good hand and showed me where to place it on her body. I liked that she closed her eyes and showed me how to touch her.

Beneath her singlet.

Beneath her shorts.

Beneath her underwear.

Soft and delicate, and fast and slow.

I liked the noises she made. I liked the way her skin seemed to glow against the soft light of her lamp. It didn't go too far—at least, not the ways Gavin had described to me in lewd detail at his parties. But it went far enough that I now felt like a small piece of my soul belonged to her, and would belong to her, forever.

Afterwards, when we were both dazed and sweaty, she was tracing gentle patterns over my skin. I felt her whisper on the back of my neck. "Did you mean to say that?" she asked.

I knew exactly what she was asking. "Yes," I said.

I felt her lips curving into a smile. "Are you sure?"

"Yes."

I liked that she needed to clarify the obvious.

"You're sure?"

"I love you, Jasmine Morè."

I turned over and kissed her again, and I liked the startled giggle that bubbled up from her chest. I liked the fact that she was both serious and playful. An adult and yet a young girl. Confident, yet shy enough that she always seemed disarmed by my movements.

I liked that, for a brief, shining moment, I actually felt like I could do this. I could be this guy. I could be *Rosemary Boy*—or at least, find a way to tolerate it. Because people like her existed. People who actually saw me for who I was and not just who they decided I was. That was a real struggle of mine in my new world: everyone had their own versions of me inside their heads. And I could *feel* it, the moment I met somebody, the moment I said something that didn't quite align with how I truly felt. How did anyone endure that? How are you ever meant to know yourself when every interaction spawns a new version of you in someone's mind? How do you keep track of all these versions? How do you forget them? Enough people start to see you as somebody else, and you start believing them.

The more I thought about it, the more I wondered if maybe that's what love is—when the way you *imagine* someone sees you matches the way you see yourself.

The next morning was a delicate dance. I needed to get back to Brett's place early enough that he wouldn't know I'd been gone, and then I needed to somehow rid myself of the natural glow that seeing Jasmine emanated from my skin.

The funny thing was that Brett *also* seemed to have this glow. We met each other in the kitchen that morning, and there was this strange, intangible buzz in the air.

We stared at each other, almost like we were sizing each other up. "Good morning," he said.

"Morning," I replied.

We packed our bags. We were only staying in Perth for one night, so there wasn't much to bring. We also didn't want to arouse further suspicion by bringing anything more than carry-on luggage between us. Ms Morè and Jasmine had also packed light, so the four of us piled into Brett's Honda Civic at about 8 a.m. that morning. I wore dark sunglasses and a beanie that I tucked all my hair into, and Jasmine kept laughing at the fact that I looked bald. I also wore a baggy hoodie that was slightly too warm, even for winter temperatures, but we didn't want to take any chances with me getting recognised at the airport.

So far, we'd made it safely through the security check. I'd been nervous to take off my beanie, but I'd kept my head down and put it back on the moment my bag had been cleared. I'd also worried, for a moment, that my nerves were going to tip off one of the airport security officers, and they would pull me aside for a secondary exam. They'd take one look at my anxious fidgeting and assume I was up to something illegal, when really, I was just trying to make it through the airport so I could visit my kidnapper in prison without attracting attention. And that was… totally legal now that I was 18, albeit a little bit strange.

We sat in the back of a café and waited for our gate to open.

I hoped that anyone who saw me hunched over the table would assume I had flight anxiety. I hoped they wouldn't assume I was worried about my prison visit being cancelled if any of them were to recognise me and alert the media. What if there was a random journalist on board who recognised me? What if everything went smoothly, but someone from the prison tipped off a news channel to make some money? I'd made the booking 24 hours ago, so their staff would know that I was visiting Angela. What if we turned up at Melaleuca Women's Prison tomorrow and there was a team of reporters who had been staking out overnight? What if all of this was for nothing?

Once our gate opened, we waited until the final boarding call so we wouldn't have to wait in line. I watched everyone queuing up to have their boarding passes scanned, and I tried to profile them and what their careers might be. This proved futile, since everything I had come to know about the world made no sense. People weren't the carefully constructed caricatures I'd seen on TV. Real people were harder to judge, and everyone with an iPhone was an amateur journalist these days.

We made it all the way to the desk without incident, and then I handed over my boarding pass with my full name printed on it. The woman behind the counter took my pass and scanned it, and I held my breath.

"Welcome, Mr Edwards-Rose—" she said, and her eyes widened. She stumbled slightly over her next words. "Rosemary… Boarding from the rear stairs."

"Thank you," I muttered, and then continued on as if everything was normal. As if she hadn't just scanned the boarding pass of one of the most famous eighteen-year-olds in

Australia. My ticket read Julian Edwards-Rosemary, but it may as well have read *Rosemary Boy.*

"Just keep walking," Brett muttered to me as we headed down the boarding ramp.

Once we got on the plane, the young girl checking the passes was too distracted by the lady next to her to look at me or my ticket properly. "Seat 27A," she told me, still chuckling.

I pulled my beanie down further. "Thanks."

We settled into our seats—me next to the window, so I was less conspicuous, Jasmine in the middle and Ms Morè in the aisle seat. Brett was sitting in the middle directly in front of us. That meant that I could still see him, even if he couldn't see me.

It also meant that, as the plane was preparing to take off, I was able to see exactly who he was texting.

Tarini
Today 9:50 am

I love you.

<h1 style="text-align:center">Chapter 26</h1>

Brett and Ms Morè were in love. Brett and *Jasmine's mother* were in love. God, why did I have to look through the cracks of those airplane seats? Why did I have to be so nosy? Why did I have to recognise the way it made perfect sense—the way that Brett's airy, almost delirious behaviour had so closely mirrored my own over the last few days?

I knew what it looked like to be in love with a Morè. It looked like being the luckiest man in the universe.

But I also knew that this was going to kill Jasmine. The secrecy of it. The fact that it was Brett, and she was already wary of him. The fact that she already had tensions with her mother, and this bombshell was only going to broaden the rift between them. If Jasmine didn't feel like a priority before, then she *certainly* wasn't going to feel like one after this.

The plane took off and landed without incident—well, if you discounted the big Brett/Ms Morè 'scandal'. Thankfully, there were no media waiting for me in the terminal at Perth Airport. But I still couldn't stop worrying about them getting a tip-off and being outside the prison at our scheduled visiting time the next morning. If they were, our visit would be cancelled, and all of this would have been a waste. A long, expensive, anxiety-inducing waste.

I pulled my beanie down again and we safely made it through the terminal and into the hire car that Brett had arranged for us, not wanting to risk the potential nosiness of a taxi or Uber driver. I'd still never taken either, but apparently prying questions were not uncommon during those rides. I looked out the window, trying to clear my head, but all I could imagine was Brett and Ms Morè sucking each other's faces.

I also couldn't stop thinking about that woman who'd scanned my boarding pass, and whether she'd told anyone. She'd known that I was flying to Perth, but she didn't know *why*. There were a million different reasons that I could have been returning to Western Australia. I could have been homesick and wanted a holiday. I could have been travelling to Fremantle to see my old neighbours (the ones that *hadn't* turned Angela over to the police). There was absolutely no reason for anyone to assume that I was going to Melaleuca Women's Prison. No reason at all.

When we finally got to our motel, it was sometime around 3 p.m. It had been a five-and-a-half-hour flight, but WA is two hours behind Queensland, so we still had plenty of daylight left. I'm sure everyone would have loved to explore the city, but we all knew it was far too risky. If I was famous in Queensland, I was probably even more famous here. I'd spent the last seventeen years of my life just half an hour from this ramshackle motel in Perth. The chances of me running into one of the few people I knew were extremely high—or at least, somebody who knew *of me*.

Brett had gone out to buy us groceries for that night and the next morning. The first available visiting hours were between 10 a.m. and 11 a.m. After that, we were catching a flight back to Brisbane just after lunch to get us home before David's return later that night.

Our motel for the night was well away from the city centre. We wanted to stay somewhere as secluded as possible, and I was pretty sure we were the only people staying there. It was a yellow, stone building with an orange/red roof, and there was a sign claiming it had been established in 1897. Our room had two bedrooms, each with two single beds. Brett and I would be staying in one room, and Ms Morè and Jasmine in the other. This was the arrangement that made the most sense *in theory*, but after learning about Brett and Ms Morè, the whole thing felt bizarrely ironic.

"My goodness. Julian! What happened to you?"

"I'm fine," I told Ms Morè. I'd been fidgeting with my bandage. "Just…uh, cut myself."

We'd just sat down in the living room to wait for Brett, and her cool fingers coiled around my wrist. "How'd you cut yourself? This looks like a deep wound—"

"He said he's fine, Mum."

"He's not fine. He's bleeding. Who…?" Ms Morè looked at Jasmine. "Did you do this?"

"Yes, and I did a good job, before he decided to re-open them."

I grimaced. I must have done it lifting my bag into the overhead locker on the plane. I was in such a hurry to get to my seat, to get out of everyone's view.

"They need to be restitched," Ms Morè said. "How did it happen?"

"I fell," I said, snatching my hand back.

Jesus Christ. If there were points for the most suspicious answers… I was hitting each question out of the park with a baseball bat.

Jasmine seemed to share that sentiment, if the glare on her face was anything to go by.

"Okay," Ms Morè said. She glanced between the two of us, and I could almost hear her mind whirring. I wondered if she suspected that there was more to our friendship—if she'd witnessed me sneaking out of their house at 5 a.m. this morning. "Well…" she said slowly, "would it be okay if I took a look at it?"

"Okay," I said, just as Jasmine said, "*No.*"

"Jules," Ms Morè tried again. "May I please take a look at your stitches?"

"Okay," I repeated, and Jasmine just rolled her eyes. She turned on her heel, and I watched her disappear into her and Ms Morè's room. It should have been *our* room.

Ms Morè ducked out to reception to get a first aid kit. When she returned, the two of us sat on the floor beside the coffee table.

I held out my hand. Ms Morè had the same gentle touch as Jasmine. She had the same long fingers—piano fingers—and the same bare fingernails. As she fixed me, I had this overwhelming ache in my chest. I imagined a mature-aged Jasmine—a Jasmine whose softness was embraced instead of challenged. A Jasmine who didn't feel at war with the world.

"I'm sorry about Jasmine," she said, as if reading my mind.

"It's okay…"

"I don't know what's gotten into her. I mean, she's always been headstrong, but it's different lately. It's like she's a beehive that someone's come along and kicked."

I just shrugged—as much as I could, given the fact one of my hands was being prodded at with a needle.

"How are you feeling?" Ms Morè asked me, changing the

subject. "Are you excited to see Angela?"

"I'm a little scared," I admitted.

"Well, I think that's a perfectly normal way to feel."

"I'm not scared of Angela," I said. It seemed important to clarify that.

"Why are you scared?"

I cleared my throat. I glanced toward Jasmine and Ms Morè's room, making sure the door was closed. I don't know why I was so nervous to talk about this stuff around her.

When I spoke, my voice was barely above a whisper. "I'm scared that…I'm going to look at her, and it's going to feel exactly the same. And that's wrong." I wanted to stop talking, because I felt like maybe I was going to cry. "I love Angela, but she isn't really my mum."

Ms Morè hummed. It was in time with a particularly deep stitch, almost like she was trying to soothe the pain.

"And Pam isn't my mum either, because she never was."

"What defines a mother, Jules? Blood?"

I swallowed the lump in my throat. "I don't know. I guess… the person who takes care of you. Who feels like home."

"Does Angela feel like home?"

"The papers all say she's evil."

"But how does she feel to you?"

Her words tripped something in me. "Like home."

Ms Morè hummed again. But she wasn't stitching into my hand this time. It felt like maybe she was just holding it. "Then the papers can say what they want, but they can't tell you that the place where your heart lived for seventeen years is not your home. It may have been wrong, but the heart does not operate on logic, Jules. You can't blame your heart for not knowing better."

Ms Morè ran her thumb over my knuckles. When she spoke next, it was in a whisper, like she also had a lump in her throat. "This world is big, and beautiful, and terrible and cruel, but you mustn't let it get to you. You mustn't let it tell you how to feel."

On our way to Melaleuca Women's Prison, I felt like one of those guilty people in movies who are worried they're being tailed by police—only, instead of police cars, I was looking for news vans and inconspicuous sedans. It was completely absurd, but these days the media chasing scared me even more than the thought of police.

When we finally got to the prison, there were no cameras, and I nearly broke down in tears from the sheer relief of it all. But in that moment, my media anxiety gave way to the crushing anxiety of this situation: the fact that I was going to be entering a prison. The fact I was going to be seeing my mum after nearly half a year apart.

I couldn't tell if the prison officials recognised me, mainly because they had to have the best poker faces of any profession. I imagine you need a natural level of stoicism when it's your job to look after potentially dangerous people.

The security screening for social visitors was extensive. We had our hire car searched in the prison car park, and then we were individually scanned by handheld metal detectors and drug detection dogs. We were also frisked by officers of the same sex, and I had to remove my beanie and hoodie so they could be inspected by the Superintendent. Jasmine and Ms Morè's bags were also searched, even though they weren't going beyond the screening point. Like Brett, they would have to wait outside, given the fact that I was the only person who had applied and been approved six weeks ago.

A part of me was disappointed that Jasmine wouldn't be meeting Angela, but the visit was going to be strange enough given all the extra precautions I'd had to agree to as part of my visitor approval. Since I was technically a victim of Angela's crime, our entire conversation was going to be recorded, and there would be a prison officer standing nearby.

I hoped all of this wouldn't be too overwhelming for Angela. She knew I was coming, but I still hadn't spoken to her in almost six months. I hadn't physically seen her since January. Someone who had been my entire world. Someone who I'd never spent a full day without.

It's funny, though: when I finally did see her, and when we finally did speak, it was like no time had passed at all. Maybe because she had never left my mind—and in that way, we'd still been together.

She looked smaller, though. I knew that. She had lost the soft belly that had once protruded beneath her sundresses. She looked gaunter around the face, and her cheekbones were missing their usual rosy blush. Her sadness had seeped into the skin beneath her eyelids, casting them a dark shade of brown. There were strands of grey in her hair, and I realised just how religiously she must have been colouring her hair on the outside, because I'd never noticed them before.

My whole life, I'd been afraid of Angela getting old, of her ending up in a place like Beacon Heights. Now, a new fear enveloped my body: the fear of her getting old behind bars.

Of her getting old without me.

I tried to shrug off those thoughts. I tried to temper those fears with more positive things, like the fact that she was alive. The fact that I was able to visit her. The fact that she was wearing blue, just like the last time I'd seen her in Fremantle. I focused on the Olympic blue of her jacket, and not the words 'CORRECTIONAL CENTRE ISSUE' that I knew were plastered on the back.

I looked behind me, and there was a stern-faced prison officer, arms folded across his chest.

Angela broke down even before she got to our table. We were allowed to hug once at the beginning and end of each visit. *A brief embrace. No holding on.* I tried to hold on, but she wouldn't let me.

"We don't want to get in trouble," she whispered in my ear, but I didn't care. She smelled the same, but also different—like honey and a new, foreign laundry detergent. Like Mum, but also faintly of grease.

"Sorry," she said. "I've been working in the kitchens. I probably smell like a deep fryer."

I imagined her being a mother in here. I imagined her feeding people. I imagined her sweeping around these dingy kitchens and making sure people were looked after.

The Double Life of Donna Jones.

We sat down across from each other. I stared at her, and I tried to imagine a younger, more desperate woman. The articles had said she had orange hair when she'd worked as a nurse. I'd only ever known her with messy brown hair, like mine. I couldn't help but see myself in her. We looked more alike than Pam and

I did. We held ourselves the same. That must be one of the most beautiful parts of love—the way it reflects two people back to each other.

Mum reached across the table. I held her slender, freckled hand in mine. I had to use my left hand, since my right one was injured.

"What happened?" she asked me.

"Long story." I hid it beneath the table, and I took a deep breath, trying not to cry. "God, I've missed you."

Her face crumpled. She looked so vulnerable, so terrified. It wasn't hard to envision her eighteen years ago, taking me from that nursery. "You don't hate me?" she asked.

I stared at a smudge on the metal table. "I should," I whispered. I resisted the urge to elaborate, to look for the right answer. I just spoke from my heart. "…But I don't."

It's hard to hate someone you love.

She closed her eyes, like that information was deeply relieving. "How is it?" she asked me, opening them again. "How is life with your mum and your family?"

I gritted my teeth together. God, this was harder than I thought. A part of me wished I did have Jasmine beside me, just to encourage me to keep it together. The other part was glad that I could just break down in private.

"Oh, Jules…" Mum said.

"It's o-okay," I told her, hiccupping. "It's okay."

"Is it?"

I shook my head. Tears were blurring my vision, and her hand was like a lifeline tethering me to the moment. "It *will* be okay."

"They don't know you're here, do they?"

"Pam does," I whispered. She'd actually sent me a text earlier that morning, wishing me luck. Telling me that she loved me. I could hardly believe that she'd been so supportive, but a part of me wondered whether she was doing it out of fear. If she didn't keep me happy, then maybe I'd talk to the media. Maybe I'd tell them about David.

"Pam is a good woman," Mum told me, and it was so jarring hearing those words coming out of her mouth that my brain momentarily short-circuited.

"What?"

"She loves you, very much."

I stared at her. I could hardly believe we were having this conversation. "How do you know that?" I asked her.

"Because she's your mother."

"I don't know her."

"But she's still your mother."

You're my mother, I thought, even though it was wrong. I just sat there, tears in my eyes, my legs trembling. *You're my mother.*

"I was never meant to be your mother, Jules." Nothing she was saying made sense, but she seemed insistent on saying all of it, almost like this was going to be our last conversation. She was glancing around us, like she was waiting for someone to bust in and break us up. How many minutes had passed? Were we running out of time? It felt like we had only been sitting there for thirty seconds. "I was never meant to be your mother, but I'm glad that I was. I just hate how many people I hurt in the process, especially your mum. Most of all, I hate how complicated I've made things for you… But I just loved you too much to turn back."

You saved me, I wanted to tell her. *I only hurt now that you're gone.*

"I've turned your life into a spectacle, when I only ever wanted you to know peace. I only ever wanted to protect you from the world, and now I've infected you with it like a disease."

I wanted to go back. I wanted so desperately to go back. I wanted to crawl inside the cavern of our memories and stay there forever. I wanted her to take off that prison uniform and put on one of her sundresses. I wanted to take her outside to meet Jasmine. I wanted our old life, with no social media, and no cameras, and no big, crowded spaces. But if we were still living our old life, then Jasmine wouldn't be in it. There would be no Brett, no Pam, no Reg, no Ms Morè.

"It's not all bad," I told her, and I spent the next forty minutes filling her in on as much of my new life as I could. All the good things, from Jasmine, to Beacon Heights Nursing Home, to my unexpected friendship with Chelsea, to Tanner and James and how nice it felt to be someone's big brother.

"They're lucky to have you," Mum told me. "You were everything I ever wanted, Jules. You still are."

Her words brought fresh tears to my eyes. "How…?" I asked her. That's all I could manage. Just that one word, and a mountain of unspoken questions. *How do I live without you? How do I ever love someone the way I loved you?*

"One day at a time, honey. One day at a time. That's all you ever have in this life. That's all that's ever expected of you."

I rubbed my eyes with the back of my bandage. I was still holding Mum's hand. "The articles…the things they say about you…"

"I know, sweetheart, I know. But just remember, Jules: there is always more to the story."

I looked at her. What did she mean by that?

A speaker droned overhead: *visiting hours will end in five minutes*. How had it been that long already? How had it already been an hour and yet I hadn't said half of the things I wanted to say?

Mum squeezed my hand. "What is it, honey?"

I licked my dry lips, chapped from the sun. I was fraught with curiosity and crippled by fear. My heart couldn't move.

"Say it, baby."

"Do you regret it?" I asked her. "Taking me. Do you regret it?"

She looked deeply affected by the question. Her gaze softened, and her hand twitched in mine.

"I get it, if you do." I glanced around the room, at the metal tables lined either side of us. The myriad of broken pieces. This place was Mum's broken cake dish. There was no other way I could think to explain it.

"Jules…"

"I get it. You lost your whole life because of me."

"No, Jules. You don't get it." She grabbed my other hand, and she squeezed them both. Her grip was icy but warm, gentle but crushing.

Other prisoners were standing up around us. It was time to go, but I wasn't ready to leave.

We embraced: *one hug permitted at the beginning and end of each visit*. You're not meant to hold on, but I did.

"You gave me my whole life," she whispered into my hair. "You did."

Chapter 27

There is always more to the story.

Mum's words replayed in my head as I walked out of the prison. As I left that dark, cramped space and re-entered the brightness of the outside world.

They replayed in my head as I got into Brett's car, and no one said a word to me—not a single one. They replayed as we walked through the airport terminal, and I was so dazed that for a moment I forgot who I was. I forgot to put my beanie back on after going through security, and Jasmine had to gently place it on my head. She swept my hair beneath the edges with soft, careful fingers, and our eyes locked, just for a moment.

"Come with me," she said quietly.

Brett and Ms Morè allowed us to disappear into a café together. They stayed at a row of tables that were still in sight. Jasmine and I sat at a dark booth in the very back, and she ordered us two chocolate milkshakes. She drank hers immediately, but mine just sat there, the moisture from the cup dripping onto the table. I reached for a serviette and began lapping it up.

After a while, I started tearing up pieces of the serviette. I don't know why, and I was aware of how it made me look, but I didn't stop. It was giving me something to do.

I laid the pieces out on the table, lining them up nicely. Jasmine just stared at them.

"Jules," she said.

The serviette was almost gone now, almost completely shredded into little snowflakes. I started tearing another one.

"Jules."

They were all over the table. A silent snowstorm. I started placing some on my knee.

"Jules!" Jasmine said. She grabbed my arm. When I looked at her, she was crying. I'd never seen her cry before. And I would have felt bad for her, if I was in a different state. I would have felt heartbroken that I had made her feel that way.

"This isn't helping," she said, but she was wrong. It was helping, a little bit.

"You look crazy," she said next, and *that*—that wasn't helping.

"I'm sorry," she said, and she was. Immediately sorry, and immediately forgiven.

A few minutes passed. The serviette pieces were everywhere now. All over me. All over Jasmine. We were both crying for a while, and then it was just me, and then it was just her, and then it was no one.

She hung her head, wiping her nose. "I just don't know how to make it better," she muttered.

"You've done more than enough," I said. My voice was light, almost happy-sounding. The wave had passed, and the sadness had withdrawn into its dark little corner. It was almost immediate, sometimes. The relief. Like emerging from the ocean after being tossed around.

Jasmine looked up at me. She was beautiful when she did that—when she looked up, when she looked anywhere. She held my hand and brought it to her face.

"Jules," she breathed.

"I know," I said.

She turned her cheek into my palm. I wondered if Brett and Ms Morè were watching us, but in that moment, I don't think either of us cared.

I started stroking her hair. "I'm always worried I'm gonna scare you off."

"What, are you going to chase me or something?"

She was joking, but I didn't want to joke anymore. Not right now. "No."

"Shave a mullet? Wax your eyebrows off?"

"I'm trying to be serious, Jas."

Her smile faded. My least favourite sight.

"You're just, you're the best person I've ever met," I said.

"So are you—"

"Yeah, but it's different. You're young."

"We're the same age—"

"You're going to meet someone. A lot of someones. And they're all going to be the best person you've ever met."

It wouldn't be that way for me. I just knew it. After her, there would be nobody.

"I like *you*, Jules. You Muppet."

"Yeah, for now."

"For always." She leaned forward and she kissed me. Sometimes I thought that was all it would take, one kiss. One kiss and I'd never feel that way ever again. They say no one else can fix you, but how nice would it be if they could?

Brett and Ms Morè were definitely watching us, and they definitely knew that we were in love, and we definitely didn't care. I'll always remember that moment. It was one of the first moments I can remember *choosing* something in my new life, regardless of what anyone else thought.

I could hardly believe that, in less than eight hours, I was going to be so angry at Jasmine that I couldn't imagine ever talking to her again.

There is always more to the story.

Pam's house was eerily quiet.

Pam is a good woman.

There were no signs of life. David was due to return any minute, and the house was as spotless as those Clarendon display homes I was always seeing in magazines.

She loves you, very much.

The kids must have been staying with David's mother. They'd been doing that more and more, and I wondered if she knew what went on between Pam and her son. If she knew what kind of man she'd raised.

Brett and Ms Morè had seemed reluctant to drop me off. A strong part of me suspected that they knew what was going on, just like I suspected the two of them had been in love for a very long time. Jasmine just hugged me goodbye, unconscious of both secrets. I stared at her as I pulled back, and I tried to commit the peaceful look on her face to memory. I knew it couldn't last. Nothing ever does.

Pam slowly emerged from the bathroom. She descended the staircase and locked eyes with me, and her entire body seemed to soften.

"Jules…" she said.

We both hovered for a moment, like we were unsure how to proceed. Then she broke the tension and rushed forward to hug me.

"Are you okay?" she asked me.

I buried my face in her shoulder. She smelled like the Black Opium perfume I'd seen in the bathroom cabinet, which she always seemed to wear when David was returning home from a trip. It was a heady, adrenaline-rich scent that smelled like black coffee. She also smelled like bath salts and too many glasses of red wine—a rivalry of scents that didn't make sense.

"Yes," I whispered. "Are you?"

She nodded. She was wearing a black silk robe that was tied at her waist. "How was…?" she started to say, but then the front door was being unlocked.

David entered wearing his usual button-up shirt and dress pants. It was almost 9 p.m., and I imagined he'd be agitated after a late flight. He stowed his leather suitcase and matching carry bag by the corner of the door, and I held my breath, unsure of how to greet him.

"Welcome home, honey," Pam said, and I was relieved to have someone break the tension. "How was your trip?"

David sighed. He still hadn't looked at either of us. He was leafing through a handful of mail he must have collected on the way in, and I just hoped it was a stack of junk mail and not bills. "Where are the kids?" he asked.

"They're staying at your mother's," Pam said. "I thought you might want to come home to a quiet house."

David grunted. I wondered whether I should just sneak off to my room, but then he finally glanced up at me. Being the target of his gaze was not unlike staring down the barrel of a gun. Or, at least, how I imagined that would feel.

"How are you both?" he asked.

I swallowed. "G-good. I'm good."

"That's good. Still on school holidays, yeah? How's the old folks' home?"

"Good," I said. "Really good." I couldn't think of another word.

David nodded, setting down the stack of mail. He must have had his keys in his hand, too, because something landed on the table with a harsh *clang.* Pam and I jumped.

David just yawned, stretching out his shoulders. "The trip was good," he said. "Productive. The conferences were well-run. A lot of people told me they took a lot from my speech."

"That's wonderful," Pam muttered, at the same time I said, "That's great."

"Melbourne's too cold, though. Far too cold. Too many people. I missed home." He finally set his gaze on Pam. "I missed you."

I watched in a strange daze as he moved forward and scooped Pam off the last step of the staircase. He growled lightly. He kissed her on the mouth. He tucked his face into her neck and breathed her in like she was oxygen.

The sight settled uncomfortably in my stomach.

"I couldn't wait to get you in my arms again," he told her.

"I missed you, too, sweetheart."

I cleared my throat as they kissed once more, and then I excused myself upstairs. I could hear them giggling on the staircase even as I went into my room, and I didn't know how to feel about it. Was I wrong about David? Was he not really as bad as he seemed? Is this just what a marriage looked like?

At the very least, I understood what was appealing about him. He was strong. He was attractive. He was a provider. He was what all those *manosphere* bloggers I'd seen floating around the internet called a *high-value man*. Pam loved him. That much was obvious. And she was no more in control of loving him than I was of loving Angela.

I sat on my bed. I remembered Jack's journal, and the way that he'd described Pam and David's relationship. He'd described it that way for a reason. Was a man really high value if he terrified his partner? If he had to break other people to gain his power?

He wanted her broken. And now she is.

That can't be a high-value man. A high-value man doesn't take more than he gives.

I opened Jack's journal again. I reread the poems about David and Pam.

All That You Will Ever Be

There is a reason
women were not made to be homes.
Because human flesh
does not have the structural integrity
of a hundred-year-old cathedral,
the walls of which can withstand
the cries and sins of millions.
There is a reason
she was not made to be your home.
Nor I, nor her, nor him.
What you are searching for

is not love, but a steel warehouse
strong enough to wither
all that you have been,
and all that you will ever be.

My mind was racing, and I tried to replace the image of David nuzzling Pam on the staircase with the image of him smashing that plate. I imagined a frightened Tanner in her Moshi Monsters pyjamas that night, and James in my bed with his hands over his ears.

Just as I was beginning to read a new poem, a familiar set of words stood out on the adjacent page.

A name.

It was short, but it still dug into my chest and carved out my heart.

It was vague, but it still left claw marks.

The Rose

Jasmine Morè.
The fire in her heart
emboldens the rose,
so delicately perched.

Chapter 28

I stared down at my hands. One was bandaged, one was smooth. Inside, everything ached. Someone signed in at the reception desk, but I didn't recall who it was. The telephone blared, and I picked it up, but I don't remember what I said beyond, *"Hello, Beacon Heights Nursing Home, Julian speaking…"*

All I could think about was Jack's poem.

All I could think about was Jack and Jasmine.

When she finally came into work, she looked like she'd been crying. "So," she said, setting down her bag. "Turns out Mum and Coach Finlay are having sex, or they're in love, or something equally repulsive."

I stared at her, at the rose in her hair. *So delicately perched.*

"Apparently, it's been going on a while. The craziest thing is I think what happened to Jack is what finally brought them together. Like they realised life was too short or something." She rubbed her eyes, and I allowed my face to show my emotions, just for a moment. She'd said his name. And for a moment, I stared at her like I wanted to, like she'd just ripped all the guts from my stomach. "It's just…it's the fact that she lied, you know? And she tried to say she didn't lie. She tried that whole *lying by omission* crap, but if it doesn't work for me, then it's not going to work for her. And it's not even the lying." Jasmine started to cry again, and I stared at my desk. "She just…she's never home. She's always working, and when she's not working, she's *working*. And I guess, when she's not working, she's screwing Coach Finlay."

For the first time, I resented how I wanted to comfort her. I resented how I kept putting her happiness before my own.

"Like, why did we even have separate rooms at the motel? You should have been in my room. They should have…" She grimaced. "Ew, okay, no, that would have been a bad idea. My mum thought it was safe to tell me since she now knows that we're together, after she saw us at the airport… And I see her logic, but it's so *wrong*. For a start, Brett is like five years older than her. Brett's into sports, and my mum was a university lecturer back home. There's no way they're compatible." She finally looked at me, and I glanced back at my computer screen. "I mean, they're not like us," she said. "We're at least the same age. We work at the same place. I'm smart… You're smart. We make sense."

"Do we?" I asked her. "Make sense?"

She frowned at me. "What are you talking about? And why don't you seem surprised by any of this?"

The fire in her heart/emboldens the rose/so delicately perched

"Nothing," I said, aimlessly scrolling through a Word document. I started clicking my mouse just to punctuate the silence.

"You're being really weird, Jules."

"Yeah, well, maybe that's because you're crying to me because your mum is dating a really good guy, and my mum's in prison. And my other mother is dating a really crap guy, one who hits her."

Jasmine was silent for a long time. I could almost hear her

mind whirring. "What?" she finally whispered.

I shoved my mouse away from me. I didn't want to talk about this. *Fuck*, I didn't want to… I swivelled around in my chair, and I grabbed Jack's journal from my school bag. We weren't back at school yet, but I still used it to carry all my things. Besides, it had the perfect compartment for the journal right at the back, almost like Jack had bought it for his own school bag.

I opened the journal to Jasmine's poem. By that point, I knew exactly where it was without even searching for it. I knew the exact heft of pages either side—60 per cent left, 40 per cent right. It seemed to fall open naturally and without any calculation on my part. Just like my heart, the spine had been trained to remember.

I slid it on the desk in front of her. It knocked into the sign-in sheet, and the pen rolled off the clipboard and onto the floor with a dull thud. Bill was sitting on a chair next to the phone, mindlessly reviewing his patient files. He didn't even flinch.

Jasmine's eyes widened. She read the words, and then she seemed to reread them.

"Who's…?"

"Jack's."

Her lips pressed into a thin line. "Where did you get this?"

"Does it matter?"

Jasmine's gaze kept running over the poem, and I had an urge to close the book. I hated to think I was fuelling whatever had been between them. It was pathetic, and irrational, but I felt like I was losing her more and more with each passing second, like she was going to dump me for a ghost. I couldn't write like that. I couldn't take the rose in her hair and turn it into something whimsical.

"I know what this looks like," she said finally.

"Well, maybe you could tell me," I said. "Because I don't really know. All I know is that, in the car park that afternoon, you told me you'd never gone near him. You told me he was a bad person."

"I never said that. I said that he wasn't always nice to people."

"Okay, but you did say that you'd never gone near him."

Jasmine grimaced at the poem, and I could see it happening in real time. I could see her walls going up. She couldn't even look at me.

"That wasn't true, was it?" I huffed out a laugh. "Of course it wasn't. Look at you."

"We just kissed, Jules. Once. Around Easter... Jack and Chelsea were on a break."

The image of the two of them bled through my brain.

"You said you didn't like him," I whispered.

"I didn't say that. But no, I didn't like him *that way*—"

"You kiss me. You don't like me either?"

"You don't have to like someone to kiss him. But that doesn't mean I don't like *you*. Jesus, Jules...You're being ridiculous."

"How?"

"You're acting this way over a *kiss*. You're acting like a child."

I tried not to flinch. I knew that she was just being this way because she was mad about Brett and Ms Morè, but still, hearing her talk like that hurt me.

"That's not even the point," I said. "You lied to me. After you told me never to lie to you. *You* lied to *me*."

"I didn't. I just..."

"Lied by omission."

Her eyes flashed. I had her, then. I had her and she hated it.

"This isn't the same thing," she said.

"No, it's worse."

"It's not worse. You're just…jealous, so you're emotional, and—"

"Of course I am! I… I'm in love with you, Jasmine. You are mine."

"So that's what this is about," she said. "You wanted something that wasn't Jack's. It's why you couldn't be with Chelsea, because everyone links her to Jack, and now you think I'm linked to Jack, and you can't stand it. All you care about is what other people think of you. You were always so worried that was going to scare me away… You never cared about what I think."

I stared at my keyboard, my eyes burning. "I couldn't be with Chelsea because I love you," I muttered. "It had nothing to do with anyone."

"That's not true."

"Yes, it is," I said, but I was losing conviction the more we argued. Even now, I was looking around us, wondering if anyone could hear us fighting. There was just Bill, and he still hadn't even glanced in our direction.

Had I pursued Jasmine so relentlessly because she was one of the only people who seemed indifferent to Jack? Had I seen it as a challenge? A challenge to prove to myself that I wasn't my brother? That I was my own person? All love stems from some desire for validation, but had I been ignorant to what kind of validation I was seeking?

I thought back to Jasmine's words after I told her I loved her.

And you...you know what love is?

"I'm not yours," Jasmine told me, closing Jack's journal. "That's not how love works, Jules."

"Why not?"

"Because people can't belong to each other."

"I belong to you," I said. I blinked away my tears. "I belong to you, but you don't belong to me."

Jasmine just sighed.

"What, does that make you angry?" I asked her.

"Yes, it does. I don't want anyone to belong to me. Not even you. I don't want to be responsible for somebody that way."

Her words were cigarette burns in my chest. "Well, I'm sorry."

"Jules."

"No, Jas, it's fine."

"You're just… We don't think the same. I'm not a romantic. I'm a realist. And maybe it doesn't work. Maybe *we* don't work. Maybe I'm too… real for you."

Stupid home-schooled romantic. You don't know how the real world works.

I turned back to my computer. I started mindlessly opening new tabs, trying not to cry, trying not to let her see just how deeply her words had affected me. I thought I'd made progress. I thought I was becoming a real person, and not just some sheltered freak who had never known the true state of the world.

I kept clicking on random webpages. I opened random links. Somehow, I stumbled onto a news forum called The Riverfront Report, and I clicked on their most recent story. They'd reposted it from PNN, a Perth news site.

Fuck.

PERTH NEWS NETWORK

Julian Edwards-Rosemary Visits Kidnapper at Melaleuca Women's Prison, Raising New Questions

JUNE 27, 2017

JULIAN Edwards-Rosemary, who was kidnapped as a newborn and recently reunited with his biological mother and her family, was spotted visiting his kidnapper, Angela Edwards, at Melaleuca Women's Prison in Perth over the school holidays. Edwards, who legally changed her name from Donna Jones just two weeks prior to the kidnapping, is currently awaiting extradition to Queensland for her crime.

The surprising encounter was witnessed by a fellow visitor who recognised Julian and Edwards from news reports. According to the source, who was visiting his uncle at the prison, Julian was engaged in an intense conversation with his kidnapper. What shocked the witness the most was overhearing that Julian had the blessing of his biological mother, Pamela Rosemary, to be there.

"Julian and Angela Edwards were holding hands and crying. It didn't seem like a visit between a victim and his kidnapper—it felt like a reunion between a mother and her son. It was hard to believe, especially after everything that's happened," said the witness.

Pamela Rosemary, who tirelessly campaigned for the return of her missing son in the early years following his kidnapping, has been notably silent for more than a decade. The fact that she apparently supported this meeting between Julian and the woman who stole him from her is raising eyebrows—and questions.

Why would Pamela approve of such a reunion? Did her husband, David Leman, Julian's stepfather, know about it? Many are left wondering if Pamela will finally break her silence and explain.

I'd gone completely silent. My head was spinning. My heart was about to fall out of my chest.

"What?" Jasmine asked me. I could hear the concern in her voice. It was as if we'd momentarily paused our argument, and she was ready to fight whatever had frightened me.

She came around to my side of the desk and read the article.

"No," she said. "*Shit.*"

I'd been so worried about that flight attendant at the airport. I hadn't even stopped to consider that other visitors to the prison might have recognised me. I'd been so blinded by Mum, by the fact that she was actually in front of me and not just a photograph in an article. She wasn't just a memory.

"Okay," Jasmine was saying. "Okay. It's okay…"

"It's not," I said. "They mentioned Pam knowing. They mentioned David. This is going to humiliate him."

Jasmine's eyes flashed. She understood now. She knew the ramifications. "What do we do?" she asked me.

"I have to go home. I have to…I have to talk to Pam. He's probably still at work. Maybe he hasn't seen it yet."

She nodded, already picking up her bag. "I'll drive you."

I'd never been in Jasmine's car. It was a 2007 Honda Jazz. White, like the rose in her hair. Vintage, like her soul.

It was still daylight outside—somewhere between 5 and 6 p.m.—and it had begun to lightly rain. Jasmine's radio didn't work, so she had a stack of pre-loved CDs in the centre console.

She picked one at random—Coldplay—and the old stereo ate it up, grateful to be fed. The music filled the car, warm and crackling. The perfect antidote to the rain. The perfect antidote to the silence.

I stared out the window, at the raindrops streaking horizontally across the glass. We didn't talk the entire way there. We didn't need to. We'd already said too much. The only good thing was that the article hadn't mentioned anything about Jasmine, Brett or Ms Morè.

When she pulled up outside my house, I started to get out.

"Jules?" she said.

"Yeah?"

"I'm sorry."

I turned to look at her. "I'm sorry, too."

She pulled me into her chest. We pressed our foreheads together.

"I should have told you…" she whispered.

"It's okay."

Her hand found mine. Palms flat, fingers intertwined. Regardless of what happened beyond that point, I knew that there was a life between our hands. A life that I could love.

"You're my best friend," she told me.

"I know, and you're mine."

"Go home," I told her. "If you don't hear from me in an hour, call Brett."

"But Jules…"

"Go," I pleaded with her.

She bit her lip, tears falling from her eyes. I wiped them with my bandaged hand and watched as she pulled herself together.

I got out of the car and then watched her drive away. I had to be sure she was completely gone before I could go any further.

The house appeared empty when I walked inside, but I knew Pam was an expert at making herself small, making herself quiet.

"Hello?" I called out.

No answer. I ventured deeper into the house. The sky was a white-washed grey, and it filtered into the darkness of the house, painting the furniture with a strange glow.

"Pam?"

The news article flashed across my mind in vivid monochrome. I imagined it spiralling out of control, pouring onto the radio, onto TV news channels, onto some arsehole's social media page. A dozen different mediums. A dozen different ways to provoke David.

"Pam? Are you home?"

There was nothing but silence. The entire house was still. The kids were still at David's mother's place, and I wondered whether Pam had done that on purpose. If she'd predicted this media shitstorm. If she'd felt it rolling in the air like thunder in the sky.

I continued down the hallway to David and Pam's bedroom. I had never been in there before. I had hardly even been down this part of the house. It seemed to get colder with each step I took, like the space hadn't been lived in for a long time. There was only an empty photo frame on a wall—a frame that I remembered seeing at the wake, and that had once contained a photo of Jack.

I turned on the light in Pam and David's room. It was immaculate, just as I'd expected it to be. The carpet was a perfect light almond colour. The king-sized bed was pristine and expertly made, with a half a dozen different pillows of varying shapes and sizes. There was a white antique dressing table by the window. The wood looked like it had been repainted several times. I went over to it. I'm not sure why. I sat down at the accompanying wooden chair. You could see into the backyard from here. I wondered how many times Pam had sat here throughout the day. There were ring stains on the surface that I knew matched her coffee cups.

I opened the first drawer. Again, I'm not sure why. Maybe I just wanted to know her. Maybe I was tired of all the blank spaces in my mind. I recalled the beginning of a poem from Jack's journal.

Pamela

The more I ask
The more you lie
The more I drift
The more you cry

The drawer was full of makeup. Lipsticks. Fluffy little brushes. The next drawer was full of random miscellaneous items. Gel pens. An old phone. Various stacks of paperwork. The third drawer was a little stiff, just like Jack's drawer had been—the one that contained his journal.

I jerked it open. There was nothing interesting inside it, except for an old jewellery box. I pulled it out and sat it on the table. I wondered if Pam had received it as a child, maybe from her own mother. She wasn't close to any of her relatives—*our* relatives. But maybe she'd decided some things had sentimental value, even despite their origins.

I scooped out some of her jewellery. There was a cream envelope at the bottom of the box that blended with its velvet interior. I opened it carefully, and my heart began to pound. I recognised the handwriting immediately.

Angela's.

April 5th, 2011

Dear Pamela,

You do not know me. I'm writing this letter to you because I can hardly live with myself for what I have done to you, for the pain that I have caused. Twelve years ago, I did what is both the worst and greatest thing I have ever done. I took your son.

Since then, I am sure you've wondered what sort of a monster I am and read several theories. That I'm a desperate woman who longed for a child of her own. That I'm a man who took Nicholas as part of an illegal adoption operation. That it was a random act of opportunity. That I'm a depraved individual who harboured sinister plans for your son. That I was motivated by a personal vendetta against your family.

I am writing this letter to dispel the rumours, and to offer you some semblance of peace. I have attached some photos of Nicholas, alive and healthy. Though I do not call him by that name, I understand that this is the name you chose. I would have honoured this choice had it not been for the threat it would pose to our discovery. I realise that sending this letter also poses a threat to us, but I simply could not live another day crippled by my own inaction, by my failure to make things right—at least in this small way.

I want you to know that I am riddled with guilt every single second. Not a day goes by that I don't see your face and realise what I took from you. Even though I am beyond redemption, I wanted you to know the truth, or at least as much of it as I can safely share with you. I am a woman. This crime was not random, nor was it carried out for any nefarious reasons. I love your son more than I can stand to explain.

When I was 21, I lost my baby, and later, I had ovarian cancer that required a hysterectomy to remove it. None of my eggs were salvageable, and ovarian cancer is very often a death sentence. All I ever wanted was to be a mother, and I saw an opportunity to live out this dream before I died. You were single, and barely 21. You were also having two babies, and that's why I decided to take one.

I'm so deeply, terribly sorry for what I did to you. I know that I am beyond absolution. I never expected to live this long, but I am one of the lucky ones. My cancer went into remission and has not returned (yet, but ovarian cancer has a nasty habit of returning, even after a hysterectomy). I never expected to face the inexorable guilt of my actions twelve years down the line. But the love that I have found with your son has brought new meaning to what was once the rotten remnants of my almost expired life. He is everything to me. I would sooner die than be parted from him, and that day is likely to come sooner for me rather than later. When it does, he will be your son once again, I will make sure of that.

Sincerely,
A mother

Chapter 29

I looked inside the envelope. There were two small, square photographs. Two small, square photographs of me.

If not for the letter, I would have assumed they were photographs of Jack. A smiling, twelve-year-old Jack. Except Jack didn't have bleached blonde hair for the majority of his childhood.

I stared out the window at the darkening backyard. So many words were fighting their way to the surface, but I buried them, just like Jack buried the truth in his journal. I buried the screaming, smothered it with silence. I just sat there. Frozen.

"Jules…"

I didn't acknowledge Pam. Not even as she stood behind me and gently rested a hand on my shoulder. We stayed like that for a long time. We watched the sun dip below the horizon, and the darkness enveloped the house like a cold blanket. It was still raining gently, and I briefly wondered if David would be home soon.

It didn't matter. None of it seemed to matter.

"You read the whole letter?" she asked me.

I nodded.

"Are you angry with me?"

Slowly, I turned to look at the floor beside me. I could see her white sneakers. I wondered where she'd been, if she'd just gotten home. I shook my head.

"Anything you want to ask me, anything you want to know…

You can ask me. I will tell you the truth. One hundred per cent."

I thought about it. All the things I wanted to know. Weirdly, I couldn't think of a single thing. A numbness had spread throughout my body. It had started in my chest but had quickly pervaded my mind. I couldn't think, only stare at random points on the floor. The faded brown mark on the carpet. The gold eyelets of Pam's sneakers.

"I can talk, if you'd prefer."

I nodded.

I heard Pam sitting behind me on the bed. I stared out the window again.

"I was never close with my family. I'm sure David's told you about that. It was true, but…they weren't bad people. They were just bad parents. I was an only child, unplanned, the product of an unhappy union. They couldn't keep themselves happy. How were they meant to teach me? And it *is* a skill, Julian. Being happy is a skill, and it's one of the most important ones you can learn. If you don't learn it early enough, you get set up for a very hard life, no matter who you are.

"When I received the letter, I don't know how, but I knew that you were being taught how to be happy."

I swallowed the lump in my throat. It was completely dark outside now. I could barely see the outline of Tanner and James' green and yellow swing set.

"James was one at the time. He wouldn't stop crying… I'd just found out I was pregnant with Tanner. David had just hit me so hard in my stomach that my lungs burned when I cried. He had just blown the last of our settlement money on his third failed business. I confided in Ray, but he told me that it was just the pressure of the situation. That I had to cut David some slack after everything I'd put him through over the years. The media circus, and the constant scrutiny of our lives and our actions, and how we were using our settlement money. The friction between him and Jack, and the lack of control of not being his biological father. His jealousy of you and how you haunted me. The fact that I refused to take his surname so that I didn't separate myself from the two of you."

"That's why Ray was at our house late that night," I said finally. My voice sounded scratchy, like I hadn't used it all day. "He was making sure you weren't going to talk."

"With the renewed media interest, I think it worried them both. David was even good for a while. But…"

"Some people never change," I whispered.

Pam was quiet for a moment. I wondered if she was only just *truly* realising that now.

"Were you mad at her?" I asked. "Angela? Were you angry at her for what she'd done?"

"*Of course,*" Pam said. "I read that letter, and my entire body burned. I was simultaneously furious and elated. There was a hole inside of me the day that you were taken, but the relief that filled my body at knowing you were alive, at knowing I would one day get you back…" She sighed. "But as quickly as the hole was filled, it became empty again. It became empty once I looked at my life, and I realised that I wouldn't be getting you back for your welfare. I'd be getting you back for mine."

"You trusted her?" I asked. "One letter, and you trusted her?"

"I trusted what I saw in those photographs. I trusted the happiness that I saw in your eyes. I trusted that she was giving you something I wouldn't have been able to, that I feared I couldn't give Jack or James or the baby I was carrying."

I rubbed my eyes. Tears had fallen down my cheeks—tears that I hadn't even been aware of until I'd blinked. I felt so removed from this moment, like I was merely observing the conversation between Pam and myself.

"I was broken, Jules." *He wanted her broken. And now she is.* "I didn't know how I was going to look after the two children I already had, much less a pregnancy and the media frenzy of your return. I swear, if I wasn't pregnant, Jules, I would have…"

Other people might have assumed she was going to say, *I would have acted differently.* But I knew what she was really saying. *I would have ended it all.*

"I felt like that terrified twenty-one-year-old all over again, alone and not knowing the right move. The world had already turned on me because David had made me retreat from the media. He'd made me stop looking for you, to accept the fact that you were gone, even though I never truly did. Not truly."

"What made you keep quiet?" I asked her. I almost turned around to look at her, but something kept me frozen.

"I thought about when I first found out that I was pregnant with the two of you. Your father, Wade, had passed away. We'd had a small love affair, nothing to stop time, but it still ripped me apart when I lost him. My parents didn't approve. I was alone. I had no money."

Nausea rolled through my stomach. *Wade.* Pam had never mentioned his name before, or the fact that he was any more to her than a stranger on holiday. I wondered if David had encouraged her to downplay their relationship throughout the years, or if Pam just wanted to keep their love to herself. I wondered if anyone actually knew the truth but me.

"I had even seriously considered giving the two of you up for adoption, right up to the last minute."

Adoption. She'd never mentioned that before, either. Not to me. Not to the media. Not to anyone.

"I hadn't met with any parents or agencies, but I didn't think there was any way I could make things work with twins on my own. But then I had you." Pam started to cry then, and my heart continued to break, even though I was convinced it couldn't break any further. "There you were. Eight pounds. Brown eyes. The name Nicholas sprung to my mind before the nurse had even placed you in my arms. But I still had work to do. I still had another one to go.

"Then I found out you were gone," she continued. "That's when I really knew how much I wanted you. And I think that was my punishment. I think that was the universe's way of teaching me a lesson, if you believe in all that stuff. It was getting retribution for how ungrateful I'd been. I was never good at being happy, and now I didn't get to be.

"In a strange way, it took your kidnapping to make me realise how much I really wanted you both."

I shook my head. Finally, I turned to look at her, and it was as if the floor had been ripped out from under me.

There was a bruise on her right eye.

"Pam…" I said. "Mum, you can't keep doing this. It'll kill you."

But it wasn't *her* doing anything. It was him.

"You deserve better," I tried. "You deserve to be happy. It's not that hard, Mum. I promise it's not that hard. I can teach you."

Pam broke down crying. She pulled me forward and into her arms, and I'm not sure how long we stayed like that for. Trembling and sobbing into each other's shoulders.

"Did he do that because of the article?" I asked her.

Pam pulled back, frowning at me. "What article?"

The dark, grisly voice emerged from nowhere: "Tell her, Jules."

Pam and I jumped to our feet. David was looming in the doorway like a contorted shadow. His hands were balled into fists, and that's when I realised that David hadn't hit Pam because of the article. He hadn't even seen her yet. David had hit Pam last night, the same night that he'd embraced her on that staircase and gushed about how much he'd missed her.

My stomach churned. *Some people never change. Not even for a night.*

He stepped deeper into the room and I didn't think. I just put my body between his and Pam's. The room was shaking. Oceans were tipping behind my eyes. And I did the Rosemary thing. I swallowed my pain, gritted my teeth…and I stared down the snarling monster in front of me.

If there was one thing this family gave me, it was the ability to *endure*.

David stopped, like he wasn't prepared for me to intervene. He stared at me, and then at Pam, and then he did something I never thought I would see him do.

He started to cry.

"Baby," he said. "Sweetheart, I'm so sorry."

For a moment, all the blood drained from my body. I felt lifeless standing there, like if someone opened the window I'd merely blow away. I was in so much shock that I didn't know what to do. And then I realised: he wasn't sorry, he was *scared*.

"Pammy," he said, because he knew he'd lost her. "Let's talk about this."

"I love you," he moaned, because he really was trying everything.

"It's you and me, baby," he lied, because that's all he had left. Lies.

He was on his knees now, and I felt Pam stepping out from behind me. For a moment, I was terrified that she was going to kneel down to him, to comfort him. I thought maybe he had fooled her.

But she merely took off her wedding ring and placed it on the dressing table.

Distantly, I could hear Brett knocking on the front door. I knew that it was over.

It was finally over.

BRISBANE BULLETIN

Pamela Rosemary and Julian Edwards-Rosemary Break Their Silence, Reveal Domestic Abuse and Request Privacy

BY JOHN ANTHONY   **JULY 3, 2017**

AFTER years of silence, Pamela Rosemary and her son, Julian Edwards-Rosemary, have issued a statement alleging domestic abuse that Pamela has endured from her husband, David Leman.

The alleged abuse, which began in late 2000, was both physical and emotional. Initially supportive of the search for Julian, David allegedly grew tired of the media attention, wanting Pamela to focus solely on him and their new family, including their biological children, Tanner (5) and James (7). He is said to have created a toxic family dynamic that may have contributed to the reckless driving and untimely death of Julian's twin brother Jack.

Pamela has once again asked for privacy as she and Julian begin to heal. She also revealed her decision to allow Julian to continue visiting Donna Jones, the woman who kidnapped him, in prison—a move that still confounds many. Pamela offered no further explanation beyond stating that it is Julian's wish to maintain that connection, and she does not want to deny him of it.

Their statement also revealed that Pamela and Julian received a generous but undisclosed financial payment in exchange for an exclusive interview with Channel 6. They plan to donate much of this money to domestic violence charities across Australia. This act of generosity reflects their hope that other victims of domestic abuse can find the support and resources they need to escape situations like the one Pamela allegedly endured for so long. David Leman has since been charged with domestic violence and faces legal action, with a court case expected soon.

The Rosemary family's story has long captured public attention, but these new allegations have added layers of complexity and tragedy to the already sensational narrative. Despite the heartache and losses that they have endured, Pamela and Julian are focused on rebuilding their lives and finding peace after years of silence and suffering. Their decision to speak out about the alleged abuse has not only brought clarity to their story but also highlighted the importance of supporting victims of domestic violence across the country.

Chapter 30

The day Pam told the truth about what happened, there was a lightness to her that I'd never seen before. She had always been beautiful, even at her lowest. But nothing compared to the beauty of her freedom.

Granted, we never told the full truth. We both decided that, like Angela's letter, some things were best left kept in the bottom of a jewellery box. Just like Pam's relationship with Wade, some things were best kept safe.

She showed me his photograph one day when we were packing up the house. We weren't moving far—just to a four-bedroom apartment slightly more east—but it still felt momentous. For Pam, it would be the first time she'd lived somewhere without David. She had just started a job as a receptionist, and it would be the first time she was living as a financially independent woman. There would always be opportunities to make money from future media interviews, but I think the two of us were happy to stay out of the media for a couple more decades.

In the new house, the first thing we did was put up the photos of Jack that David had removed after the wake. He'd never allowed many apparently, and far fewer than the photos of James and Tanner. Now they were everywhere. There wasn't a single room without some kind of tribute to him.

We also added some photos of me with James and Tanner, and one that the media had taken of Pam and I when we'd given our statement. I was sitting on a chair, and she was standing behind me with her arms locked around my shoulders. We looked like characters in a Lifetime movie. And for the first time, we also looked like mother and son.

When Pam put up the photograph of her and Wade, the one that she'd shown me back at the old house, I nearly broke down in the hallway. I finally knew who my real parents were. I finally knew their names *and* their faces.

It was a lively photo of my father with his arm around a young, sun-kissed Pam. Beneath the photo, it read, 'Wade and Pam, 1999'.

He was handsome, my father. *Wade*. That kind of strong, classic, decathlon-winner handsome. He had a mop of brown hair like mine, but it was parted down the middle like those Hollywood heartthrobs you saw in old movies. He was fit, happy…

"You look like him," Pam told me. "More than Jack did. I always thought that. Jack looked like me. You looked like your father."

"Jack and I were identical."

She smiled at the photograph. "Not to me. Never to me."

I stared at the wall. It contained images of our entire family—well, bar one. I knew it was pointless to imagine a photograph of Angela on these walls. Despite Pam's grace, and her willingness to still let me visit her, it was an insult to expect Angela's face to ever be on these walls. I kept a photograph of her in my wallet, and the only person who knew it was there was me. *You have to keep a room in your heart for you.*

About a week later, I received a letter from the Director of Public Prosecutions. In a very formal and matter of fact way, it advised me that Angela was being extradited to the Brisbane Women's Correctional Centre at Wacol in August. The letter also explained that she would be appearing at the Brisbane Supreme and District Court in September, and offered me the opportunity to provide a written victim impact statement for the judge to consider before making the sentencing decision.

For a few fleeting moments, I thought I had a chance to tell the judge all the good things about the woman who raised me, but my heart sank when I read the statement instructions. I could talk about any physical and emotional impact of Angela's crime on me, but my statement couldn't contain 'your opinion of the personal character of the defendant or what sentence they should receive'.

That sealed it for me. I declined to make any victim impact statement at all. I don't know if Pam did. I didn't think it was my place to ask her.

Angela pleaded guilty when she appeared in court in September and received the maximum sentence of fourteen years. Neither Pam nor I attended, and we made no comment when inevitably contacted by the media. I broke down when I saw Angela in handcuffs on the TV news being transferred to and from the prison van, but thankfully the media were barred from getting close to her. No cameras were allowed inside the court.

It was a long, tense discussion, but Pam had allowed me to continue seeing Angela on one condition.

I had to go back to counselling.

And I agreed, but I had my own conditions.

Pam had to return to counselling too.

The rest of the school year passed relatively quietly after that. Sure, there were a few nosy students wanting to know about why Pam was allowing me to see Angela—mainly *Gavin*, but I was getting better at deflecting my answers.

In September, things started to get crazy again with graduation prep. Exams had been rigorous, and there was something called a Queensland Core Skills Test that Elijah had briefly explained to me at the start of the year. I knew it was important and dictated my eligibility for certain university courses, so he'd encouraged me to take it. I swear, passing it had been almost as difficult as talking to the media with Pam, but it too had been a necessary evil.

When all the hard stuff was finally over, I was able to celebrate with Jasmine at our Year 12 formal. She'd worn a navy, purplish dress that went right to the floor, and I'd stolen her dad's rose corsage from her dressing table and presented it to her in a white box. She'd loved it so much she cried.

As for work, I was still at the nursing home, and I'd also become Reg's personal stylist. His venous insufficiency meant that his legs were constantly bleeding through his compression socks, and it often ruined his shoes. He was also steadily declining into middle-stage dementia, and that often affected our conversations.

"These will work," he said, velcroing a new pair of slippers. "Thank you, Jules."

I nodded. It was difficult to please a man like Reg, but I had it down to a tee. *Strong coffee, extra-wide slippers with adjustable fasteners, and a vocalised hatred for the institution.*

"If only the damn doctor would visit you more than once a week." I folded my arms, leaning back in my chair. "Beacon needs to contract more GPs. One doctor for the entire facility? It's madness."

"You're telling me. *Damn Beacon…* A miserable place to die indeed." Reg shook his head, picking up his coffee. "A miserable place, but with the exception of you, Jack."

My heart twinged, but only briefly. It was getting easier to forgive this little blip.

Some days I was Jules. Some days I was Jack. But that was okay. I no longer loathed the comparison; in fact, a part of me welcomed it. That same part of me that was learning to love someone I never knew, and to accept the fact that he lived on inside me.

Maybe I would always be *Rosemary Boy*, but I got to decide what that meant. With each news article that was released (the media machine had *devoured* a new criminal spinoff of The Rosemary Story), it was getting easier to separate myself from the character they'd created. A caricature of grief and dreadful circumstance.

I was more than that. I *would be* more than that.

Julian Edwards-Rosemary was a son to two mothers. He was a friend to a small but valuable tribe of people. He was a brother. He was also on track for a career in occupational therapy, so he could help more people like Reg, and stop people falling without being sued.

There was a brief knock at the door, and then it was swinging open. "Reg, there's Christmas activities down in the—" Chelsea's eyes widened. "Oh. Sorry. I…I thought he was alone."

"Sorry," I said. "We were just catching up."

"Screw your festivities," Reg bellowed. "I'm having coffee with Jack, and you can't make me venture out into the jolly bowels of this facility!"

Chelsea glanced at me, frowning slightly. Some days, I think that Reg's mention of Jack affected her more than it affected me. After all, I was learning to love Jack. Chelsea was learning how to forget him.

I squeezed Reg's knee. "Come on, old man. It's Christmas. Let's go out there for a few minutes. If it makes us sick, we can come right back here."

Reg grumbled, but he eventually gave in and let Chelsea wheel him out of his room. I trailed behind quietly, hands in my pockets.

"Can we go back yet?" Reg asked me.

"Not yet. Look."

The reception area had been completely transformed. Jasmine and I had spent all last week hanging tinsel and *jollying these bowels*, as Reg would say.

"Well, bah humbug," he muttered.

Chelsea stationed him in the centre of the crowd, ready to listen to the afternoon's Christmas carols. Instead of hiring actual performers, the facility turned the microphone over to the residents. It was amazing, the things they remembered. Even when their minds were decaying, they could remember entire songs. In Pip's case, she could hardly recall her family members' names, but she could sing a haunting rendition of 'Silent Night' without incident.

I should have gone back to the reception desk, but I didn't.

Instead, I sat beside Reg and Chelsea. It was Christmas Eve, after all.

"How's uni?" I asked her.

"Full on," she said.

Chelsea had made great strides over the past year. Her grades were so good that she was able to undertake university-level courses while still completing grade twelve. She chose to study psychology, which seemed like a natural progression considering how worldly she was already. It was so obvious now that she was Reg's granddaughter—that the nuggets of his wisdom had been firmly implanted in her mind.

"You still want to be an OT?" she asked me.

"I'm not sure," I told her. "I think so."

"You think so?"

"I guess it's hard to know," I said. "My dreams before all of this were so different. Angela bought me superhero toys when I was younger. I convinced myself I wanted to be Iron Man."

Chelsea laughed. "That *is* different."

"Then, when I got a little less delusional, I wanted to make films. Great films like the ones that kept me company. Films that taught me about the world and made me think. Films like *The Truman Show*. That's what I wanted to do with my life."

"So why don't you do it?"

I looked at her, like she was talking nonsense. "I don't know the first thing about filmmaking."

"So, start learning."

"It was just a dream," I told her. "When you're a kid, dreams are like toys."

"Yeah, they are. And through the years, we owe it to our

childhood selves to take care of our toys."

"Maybe…" I said. "Or, maybe, when a person gets older, they have to put away their toys. Maybe they have to put away their dreams, you know… The ones that aren't cute anymore. The ones that are just costing them money, costing them their dignity."

She shook her head. "I don't believe that. You have to keep going, Jules, and you have to keep caring about your silly, childish dreams, because no one else will. And you owe it to him. You owe it to little Jules to take care of his toys."

Little Jules. I hadn't thought about him in a long time.

"Besides, there are so many ways to help people," she said. "There's physically assisting them in places like this, and then there's creating pieces of art to take them *away* from places like this. Both are just as meaningful."

I turned my gaze back to the makeshift stage. Pip was halfway through her song, and she looked more joyful than I'd seen her in months. I thought about all those nights she'd bring out photo frames of her children to watch *Rear Window* with her in the foyer. I thought about the contented smile she always fell asleep with.

"I'm really grateful for you," I told Chelsea. "I'm grateful that you forced us to be friends."

She let out a startled laugh. "Well, I'm grateful you took my phone calls, even when all I did was sob."

I stared at her, at the slight dimple in her cheek. I'd never noticed it before. But there were a lot of things I'd neglected to notice about Chelsea.

"Jack loved you too, you know."

She glanced at me, her smile fading.

"If you were…you know, if you were confused about that.

You shouldn't be. I know he wasn't perfect, but he loved you, Chelsea. He did."

"How…?" Her gaze flickered to the space between us. "How do you know?"

I reached into my backpack. I pulled out Jack's poetry book and, after a moment of hesitation, I pulled out one of the pages toward the end. I folded it and then handed it to Chelsea.

"It was one of the last poems he ever wrote," I told her. "And it was about you."

I heard Chelsea swallow. She took a deep breath, and then she unfolded the piece of paper.

Fresh Hands (Chelsea)

Little words rush between us at first glance.
Who will be first to make the other laugh today?
Fresh light means fresh hands—
encircle me like the smooth skin of water.
Hold me to the bed
with the softness of an anchor.
I have to go to work. I have to go to work.
But where will you be when I'm thrust into those
paltry sights? Not going about your day
as I go about mine—
rather, with me, still,
in the back of my mind.
Five more minutes. Five more minutes.
What am I working for
if not the luxury of being late?
I can never be early
when there is always time
to be late with you.

Chelsea held the page for a long time. Finally, she took another deep breath and then handed it back to me.

"You keep it," I told her.

"Are you sure?"

"Of course."

She folded the page gently, and she stored it away safely in her handbag. She directed her gaze back to the makeshift stage in front of us—to Pip.

Silent night, holy night
Shepherds quake at the sight
Glories stream from heaven afar
Heavenly hosts sing hallelujah

When I looked back at Chelsea, tears were slipping down her cheeks. She didn't wipe them, and I pretended not to notice.

"I think…he needed somebody to tell him that it wasn't his fault," she whispered. "Everything that happened with Pam. Everything that happened with David."

I nodded, looking back at Pip. Her words nestled uncomfortably in my chest.

"I wish somebody had told him that. I wish *I'd* told him that." I felt Chelsea staring at me. "Sometimes, when I look at you, I trick myself into thinking I still can."

I swallowed. There was a lump in my throat the size of a golf ball. It was ridiculous, but… "You could try."

"It's not your fault, Jules."

I sniffed. "Thanks, Chels."

"Did that work at all?"

"Maybe," I told her. "We'll see."

I'd become remarkably good at scheduling my crying. After my conversation with Chelsea, I sat and felt the emotions rising and falling in my chest. I felt the burn spreading throughout my body. I felt it, and I acknowledged it like a dog scratching at the door: *yes, I see you. I'll let you out later. I promise.*

Chelsea took Reg back to his room, and I walked out of the facility and down toward the river. I walked by the rubbish compactors on the way and felt a phantom ache in my right hand. I kept walking.

I sat down on the edge of the jetty. My heart was engorged, and I needed it to shrink a few sizes before I could go back inside. Sometimes this took a few minutes; sometimes longer.

"You trying to escape Christmas too?"

I looked over my shoulder. Jasmine was walking toward me. The sun reflected off the rose in her hair like a spotlight, and the familiar sight loosened something within me.

"I had to get out before 'Auld Lang Syne'. That song always tears me up for some reason."

"That's a shame," Jasmine said. She sat down next to me. "Moira's version really kills."

"I'm sure it does." I smiled at her, and then I looked back out at the river. The grey-blue water was sloshing gently north, and the sound was soothing. "I used to come out here to cry on my lunch breaks," I told her. "I still do…sometimes."

"I can see that." She reached out and wiped a tear from my cheek. She left her hand there for a moment, and I leaned into it.

"Seven weeks," I whispered.

"Seven weeks, and then you'll never have to see me again."

I knew that she was joking. *I knew it*, but the thought still brought fresh tears to my eyes. I turned away, rubbing my face with the back of my hand.

"It's only a three-month internship," she said. "I'll be back before you know it."

"Not if they're smart," I said. "If they're smart, they'll offer you a job and get you to stay forever. Jasmine Morè: Senior Editor at *Victorian Quill Press*."

"I don't think people make the jump from intern to senior editor that quickly."

"You might."

"You're deluded, *Rosemary Boy*."

I smiled. She was the only person that could call me that and somehow make it sound like a compliment, like it packed the entire weight of the universe behind it. "Well, someone told me a little delusion is good."

"Can't live without it," she said, and she stared at the water. "You could come with me, you know."

I frowned. "I don't really think Melbourne's the place for me."

"Where's the place for you?"

Wherever you are.

"Here," I told her. "For a little bit, at least. There are things I need to do here."

"Well, you do have a mother here, and a second mother that you need to keep in contact with. And Brett, your pseudo stepfather..."

"Don't," I told her. "Don't try to make sense of it."

Jasmine laughed. She kicked her leg out from underneath her and it brushed against mine.

"He's marrying your mother," I told her. "So, he's kind of like both our dads. We're kind of like brother and sister."

"*Don't*," she said, but there was a smile on her face. Over the last five months, she hadn't just grown to tolerate the thought of Brett and Ms Morè together. She'd actually grown to like it.

Our legs were still pressed together. I tilted my head up to the disappearing sun. "I also can't leave Reg. I'm one of the only ones he remembers now—probably because he knew me as two people. It's harder to forget two faces than it is to forget one."

"I never saw you as two people, you know."

I looked at her. She was staring down at our legs.

"Despite everything. Despite what you may think."

"How did you see me?" I asked her. *How* do you *see me*?

"I think you have just about the worst haircut I've ever seen on a guy."

I laughed. It was the first time I'd laughed in a few days—since Reg spilt a blob of cream on his new silk shirt.

"Will you visit me?" Jasmine asked.

"Of course."

"And will you get out of here?" she asked me. "When the time is right?"

I looked at her. "Of course."

She held my hand. "Jules…" she said. She took a deep breath. For the first time, I didn't press her. I didn't initiate. I just sat there, silent. Waiting.

"I've never loved anyone," she said finally. She straightened her shoulders, like she'd just taken off a heavy coat. "I thought I did, once… But then I met you.”

I squeezed her hand. The water sloshed around us. A plane hummed overhead.

“Everything I thought I knew before changed, and everything I didn’t know was suddenly very clear to me.”

“Is that your Jasmine way of saying you’re in love with me?”

She laughed. “That’s my way of saying you were an insufferable git, but you taught me things.” She squinted out at the lake. “*And* I’m in love with you.”

“You always have to do that, don’t you?”

“Yeah, I do.”

I smiled at her. “I love that about you, you know?”

“Yeah, I do.”

EPILOGUE

Pam was teaching me to drive. There seemed to be something healing about it for the both of us. Maybe because Pam had never taught Jack to drive, and Angela had never taught me.

It was a mother/son experience Pam and I had both given up on, perhaps. It was especially hard since the memory of Jack's death was so visceral whenever we were in a car. He was there with us. We could both feel it. And there was something haunting about it, but also something deeply comforting. It was a second chance, an opportunity to do things right. There were still so many questions surrounding Jack's death that night, but I now knew that he'd fought with David right before he left. According to Pam, she'd gone to bed early but woke suddenly when she heard the front door slam closed. David and Jack had been fighting over the new night light Jack had bought Tanner.

Now, of course, Tanner was allowed to have the night light on without consequence, but I still went in there every morning out of habit. It didn't feel like an obligation anymore, but rather an acknowledgement of Jack's love for our siblings. Of everything he had fought for.

As I drove Pam's old Ford, I noticed the glimmer in her eyes. The *life* that flashed behind them every time we hit a little speed bump, or I took a corner too fast.

"Careful," she said. "Careful…"

We pulled into a café, parking well away from anyone. It was New Year's Day, and not many people were out today. We sat at a table at the back.

Pam took off her sunglasses, and I noticed the clear skin beneath her eyes. She took a long sip of her latte, and the image soothed something in me. I felt the warmth of her drink permeating throughout my body as if I'd drunk it myself. That's when I realised: it was the first time I'd actually seen her drinking coffee from a coffee mug.

"Thank you," I told her.

"Don't thank me," she said, stirring her coffee. "I'm a terrible teacher. You'll be lucky to pass your second go—"

"No. I meant, *thank you.*"

She peered up at me. Her shoulders were hunched, and her fingers seemed to tighten around her mug.

"Thank you for letting me stay with Angela." I stared down at the table. "Thank you…for letting me have a better life."

Pam stayed completely still, but I could *feel* it: the words reaching inside her and untangling years of knotted cords.

She swallowed hard. "Thank you for coming back. Thank you for…thank you for staying."

"You're welcome," I said, like I'd had any choice in the first part. But the second part, the second part I *had* chosen.

Pam's voice started to shake. "I love you, Jules. I always have."

"I love you too, Mum."

We sat in silence for a long time. We were both trying not to cry and doing a terrible job. We just drank our coffees and put on our sunglasses.

It was new, the Mum thing. I'd tried it a couple of times when our throats weren't clogged with emotion, when I wasn't imploring her to make a decision. She served me cereal. *Thanks, Mum.* She congratulated me on my high school graduation. *Couldn't have done it without you, Mum.*

I thought it would feel wrong, like maybe I was cheating on Angela. But it felt strangely cathartic, like two dusty puzzle pieces finally fitting together. And I was *happy*, despite all that had happened. Despite the sensationalism of my life.

Sure, there was still lots to worry about. David's domestic violence trial was yet to start. My other mother was still in prison. The media attention hadn't really let up. But being happy is a skill. And Angela always used to say, *To be happy, you have to get really good at looking at what you've got.*

And I really did have a lot.

ACKNOWLEDGEMENTS

I started this novel back in 2022, and much like Jules, I encountered many people who made the journey slightly less bumpy. I'm endlessly grateful to each of you:

To **Bonita Mersiades**, who read this manuscript and agreed to publish it without hesitation—thank you for your trust. I'm honoured to be one of your authors under the Popcorn Press fiction imprint. I would also like to thank Asher Reed for the book's cover design and Ana Nedeljković for its internal design.

To my agent, **Belinda Bolliger**—your thoughtful notes and unwavering belief in this story meant the world. You championed this book from the moment it landed in your inbox.

To **Jasmine Barui**, my friend and fellow writer, thank you for sharing your knowledge and letting me pick your brain about the caste system. Your insight enriched this story and the Morè women.

To **John Jacobson**, whose wisdom has guided me for over a decade. You gave me feedback on a short story when I was sixteen—and have been reading everything I write ever since. Thank you for always believing in my words.

To **Tenille Duncan**, a constant well of creativity and motivation. You've always encouraged me to go after what I want, even when I turn up to your house filled with doubts.

To **my dad**, who cares about my words more than anyone. This dedication is no token gesture—you were the first person to read this book and the first to believe in it. You grounded the sensationalism of this story into something real and accessible.

Thank you for reminding me of its heart: a young boy discovering the big, beautiful and terrifying world around him.

To the rest of my family:

My **sister**, for brainstorming with me one afternoon when I hit a wall. I don't think any of those ideas made it in—but I love you for trying. My **brother**, for letting me stay at your place in Cairns for two weeks and do nothing but write, eat and complain. And my **mum**, who's been encouraging my writing since I was twelve, and who still takes care of me when I need it most.

To my sweet **Jamie**—thank you for always showing up. Sitting beside you on the lounge as we acted out a chapter together will forever be one of my favourite memories. You couldn't wait to read this book, and I couldn't wait to watch you while you read it.

And finally, to *you*—my readers. Whether you found me through *Boys on a Train*, or stumbled upon this book by chance, thank you for being here. This story—and everything I go on to write—will always be for you.

ABOUT THE AUTHOR

Amy Coomer is an author, actor and producer based in Queensland, Australia. Her debut young adult novel, *Boys on a Train*, has reached readers in over thirteen countries and appeared on multiple Amazon bestseller lists.

Rosemary Boy is her second novel.

To learn more, visit www.amycoomer.com.

MORE BOOKS FROM POPCORN PRESS

Abebi

Anna Black – this girl can play

High Heels and Low Blows

Light and Shadow

RIPPA!

The Yawning Giant